LIVI MICHAEL is an award-winning writer of novels for adults, young adults and children. Her short stories have appeared in several magazines and anthologies. She runs a podcast about short stories with writer and translator Sonya Moor.

livimichael.co.uk

Elizabeth
AND
Ruth

ALSO BY LIVI MICHAEL

FICTION
Under a Thin Moon (Secker and Warburg, 1992)
Their Angel Reach (Secker and Warburg, 1994)
All the Dark Air (Secker and Warburg, 1997)
Inheritance (Viking/Penguin, 2000)
Succession (Penguin Random House, 2014)
Rebellion (Penguin Random House, 2015)
Accession (Penguin Random House, 2016)
Reservoir (Salt, 2023)

YOUNG CHILDREN'S FICTION
Frank and the Black Hamster of Narkiz (Puffin Books, 2002)
Frank and the Chamber of Fear (Puffin Books, 2003)
Frank and the Flames of Truth (Puffin Books, 2004)
Frank and the New Narkiz (Puffin Books, 2005)
43 Bin St (Orchard Books 2005)
Seventeen Times as High as the Moon (Orchard Books 2006)
The Goose Girl (Collins 2016)

FICTION FOR OLDER CHILDREN
The Whispering Road (Puffin, 2005)
The Angel Stone (Puffin, 2006)
City of Dogs (Puffin 2008)
Faerie Heart (Puffin 2009)
Malkin Child (Foxtail 2012)

COMMUNITY THEATRE
Singers not Sinners

Elizabeth
AND
Ruth

LIVI MICHAEL

CROMER

PUBLISHED BY SALT PUBLISHING 2026

2 4 6 8 10 9 7 5 3 1

Copyright © Livi Michael 2026

Livi Michael has asserted her right under the Copyright, Designs and
Patents Act 1988 to be identified as the author of this work.

*This book is sold subject to the condition that it shall not, by way of trade or otherwise,
be lent, resold, hired out, or otherwise circulated without the publisher's prior consent
in any form of binding or cover other than that in which it is published and without a
similar condition including this condition being imposed on the subsequent publisher.*

This book is a work of fiction. Any references to historical events, real people
or real places are used fictitiously. Other names, characters, places and events
are products of the author's imagination, and any resemblance to actual
events or places or persons, living or dead, is entirely coincidental.

First published in Great Britain in 2026 by
Salt Publishing Ltd
12 Norwich Road, Cromer, Norfolk NR27 0AX, United Kingdom

GPSR representative
Matt Parsons matt.parsons@upi2mbooks.hr
UPI-2M PLUS d.o.o., Medulićeva 20, 10000 Zagreb, Croatia

www.saltpublishing.com

Salt Publishing Limited Reg. No. 5293401

A CIP catalogue record for this book is available from the British Library

ISBN 978 1 78463 368 4 (Paperback edition)
ISBN 978 1 78463 369 1 (Electronic edition)

Typeset in Neacademia by Salt Publishing

Printed and bound in Great Britain by Clays Ltd, Elcograf S.p.A

To my sons, with love

PART I

CHAPTER 1

Elizabeth

ELIZABETH GRIPPED HER umbrella as the small carriage jogged over the bridge. Smoke from a hundred factory chimneys poured over the river, flakes of soot and ash drifted down. The usual smog had formed like a damp cloth, blotting out the light. It was perhaps the worst day she could have chosen for visiting the New Bailey Prison.

She could see its ghostly outline through the mist. So many new buildings had accreted onto it, in successive degrees of ugliness, that it had lost all its original shape. But it remained menacing, like the city of Dis in Dante's Inferno, *a place mute of all light, in grief's abysmal valley.*

Jim pulled the carriage up, then stepped down, grunting, to help Elizabeth. Holding onto his arm, she stepped over a pool of brick-coloured mud. Then they stood together, staring at the prison gates.

'We could always go back,' Jim said.

But what would she say to Thomas? *The girls are so grateful to know they're not forgotten*, he'd said.

'Just wait for me here.' She waved the umbrella to one side then the other in an attempt to close it. It was her husband's umbrella in fact and it wasn't *wieldy*, if that was the word. Its thick wooden spokes resisted closing.

'Well, I'm hardly likely to leave you,' Jim replied, though she saw him glance towards *The Nag's Head*.

'I won't be long,' she said a little sharply, but since she didn't know how long she was likely to be she could hardly condemn him to sit outside in the rain. Umbrella finally closed, she gathered her skirts, stepped over another puddle and rang the bell.

Inside she followed a wardress along one whitewashed corridor after another. The wardress was sturdily built but her shoulders were curved like the arc of a bow, straining the grey serge of her prison uniform. She hadn't offered her name and showed no interest in Elizabeth's, but the badge on her blouse read *Miss Jamieson*. She led the way without speaking so only the smells helped Elizabeth to navigate; fatty, boiled meat from the kitchen, and the pungent reek of some substance used to scour the floors.

As they approached the central atrium she could hear a scraping, shushing noise. Rows of kneeling women were scrubbing the floor with identical circular movements beneath a skylight that revealed a whitish rectangle of sky. That was the final smell of course, the prison perfume of stale, unhopeful human. Subtly different from the stench of poverty and despair in the slums.

The kneeling women didn't look up as she passed, but the set of their shoulders, a momentary alteration in the rhythm of their work, registered her presence.

Elizabeth had written to the Matron, Miss Jopson, who had replied that she was *indeed honoured to welcome such a celebrated authoress into her humble institution* (there it was – the sharp pang of shame and pride that stung her whenever her literary reputation was mentioned). And then in the next line, *There are many varieties of misfortune within this penitentiary, but I hope I need not assure you that anything heard or confessed here must stay within these walls.*

Elizabeth had felt a prickle of outrage. She wasn't looking for material – why did everyone imagine she was?

The letter went on to say she was welcome to visit the prisoner at the specified time, but since the cells were in the process of being cleaned an alternative venue for their appointment would be found.

So now she could only follow the wardress, wondering where that venue might be.

Miss Jamieson stopped suddenly in front of a heavy oak door that bore the Matron's name on a brass plate. Would Miss Jopson interview Elizabeth after all?

The wardress turned towards her with lowered eyes. When she spoke Elizabeth was surprised by the gruff tone and the accent which wasn't from Manchester or Salford. The Wirral perhaps? Her husband would know. 'Miss Jopson is at a meeting of the governors,' she said. 'She asks, will you wait here while the girl is brought to you?'

'Of course,' Elizabeth said, slightly flustered: *did she mean here, in the corridor?*

But Miss Jamieson opened the door onto a small, wood-panelled room. There was a desk with a high-backed chair behind it, and a lower one in front. Papers were scattered across the surface, and there was a ledger. On the wall above, there was a sampler.

Repent, therefore, and be converted

Probably stitched by the inmates.

'I'll not be long,' Miss Jamieson said, closing the door behind her with a soft click.

Elizabeth felt suddenly lost. She wasn't sure what to do about the umbrella that was still dripping, or her bonnet and cape. After a moment's hesitation she stood the umbrella next to the door. It slid to one side, grazing the wall, then rested on the door frame. She unfastened her bonnet then waited, feeling like a naughty schoolgirl in the headmistress' office. Her gaze travelled towards the bookshelf in the alcove.

A Treatise on the Prevention and Cure of Diseases by Regimen and Faith.

Disorders, Distempers and Maladies of the Female Sex.

Then a battered copy of *The Pilgrim's Progress*, and two or three smaller books with faded titles. She would have to lift them from the shelf to see what they were. Obviously she wasn't going to do that. In any case, she wouldn't be able to reach.

What was she doing here really?

If only Thomas Wright hadn't caught her off-guard.

Many of the girls have no visitors, he'd said. *Even their families, if they have any, will have nothing to do with them once they're penned up – they might as well be lost to the world.*

Then he'd told her about this particular girl, but in such a convoluted way that Elizabeth was still unsure of the details. When she'd pressed him his face had flushed almost to the colour of a bruise. Elizabeth was astonished that this father of nineteen children, whose tales of the male prisoners were nothing if not lurid, should be so abashed.

'You must ask her,' he'd said.

Pasley, he'd called her. But that was her surname, surely?

What she'd managed to gather from him was distressing, not because it was unusually tragic, but because it was tragically common. Manchester was famous for its neglected children.

And yet it was not quite usual, this tale.

Apparently, the girl was the daughter of an Irish clergyman and therefore respectable by birth (Thomas Wright had impressed this upon her) but her father had died when she was an infant. And her mother, upon marrying again, had taken her only child to an orphanage.

Regrettable but again, not uncommon.

From there Pasley had been apprenticed as a seamstress. But her employer was *a corrupt woman who had led the girl to her destruction*, Thomas had said. He would not elaborate on this.

When Pasley had fallen ill her employer had taken the unusual step of calling a doctor who had *very much abused his trust.*

Thomas' face had flushed again when he said this, and his hands shook so she was almost afraid for him. He was not a well man. And *not getting any younger*, as he would say. She didn't want to distress him. It seemed, from what he'd said, that the doctor had made some kind of assault upon his young patient.

Then, by some process that wasn't clear to Elizabeth, Pasley had ended up on the streets where she'd taken to theft, and worse.

She'd been arrested for enticement. Luring a man down an alley so that he could be set upon and robbed. The judge, aware perhaps, of the kind of circumstances that brought young girls into the dock, as well as the growing tide of opposition to transportation, had been lenient. Pasley had been given a six-month sentence.

Then, a few weeks ago she'd fallen ill again and a doctor had been called once more. Dr Billington was a man of impeccable reputation and one of the few who could be called upon to treat the institutionalised poor.

But Pasley had been so distressed by the appearance of this doctor that she'd collapsed weeping in the infirmary. And the doctor had been heard to say, *Good God, what are you doing here?*

Which could only be incriminating, although no one had questioned him apparently, to find out what he'd meant. He would not be called on again to treat the female patients, Thomas had said, darkly. The institution would not be employing him again at all, in fact. The matter had been taken to the Board.

There would be no investigation, however, since the Board had ruled against it.

Thomas wasn't asking Elizabeth to investigate the doctor. He was asking her to talk to the girl, to see if she could be helped on her release from prison. *She might speak to a lady such as yourself, a lady and a mother.*

At one time, Elizabeth would have been eager to take up this challenge, to rescue just one poor soul from the evils of the city. But that was in the early days – before she'd realised that Manchester was full of such horrors. *Behold, a great multitude which no one could count, from every nation and all tribes and peoples and tongues.*

She'd told her husband they should move, take the girls to the countryside where they could breathe clean air. But his answer was always the same: *My work is here.*

But what about me? she'd thought. *What about our daughters?*

Elizabeth made her way over to the window, her skirts brushing the desk. Through the mist, she could see small plots of land, largely desolate. It was where the girls used to grow vegetables and flowers, she'd been told. But the land had been so affected by the foul waters of the Irwell, the poisonous vapours of the dye works and tannery, that nothing would grow any more apart from rhubarb.

It wasn't the season for rhubarb, though she could see some blackened stalks, a few yellow-brown leaves. And bracken and nettles of course, that flourished on neglect.

Not like people.

She withdrew from the window, removing her bonnet finally, since it was damp. A fine spray of droplets flew from the brim as she shook it. What time was it? She imagined Jim leaning over the bar of the *Nag's Head*.

I won't be long, she'd said. Why did things invariably take longer than she'd planned? She had a dinner to arrange the following evening, and who knew what her daughters were getting up to in her absence?

Just as she was wondering whether Miss Jamieson had got lost, there was a knock at the door.

'Come in,' she said, then coughed, because her voice sounded strained, as though her throat had constricted while she was waiting. She thought she should perhaps look away, to avoid making the girl nervous, but it was too late; the door opened and Miss Jamieson ushered her in.

CHAPTER 2

She wore the same blue-grey uniform as all the prisoners, with an apron and a cap to cover her hair which had been cropped in the usual way to reduce the risk of lice. Elizabeth could see a few dark strands escaping from the cap. But it was the girl's thinness that struck her. Her bony wrists extended beyond the too-short sleeves of her dress. It would have been possible to circle one with Elizabeth's finger and thumb.

She observed all this in an instant while the girl looked at the floor and Miss Jamieson said, 'This is Mrs Gaskell, a minister's wife, come to visit you, out of charity.' Then she stood to one side of the door. Pasley's eyelids flickered, but she didn't look up.

'Do sit down,' Elizabeth said, almost adding *my dear*, but she mustn't be too informal. Instead she said, almost sternly, 'Please.'

Without raising her eyes, the girl went to the chair in front of the desk and perched on it.

There was a silence.

'I'm afraid I don't know what to call you,' Elizabeth said, sitting on the higher chair.

'Pasley,' said the girl.

'I mean your Christian name,' Elizabeth said, and for the first time the girl glanced up. Her eyes were light, her lower lip was tucked a little inside the upper. There were patches of eczema on her cheeks, but even in the dingy uniform it was clear she was very pretty. Elizabeth felt a flare of anger towards the doctor and all men who made the natural advantage of beauty the most dangerous gift the poor could possess.

'I am generally known as Pasley.'

Elizabeth glanced at Miss Jamieson, who nodded. 'The girls are usually called by their last names to avoid confusion,' she said. 'There are so many Marys and Annies.'

'What would you like me to call you?'

The girl was looking down again, at her hands. Elizabeth saw that they too were raw with eczema, the nails bitten. 'I'm quite reconciled to Pasley,' she said.

She was articulate, Elizabeth registered with a touch of surprise. But she had been educated after all. Her vowels were Mancunian, but her voice retained an Irish lilt. Manchester was full of Irish since the famine; thousands of them had been herded into the ghetto known as Little Ireland. But Pasley didn't talk like one of the slum children there or like the girls from the streets, which was a relief, since it was hardly possible to understand them.

She didn't look like a street girl either, she was oddly self-possessed despite a certain timidity. *Fourteen*, Thomas had said, but that was before her arrest; she must be older now.

When Elizabeth put the question to her she said she was sixteen.

'Just a little older than my oldest girl,' Elizabeth said. When Pasley didn't respond to this she continued, 'I have four daughters. Marianne, whom we call Polly, is fifteen. And Meta, whose full name is Margaret Emily, is twelve. So you see there are many names in our house—' She was rambling because she hadn't the vaguest idea how to proceed. But Pasley looked up again at the mention of Elizabeth's daughters and for the first time there was a ghost of a smile on her lips so she went on, 'My younger two are Florence, or Flossie, and Julia – who is just Julia so far. What did your mother call you?'

Pasley's face flushed from the neck up. She stared at the floor with a concentrated intensity.

Elizabeth asked gently, 'Have you heard from your mother?'

Pasley shook her head.

'Could you not write?'

A great tremor ran through the girl. Elizabeth glanced at Miss

Jamieson who gave an almost imperceptible shake of her head, so she said, 'But I hear you can write, at any rate?'

Still looking down Pasley said, 'Miss Vivienne taught me at the orphanage. She said I learned faster than anyone she ever knew. I helped to teach the little ones.'

'That's wonderful. It's so rewarding to teach. I teach at our Sunday school – not far from here in fact.'

No response.

'Do you like to read?'

'I used to. I don't have anything to read here—' she glanced quickly at Miss Jamieson 'apart from the Bible of course,' and Miss Jamieson nodded.

'We'll have to see what we can do about that. I have a great number of books in my house – my housekeeper is always complaining about them. She says they attract dust. I say they only attract dust when they're left on the shelf, so we must use them more regularly. But there are so many of them – I'm told we have more than two thousand.'

Pasley looked up finally, astonished. Even Miss Jamieson seemed startled.

'Yes, I know,' Elizabeth said. 'It's almost the chief reason we want to move house.'

Pasley looked down again. 'I can't imagine that,' she said. Elizabeth could have told her about their efforts to buy more books for the Sunday School or for the working men her husband taught or for the new library that would open soon. Instead she said, 'How old were you when you left the orphanage?'

Again Pasley glanced at Miss Jamieson before answering, 'Almost fourteen.'

'And you went straight to the workshop in Manchester?'

'No – I went to a dressmaker first. She was from Ireland too.'

'How long were you there?'

Again the pause, as if she was reluctant to speak.

'Mrs Fenton – the lady's – shop failed, and we had to find new situations.'

Pause. *Like pulling teeth.* 'Where did you go then?'

Pasley shook her head as though trying to shake some order into her thoughts. 'The business was bought by someone – she used to work for Mrs Fenton. She said she would take me on and treat me well. I would be well paid and have Sundays off and be cared for, she said. That was all lies,' she concluded bitterly.

'And this lady's name?'

Pasley hesitated, glancing sideways again towards Miss Jamieson, then down at her hands. Elizabeth decided not to press her. 'So, you were persuaded to go?'

'Mrs Fenton said it was an opportunity. She said there was a great demand for needlework in the city. If I didn't like my job I could soon get a different one – or even learn a different trade. In any case she couldn't support me, and so I had to go.'

Again that bitter turn of her mouth.

'Did you not like your new position?'

Pasley closed her eyes and shook her head vehemently. Elizabeth searched for the right question to ask.

'Were there other girls there?'

Pasley started to scratch at a raw place on her hand, then checked herself. Miss Jamieson said, 'You must tell Mrs Gaskell everything – just as you remember.'

'It doesn't matter,' Elizabeth began, but Pasley said,

'About twelve of us, more or less. We were all kept in the same room.

Elizabeth knew of such places, they were sadly common. A silence stretched between them, then she said, 'Did you ever think of leaving?'

Pasley said simply. 'I had nowhere to go.'

Elizabeth waited and the girl went on. 'I didn't know Manchester – and what I had seen of it – seemed like the biggest, noisiest, dirtiest place in the world.'

Elizabeth suppressed a smile. That was exactly how she would have described it. She avoided the city when she could, apart from

Sundays of course, when she had to attend chapel. That morning Jim had gone a long way round to avoid the centre but even so the throb of engines, the whistles of steam and the clanging of bells had almost deafened her. She couldn't blame Pasley for not chancing her luck on the streets.

But she was speaking again.

'I told myself, as soon as I got my first wage, I'd leave but I never did get it – there was always something I owed, seemingly – for bed or board – or because my work wasn't good enough. We never saw any wages.'

'Didn't you complain?'

'If we complained it went on the slate. Mrs Digby kept a slate for us all to show how much we owed, which was more every week. She had no intention of paying us!'

Elizabeth bowed her head. Pasley had given away the name of her employer. She tucked it away in her mind. 'And there was no one you could write to?'

'I wrote to my mother,' Pasley said. Her face flushed as she said this and tears came into her eyes but she blinked them away. After a moment she continued, 'I made up my mind to leave many times – to run away – but then I fell ill.'

Elizabeth could see she was struggling to frame the words. 'Go on,' she said.

'I fell behind with my work and Mrs Digby – she – called the doctor.'

Pasley's face flamed and she clawed at her rash. Elizabeth said gently, 'Was that the same doctor who visited you here?'

Pasley nodded vigorously, her eyes closed again.

'Dr Billington?'

More nodding.

Elizabeth leaned forwards. 'I'm sorry if this is painful for you,' she said. Pasley flinched away. Elizabeth glanced at Miss Jamieson and briefly Miss Jamieson's eyes met hers. They were yellowish, she noted in surprise. Yellow-green, like a cat's.

'Did he examine you?' Elizabeth asked, and Pasley looked so wretched Elizabeth thought she might faint but then she burst out, 'Oh Mrs Gaskell – if you knew how often I have gone through what happened – how many times I've wished it different – you must believe me – you must!'

And she covered her face with her apron and wept.

Tears stung Elizabeth's eyes. Miss Jamieson stepped forward and gripped Pasley's shoulder – not gently, it was hardly an embrace. 'Come on now, girl,' she said. 'Bear up.' Then from somewhere in the building a bell sounded and Miss Jamieson glanced at Elizabeth. 'That's the dinner bell,' she said. 'She'll be expected to go back to her cell. Not that she'll eat.'

They had hardly started, Elizabeth thought. But to Pasley she said, 'You must eat – even if you have no appetite. I want you to get well and strong for me. Can you do that?'

Without taking her face from her apron, Pasley nodded. She looked so forlorn! On impulse Elizabeth crouched down beside her, putting one hand tentatively on her arm. 'I will visit you again – if you would like me to?'

Pasley nodded into her apron again. Elizabeth wanted to say something to comfort her but there was so little comfort she could offer. She wanted to hold her, like one of her own daughters, but she could hardly do that with the wardress looking on.

Instead she pressed Pasley's arm (so thin!) and said, 'I will do everything I can to help you.'

Slowly Pasley lowered her apron. Her face was blotchy and pink, her eyes reddened. 'Thank you,' she whispered.

The click of the door sounded loud as Miss Jamieson opened it.

'We'd best be going,' she said. 'We shouldn't be late.'

Elizabeth nodded, then with some difficulty got up from the crouching position she'd so thoughtlessly dropped into. Her knees were not what they were. She straightened slowly, holding onto the table. As Pasley left the room she said, 'I'll come back soon.'

CHAPTER 3

ELIZABETH'S FINGERS FELT stiff as she tied her bonnet, fastened her cloak. She could still see the back of Pasley's neck as she followed the wardress out of the room, bent like a frail stem, the skin beneath her cap patchy and blotched.

What was she getting into?

She hadn't asked enough questions, or the right kind of questions – she knew hardly any more now than before her visit. It had ended so soon.

I'm sorry if this is painful for you, she'd said. Of course it was painful – how could it be anything else?

Did you ever think of leaving?

She'd sounded so prim, so clueless. Because she didn't know what to say.

She was too aware perhaps of the distance between her own experience and Pasley's. She shook her head at herself as Miss Jamieson returned. 'Shall I show you out, ma'am?'

They crossed the atrium together in silence, Elizabeth thinking furiously about all the things she needed to know but didn't know how to ask. They were approaching the exit before she said timidly, 'I was wondering – I mean – when is Pasley's release date?'

'January 9th.'

Less than two months away. January was the bitterest month, the hardest for those seeking employment and the most unforgiving for those who had no home. At Christmas all the hostels were full. And she would not like to see Pasley in some of them, in any case.

There were other questions she should ask, of a more delicate nature.

'And – do you know – is she fit to be released?'

No reply. Elizabeth persisted. 'Has she been examined?'

A slight shrug. 'Not that I know of.'

'So – we don't know what her illness was, exactly. Do we know her symptoms?'

Silence. But before Elizabeth could press her Miss Jamieson said, 'She complained of feeling sick, dizzy – I think she fainted once. Some of them put it on, mind.'

Put it on?

'To get out of their duties, ma'am. Spend time in the sick bay.'

Elizabeth felt annoyed but she had to tread carefully because there were more questions to ask. Could Pasley be pregnant? It was hard to believe, given the girl's thinness, her fragility. How long had she been in? Four months? It wasn't possible, surely.

Still, she would have to check.

'So you don't think – ?'

A blank stare.

'You don't have any reason to believe . . .'

'Prison food,' Miss Jamieson said. 'And the air – it takes 'em that way sometimes. And she won't eat – you wouldn't think she'd been on the streets,' she added as if to herself.

'I see,' Elizabeth said faintly. She would have to try harder. 'There's no possibility that she might be – with child?'

Miss Jamieson glanced at her briefly then away. 'Not so far as I know, Ma'am.'

What did that mean?

'Wouldn't she have been examined when she came in?'

A slight shrug, 'Depends.'

'On what?'

They were approaching the door and the wardress stopped. Light shone through a pane of glass and was reflected in Miss Jamieson's yellow eyes.

'If it looks like they might be well on and likely to give birth here, we keep a record. But if it's early and they're likely to be gone soon there's no point.'

Apart from diet, and medical care. Periods of rest from the punishing prison routine.

The wardress was looking at her as if daring her to say something. *You know nothing*, her yellow stare said. Elizabeth bit back her response. She thought again of Pasley's thinness, her fragility. She was surely not more than four months with child.

'So – you don't believe her to be – in that condition – now?'

'No ma'am.'

'But you don't know whether she has been?'

The stare turned hostile. Horrible images flitted through Elizabeth's mind, the babies dumped in the Irwell, left on slag heaps or in stinking ginnels.

If Pasley wasn't pregnant, might she have that other unmentionable consequence of her way of life? If she'd been in the kinds of places Elizabeth wasn't supposed to know about, it was difficult to imagine she *hadn't* contracted some terrible disease.

'And is she – is she – clean?'

A slight shrug. 'You'd have to ask her.'

Was that a smirk?

'I will,' she said as confidently as she could. Then, thinking about the number of doctors in her acquaintance she added, 'I can arrange for her to be examined.'

'I don't know about that.'

'Oh?'

'She won't have it. You didn't see her when that other doctor came.'

Elizabeth started to say *we need to know*, but Miss Jamieson said, 'There was some incident between her and one of the other girls. Neither of them would talk – girls in here don't talk to staff if you take my meaning – you might have better luck in that way, Ma'am.'

'What kind of incident?'

'The kind that happens when you pen girls up together. They turn into wild cats—' Elizabeth thought briefly of her own four daughters, ' - worse than the men sometimes. It wasn't my shift, Ma'am so I only know what I've been told.'

'She was fighting?' *Worse and worse.*

'Not her, I shouldn't think - she's no fighter. Though she can be stubborn. My guess is one of the others was picking on her. And between that and the not eating, the girl passed out, that's all.'

'So that's when you sent for the doctor.'

'She was taken to the infirmary - he visits them there. Visited,' she added as an afterthought.

'But you weren't there when he - ?'

'Not my shift, like I said. I only know what I've been told.'

Elizabeth closed her eyes briefly. 'I think she should be examined. It may help her, once she's out.'

No one would employ a pregnant maid.

Miss Jamieson said, 'It'll take more than that to help her.'

'I'm sorry?'

'Girls like Pasley are better off inside - she'll tell you as much herself.'

Elizabeth waited, and the wardress said, 'There are some bad people in here, Mrs Gaskell.'

Elizabeth thought of saying it would be surprising if there were no bad people in prison, but Miss Jamieson went on, 'Bad women, who prey on the younger girls, if you see what I mean.'

Elizabeth shook her head slightly.

'That's how she ended up here in the first place. They'll not rest until they've dragged her down with them, into their way of life - the street way - there's always someone looking for a young girl with nowhere to go.'

Elizabeth felt a tug of dread in her stomach as though she was on the brink of some abyss. She should ask more questions, she thought, but Miss Jamieson had already started to unfasten the bolts. Over her shoulder she said, 'She'll not last two minutes on the streets, that one. Not without help.'

'Well,' Elizabeth said, 'that's why I'm here. To help.'

Miss Jamieson shot her a look of blistering contempt. *How can you help her?* it said. Elizabeth was so startled she didn't speak. Then Miss Jamieson opened the door, and Elizabeth stepped through it, hearing it clang shut behind her.

CHAPTER 4

SHE STRUGGLED WITH William's umbrella until it opened. Then she stood with the pony, peering through the rain towards the Nag's Head.

'Poor Tommy,' she said. 'Has he left you again?'

The pony looked at her mournfully.

She'd spoken to Jim before about leaving the carriage, but he would have his excuses.

It was only for a minute.

I never took my eyes off 'un, the whole time.

She would have to speak to him about his drinking. It was no use expecting William to do it; he left the servants to her. And he was inexplicably fond of Jim.

But it was Jim's job to transport their daughters to their various engagements around the city. She couldn't have him drinking while he drove them. She patted the pony's muzzle and he butted her hand, disappointed that she had nothing for him. 'I'm sorry, Tommy,' she said.

'There you are, Ma'am,' said Jim, appearing suddenly at her side, flushed and sheepish.

'There *you* are,' Elizabeth said. Jim looked hurt.

'Begging your pardon, ma'am,' he said. 'I had to nip round the corner, as it were . . . '

Elizabeth glared at him. He knew she was unlikely to press him further about relieving himself into some drain.

Jim turned to the pony. 'You were all right, weren't you Tommy, old boy?'

She could smell the drink on him but she couldn't confront

him now, she was too tired. Thomas must have known how taxing prison visits could be, how impossible to avoid being drawn in. That was what she'd feared from the start, being *drawn in*. Yet she'd agreed to go.

Jim helped her into the carriage and set off over the cobbles. The rain increased, spilling from gutters, forming long brown pools in the streets.

Elizabeth pressed her handkerchief to her face. There was a bitter, choking tang in the air now and she could feel a headache coming on.

She remembered the look Miss Jamieson had given her, that venomous yellow stare. What could she possibly have done to offend her?

But she should be thinking about Pasley, all the questions she hadn't asked. She hadn't even found out the girl's first name.

I'm quite reconciled to Pasley.

Elizabeth shook her head. What did she know now that she didn't know before?

She'd learned that Pasley had been in a sweatshop and the name of the woman who ran it. That wasn't likely to be useful unless Elizabeth was going to report her. But there were thousands like her – you could stamp one out and others would spring up like mushrooms.

She *thought* Pasley might have been pregnant – that would explain how she'd ended up on the streets. Although Miss Jamieson hadn't said one way or the other.

It would be difficult enough to find a situation for the girl without that complication. Although Pasley was polite and presentable. She didn't seem to be hardened by her experiences like other girls Elizabeth had met. Girls prostituted by their mothers from the age of eight or even younger. Those girls had a shuttered, veiled look. They closed up like sea urchins when questioned, spiny, impenetrable.

Pasley was not like that. Perhaps because she wasn't brought up to *the life*, but only lately come upon it. But she'd been imprisoned for enticement, the prostitute's trick. There were very few ladies who would employ a former prostitute. Mainly, Elizabeth suspected, because they didn't trust their husbands.

Would they need to know?

They would find out. This was Manchester.

Elizabeth would have to tell them. She should be completely truthful from the start. It wasn't the girl's fault!

Ah, that look in her eyes when Elizabeth said she would help her! That painful, scarring hope. She couldn't let her down.

If only Pasley would confide in her! Perhaps the distance between them was too great. If she was conscious of it the girl must surely be.

As they left the city the fog began to lift. The first trees appeared, bare and black, branches dripping. Tommy increased his pace as they neared Upper Rumford Street, hurrying home.

'They didn't keep you in then,' said Meta as Elizabeth entered.

'Of course they didn't *keep me in*,' she said, irritably.

Julia, her three-year-old, ran up to her crying 'Mammee, mammee!' and tugged her skirts until Elizabeth picked her up.

'Who did you see?' asked Meta, surveying her through a magnifying glass. But of course she couldn't tell her. How could she tell her daughters that hideous story of abandonment, betrayal and rape?

Instead she said, 'Did you get that from your father's study?'

'I may have.'

'Can you put it back, please?'

'He isn't using it.'

'But he may want to use it. And then he would like to know where it is.'

'And I'll be able to tell him.'

'Mother,' said Polly, appearing from the kitchen in an overcoat and boots. 'Part of the fence has come down in the rain.'

Elizabeth tried to prise her bonnet strings from Julia's grip. 'Tell your father,' she said.

'Whatever for?' said Meta. 'He'll only compose a poem to it.'

'Or a sermon,' said Polly.

'Or make a speech to Parliament,' said Meta, 'and then in ten years' time we'll have an Act that says, *there should be no gaps in any fences.*'

'Well, it isn't my job,' said Elizabeth, struggling to take off her cloak as Julia clung to it. 'Tell Jim.'

'Jim will get very mournful and sing ballads to it,' said Meta.

'I could tell the neighbour's housekeeper,' said Polly, going towards the kitchen again. 'It's their fence too.'

'But she'll keep you there an hour,' Meta said, 'telling you her cousin's daughter has had three sets of triplets in four years and is quite *bowlegged* from carrying them.'

'Meta,' said Elizabeth. Her second daughter, who was nearly thirteen, had that fragile blend of precocity and innocence that was the gift of the young. You would never think of it as a gift until it was gone.

Pasley didn't have it.

She followed her daughters into the kitchen where there was a smell of burning.

'Cook's had a bit of an accident with the pan,' Bessie said. 'But it's all right – I've fed the children – I didn't want them going hungry.'

'Vinegar,' Elizabeth said.

'We're clean out of it. She's gone looking for some. At least that's what she said,' she added darkly. 'She's been missing all afternoon.'

It was Bessie's opinion that the new cook wasn't competent. But Elizabeth didn't want to get into an argument about her staff just now.

'I need to go to upstairs,' she said, passing Julia to her housekeeper, Hearn. Julia squawked in protest. But the headache that had been threatening since she'd left the prison was blooming now inside her skull. She had to hope it wouldn't be one of her unmanageable ones that meant she could only lie on her bed and moan.

'Shall I bring you some soup?' Bessie called after her, and Julia wailed 'Mammee!' as she left. So she felt guilty as well as unwell, climbing the stairs. Her daughters wanted her and all she could do was push them away.

She shut the door behind her, sat down on her bed, then gazed out of the window at the collapsed fence, their ragged lawn.

The garden like the rest of the house was small. Too small for them. When they had first moved in they'd had two girls and two servants. Now there were four girls and four servants. They needed a larger house. A bigger garden.

Then she remembered Pasley in her cell. She hadn't seen Pasley's cell but she could imagine it. She lay down on the bed feeling bruised, almost as though someone had punched her. Clouds of flies seemed to be swarming in her skull.

Why hadn't she asked more questions? The interview had been cut short by the dinner bell and the girl's distress but there were things Elizabeth needed to know.

Why had she left Mrs Digby's shop? Was it because of the doctor, or was there another reason?

Could her mother be contacted at all?

Did she have any other relatives?

How skilled was she with the needle?

She must establish that if she was going to find employment for her . . .

She remembered Pasley's wrists, brittle as twigs. She felt a pang thinking about them, a perilous qualm.

Thomas was bound to ask her how she'd gone on when they next met, whether there was anything she might do.

Ah, Thomas, what have you got me into?

Bessie tapped on the door. 'Soup's ready,' she said.

'I'm not hungry.'

'Are you poorly?'

'No, I'm quite well, thank you.'

'I've lit the fire in the parlour for when you come down.'

Elizabeth closed her eyes briefly. 'In a minute,' she said. There was a silence during which she could practically hear Bessie's disapproval through the door, then her footsteps retreated. Elizabeth made no attempt to move. From this angle, through the window she could see only sky.

Sometimes, as a child in her aunt's house, she had stared out of the window like this. Gazing until her mind emptied itself and everything she looked at was strange.

She was startled by another tap on the door. 'I'm *coming*,' she said, thinking it was Bessie again or Hearn their housekeeper. The door opened anyway, with the gentlest click.

'What is it?' she said, sitting up.

Light, soft footsteps, then Florence was standing beside her. She rested her small weight against Elizabeth's shoulder.

'Flossie,' Elizabeth said.

Florence continued to lean.

She would lean on her mother like this when she was writing, imagining, Elizabeth supposed, that if she didn't speak it wasn't an interruption. Usually it was because she was fretting over something and needed comfort. Now, however, Florence was trying to comfort her.

'I was just resting,' she said.

Florence's head drooped against hers. Elizabeth sighed but didn't try to move her. Flossie would never settle if she thought something was wrong.

'Shouldn't you be practising the piano?'

Silence.

'I'm not ill, you know – I've just got a bit of a headache. I'll come down soon.'

Florence lifted her hand. On it was a glove puppet of a bear. 'Mammee Bear sad.'

Goldilocks was her favourite story. She never tired of playing baby bear. Julia was always Goldilocks and Florence was Baby Bear. Which was odd, considering that Julia was the youngest. But Julia was more adventurous, happy to explore the wild wood, Florence never wanted to leave her family.

'I'm not—' But the tiny paw of the glove puppet patted her face; she hadn't realised she'd been crying.

'Oh, Flossie—' She submitted to having her face patted all over, turning it from one side to the other. 'What would I do without you?'

Florence's eyes, grey with tiny golden speckles near the pupil, gazed earnestly into her own. 'I'm *here*,' she said, as though there was no question of her ever being anywhere else.

Of all her children, Elizabeth worried most about this one. She slipped her arm around her. What wouldn't she do to protect this fragile child?

Impulsively she clasped her face. 'Flossie, my love,' she said, 'don't let anyone ever treat you badly. You mustn't - will you?'

She saw the surprise in Flossie's eyes. Incomprehension. But she nodded solemnly. Elizabeth held her tightly, almost crushing her. She was frightening her daughter. Flossie didn't understand, how could she?

Elizabeth prayed she would never learn there were men in the world like the doctor, women like Mrs Digby or Pasley's mother. But however hard she prayed it wouldn't be enough. She couldn't protect her. Three of her children had died. She hadn't been able to protect them. And no one had even tried to protect Pasley.

Tears threatened again but Florence took hold of her finger and tugged it. 'Come down,' she said, and Elizabeth allowed herself to be led from the room.

The parlour was unnaturally quiet. Polly was drooping over an unopened piano, Meta was staring out of the window and even Julia seemed subdued, curled into a chair. Elizabeth felt a pang of guilt.

'What's all this?' she said. No one answered.

'This won't do!' she said. 'Polly, I thought you were practising the Arabian piece - come on now - Meta, you can be the princess - Julia, baby, come and sit on Mammee's knee.'

For a moment she thought Meta might object, but then saw a light in her eye - she loved to dress up. She tweaked the antimacassar from the back of a chair and wrapped it into a turban around her head.

'Shall I dance?' she asked.

'Of course!' said Elizabeth. 'Let's move the furniture. Polly, why aren't you playing?'

Flossie brought her a cushion to sit on and Julia immediately climbed onto her knee. 'You have to keep still,' Florence told her. 'Mammee's not well.'

'I'm fine,' Elizabeth said firmly. If there was one thing she believed in, it was that you had to make happiness happen. You had to light a spark in the gloom or it would swallow you whole.

Julia rested her head against Elizabeth's chest and began sucking her thumb, which of course she wasn't allowed to do, but for once Elizabeth didn't object.

Meta tugged the table to one side then clapped her hands. 'Play!' she commanded.

Polly played and Meta twirled, waving her arms like snakes. Flossie clapped and Elizabeth sat back, stroking Julia's hair and laughing as Polly's piece altered seamlessly into a version of *Sing a Song of Sixpence* with exotic flourishes added in.

Outside the sky darkened; yellow leaves shook rain onto the window.

She had all this, she thought, her daughters, her husband, her house. She was sometimes afraid, impossibly afraid, that they would be taken from her.

Sometimes she could sense her other three children looking on. How bright the room would seem to them, like a small candle floating in infinite darkness.

But that was nonsense; her children were all here, her lovely, brilliant daughters; Polly playing with comic relish and Meta clumping around the room like an Arabian elephant.

Elizabeth clapped along with Flossie, then tugged Julia's thumb gently from her mouth and made her clap too. Everyone was happy when just moments before they'd been so sad. She believed her daughters' happiness was her responsibility, although William didn't.

But as she'd often told him, there was more than one way of fighting the evils of the world.

Still, she felt a little guilty for laughing. What did Pasley have to laugh about?

But she would change all that. Or at least she would do her best. Once the girls were in bed she would write to Miss Jopson again, asking for a longer visit next time. And to her friends, to begin the process of finding a place for Pasley to go.

CHAPTER 5

OH, THE FLURRY of getting everyone to chapel that Sunday! Julia had a cough that kept her awake all night so she stayed behind with Bessie. Meta didn't want to get up at all.

William left early. It was his habit to walk to Cross St in order to think over his sermon. So Elizabeth assembled their daughters with Hearn's help. Now they were lodged in their seats, with Elizabeth at one end and Hearn at the other. Jim, who had brought them, sat at the back.

The chapel was designed so that everyone had a good view of the pulpit and no one member of the congregation was seen to be more important than another. There was the usual bustle of people settling into seats, standing up again to let more people in. Then a hush of anticipation as William stepped onto the platform.

Her husband looked around the assembly with his dark, benign gaze. He waited until a spate of coughing ceased then said, 'Today my text is from Proverbs. *Possessing wisdom is better than gold, understanding, better than silver.*'

He was campaigning again for the new library, the first free public library in England which would open in Manchester. But most people had donated already, and there were some who said it would bring nothing but trouble. There they were, in fact, Councillors Acker and Strutt.

'*Without vision the people perish.*'

Elizabeth felt a spark of appreciation for him as he stood there, so free from doubt. It was almost enough to take the chill from the great room, which the tall candles with their wavering flames could not.

Outside there was an impenetrable gloom, a bitter, smoking cold.

The perpetual fog of Manchester crept in beneath the door of the chapel, through chinks in the window frames.

It's an ill wind that blows no one any good, Hearn was fond of saying. *And that's what we've got in Manchester – an ill wind.*

This after bringing in the sheets, which were dirtier than before she'd washed them, she said, streaked with grime.

'—with sight we see the world,' William was saying, 'but with vision we can change it . . .'

Meta sneezed. The whole family would doubtless get Julia's cough. Flossie was already drooping. Hearn put an arm around her, smiling ruefully at Elizabeth.

Elizabeth scanned the rows looking for people she might approach about Pasley.

The Mayor of Manchester, John Potter, was in his usual seat, glancing round to assess the level of support. He was a plump man with luxuriant hair and a fixed and perturbing gaze. The Free Public Library was his project, and he had embroiled William in it. Although truthfully, William had needed little persuasion.

Perhaps the Mayor could return the favour and do something for Pasley?

But the Mayor was said to keep a notorious woman in an apartment not far from his family home. Would Pasley be safe with him?

Behind the Mayor sat the Davenports with their fifteen children. Elizabeth smiled at them but her smile faded as she saw Edward Taylor of the Manchester Guardian, who'd been so critical of *Mary Barton* when it first came out.

Perhaps, even so, she could approach him about Pasley? He could advertise her plight, although he would have to be careful not to incriminate her in any way . . .

To the right of Mr Taylor Susanna Winkworth gazed at William with a fixed and sombre attention. Susanna was thin and sallow, with slightly equine features. No one would describe her as attractive, although she had wonderfully abundant hair. And was quite brilliant, William had said.

Once Elizabeth had overheard Susanna saying she wouldn't marry anyone if she couldn't marry Mr Gaskell. But she gave her time freely to the Sunday School and had been fervent in her support of *Mary Barton*. Also, her sister Emily taught Polly the piano . . .

Behind Susanna sat Mrs Carver from the Mission for the Destitute Devout in black silk and next to her was Mrs Fairlie (*Mrs Fairly-hard-done-by*, as William called her) in an irreproachable black serge. She ran the Home for Orphan Girls (born in wedlock) on the other side of the river. Both of them could be approached about Pasley. On the row behind was Mrs Hudson of the Dressmakers and Milliners' Association, who might also be useful, and next to her in the mauve poplin that did nothing for her complexion was her niece, Angelina, who was woefully plain and had been in love with William since she was a little girl.

Why would she not love him, this handsome, courteous man, who was unfailingly kind to her? Elizabeth should tell him to be less kind.

All these ladies were in the baking circle begun by Elizabeth. After the service they would bring the biscuits for Elizabeth to take to Sunday School and she would ask them about Pasley, whether there was anything they might do.

'Look around you,' William urged. 'There are people lying in the streets and alleys, in doorways and slums that reek of damp and despair. While others walk past, blind to their suffering, hardening their hearts against their fellow man . . . '

Elizabeth could see people thinking, *Not me, that doesn't apply to me.*

'But the righteous see with the eyes of God, with compassion, and mercy.'

That bit would apply to them, of course.

'I'm cold,' Flossie complained on being nudged awake by Meta. Hearn hushed her, tucking her cloak around her.

They were attracting glances. The congregation often seemed more interested in Elizabeth than her husband. What she wore, how she behaved, how her girls behaved, whether she yawned during the sermon, how active she was in church events (a particular controversy). No matter what she did, how hard she tried, there was a continuous murmur about her in and out of church.

When her book had come out last year the murmur had risen to a roar. Even though she'd published it anonymously the news had broken within weeks. Everyone in the congregation had bought a copy of *Mary Barton*, or at least the men did. It was their job after all to read it first and decide whether it was suitable for their wives.

Several of them had said William shouldn't have allowed her to write it.

'I suggested it,' he told them. As indeed he had.

'A new society needs vision, not blindness . . .'

Not everyone wanted a new society, of course. Councillor Acker was looking around for support now. Elizabeth sat back before his glance could fall on her.

Meta was pulling hideous faces at Flossie to make her laugh. Elizabeth frowned at her but was distracted by her husband stepping down from the platform.

'A new society,' he said, walking into the congregation, 'where the wolf can dwell with the lamb, the leopard with the kid. I doubt Isaiah was thinking about Manchester when he had his vision,' he said, raising an appreciative titter from the Misses Evans, two sisters who had inherited an immense library of books from their father along with an injunction not to read any of them.

'But nonetheless, it is here, in this city, that Isaiah's vision could be realised.' He stopped in front of Justice Day, known as Judgement Day to friends and foes alike. 'This city could be our New Jerusalem, filled with knowledge, as the waters cover the sea!'

Justice Day's long face seemed to lengthen further as William moved on to Councillor Strutt, who had said publicly that the poor could not benefit from education any more than beasts could. 'The poor need knowledge as much as the rich,' William said as the councillor scowled at him. 'If not more so.'

Don't overdo it, William, Elizabeth had told him, but he was fearless. And entirely unselfconscious. He had a kind of innocence that was almost dangerous, she sometimes thought. He was oblivious, for instance, to the kindling of Angelina or Susanna as he passed them, to the tremulous fervour of the Misses Evans in front of whom he now stood.

The Misses Evans, although devoted to William and to the library *in principle*, had raised concerns about whether it was entirely safe for ladies to frequent the same public space as labouring men. Or any men, if it came to it. 'The work of great writers and philosophers of the world must be freely available to everyone – men, women, children, of all classes,' he told them, 'to lighten their darkness.' The Misses Evans beamed at him with a single smile.

Now he stood in front of Councillor Acker. The old alderman sat up very straight as though braced for attack. 'For while knowledge can change our minds only vision can change our hearts. And it is our hearts that need to change.' He put his hand on the alderman's chest and a small shock rippled through the congregation.

Hearn glanced at Elizabeth and Elizabeth looked away. Obviously there would be trouble. Equally obviously, it would be her job to defend her husband.

Happily he seemed to have finished. He left the aldermen bristling in their seats and returned to the pulpit. Everyone stood to sing the final hymn, one of William's own. *A Sure Stronghold Our God is He.*

Their voices were raised in an approximation of harmony as they had been in congregations all over the world for nearly two thousand years. Everywhere the same discordant notes, the lagging rhythms, the single voice raised above all the others and entirely out of key. She felt an unexpected affection for it, this flawed unison; *accept, O Lord, our imperfections.*

The last note was drawn out to a quivering, inharmonious end and the last prayer was said. As wife of the minister, Elizabeth was first to stand. Then Hearn led Polly, Meta and Flossie towards the door where Jim was waiting. People rose to let them pass then began moving into the aisles, forming clusters that Elizabeth had to navigate.

But she couldn't navigate far because Councillor Acker stood in her way.

'I don't appreciate being put on show, Mrs Gaskell.'

'I'm sorry?'

'You know my position.'

She did. This was the man who had harangued her in chapel about *fomenting discord* between master and man when her novel came out. *I know I'm right*, he'd said.

How very gratifying for you, she'd replied and walked away.

She couldn't walk away now since he was at the end of the row. Elizabeth glanced towards William but he was embroiled with the Mayor.

'I'm sure there's room for more than one position,' she said.

Don't let him drag you into an argument, William had said. *And whatever you do, don't let him get started on his childhood.*

'When I were a lad,' Councillor Acker said, 'there were nine of us in a stinking room by the tannery. We had rainwater leaking in through the roof, and river water seeping under't door! Not one of us knew what a book were. If we'd've had a book, we'd've used it to stuff the gaps!'

The problem with the self-made man, William had once said, *is that he makes himself very badly.*

But she couldn't see William and the Mayor had moved on to Justice Day.

'What use are words to a starving man?' Councillor Acker was saying. 'If he were drowning, would you hold out a dictionary and read him the meaning of 'wet'? No. It's wages and houses that are needed – not words.'

'They're not mutually exclusive, surely?' Elizabeth said, a little waspishly. 'It is possible to have a home *and* books.'

But Councillor Acker hadn't finished.

'If you educate a poor man what do you get? Someone who sees what a bad deal he's got - that's what—'

'Mrs Fairlie!' Elizabeth said.

'There you are,' said Mrs Fairlie. 'I've got three boxes of biscuits for the Sunday School. Will you take them or will I get Mrs Egerton to drop them off?'

'Excuse me,' Elizabeth said to Councillor Acker, squeezing past the indignant alderman. 'How is the refuge?' she asked, and Mrs Fairlie launched into a tale of overcrowding, unpredictable supplies, *girls of uncertain character and temperament.*

'Is there any room at all?'

'We make room, Mrs Gaskell. Needs must when the devil rides, as they say.'

'Could you take one more resident, after Christmas?'

'Who did you have in mind?'

'A young girl - sixteen years old. Born in wedlock,' she added, hopefully.

'Can she work?'

'She's a trained seamstress.'

'Where's she working now?'

Elizabeth hesitated. 'She's been very unfortunate - very badly used. She is at present in the New Bailey—'

'I see!'

'But if you knew her story—'

'They've all got stories Mrs Gaskell. Make your heart bleed and your hair curl.'

Elizabeth tried a different approach. 'You must have many girls who've suffered misfortune—'

'That I have Mrs Gaskell. That's why I try to take on the ones of good character and not expose them to corrupting influences.'

'But I believe she is of good character.'

'No doubt you do. But one good person in prison's like a drop of rainwater in a muddy puddle. They can't help but be polluted - you'll see.'

'Should we not try to help them?'

'Good intentions, Mrs Gaskell – we all know where they lead.'

Elizabeth felt a rising exasperation. 'This girl has nothing. And no one. It seems very wrong to leave her on the streets, where she can be preyed upon – or worse – by incorrigible criminals.'

'There's always the Reformatory. I don't want my girls exposing to dangerous influences. They're restive enough already.'

Really? Elizabeth thought of saying. *On their diet?* But just then Mrs Kirkby-Wilkes walked by.

'Mrs Kirby-Wilkes,' she said, 'I hear you're looking for a maid?'

'I will be,' Mrs Kirkby-Wilkes said, 'Sophie is leaving after Christmas to look after her mother.'

'You won't be looking in prison,' Mrs Fairlie said.

'Prison?' said Mrs Kirkby-Wilkes.

'Thank you, Mrs Fairlie,' Elizabeth said, glaring at her.

'I'm just saying. You know Mrs Fetherington took in a prison girl out of the softness of her heart and the next thing you know, she'd let in her accomplices and the whole place was stripped – not an ounce of silver or brass left in it! No good deed goes unpunished, that's what I always say.'

'This girl is not like that,' Elizabeth said firmly. 'I would swear to her good character myself. What have we come to,' she said to Mrs Kirkby-Wilkes, 'if we can't give people a chance?'

'We need someone with experience . . .'

'What about a laundry maid?' Elizabeth persisted. The Kirkby-Wilkes had nine children who must produce a prodigious degree of washing, but Mrs Kirkby-Wilkes was backing away.

'We have a maid for the laundry,' she said. 'I'm not looking for anyone just at the moment – and when I do I will use the traditional channels.'

She disappeared into a tangle of people, gliding serenely despite the nine children and a husband who, it was rumoured, tended to stray. Elizabeth, with only four daughters, often found it difficult even to get out of the door with her hair pinned up and her corsets laced. She'd always admired Mrs Kirby-Wilkes but she wasn't entirely surprised by her response. She was disappointed in herself if anything. She would have to do better for Pasley than this.

She looked around the remaining congregation but Mrs Hudson had already gone and Mrs Carver was leaving. Mrs Egerton, however, was approaching her with a defensive smile, her daughter barely visible behind three large boxes. 'Mrs Gaskell, I do hope we can count on your assistance at the Charity Fair,' she said.

Elizabeth looked blank.

'For the Benefit of Abandoned Infants,' Mrs Egerton reminded her. 'This Thursday. You did say you were free,' she added.

She surely hadn't said that, she was never free. But she would need someone on her side for Pasley's sake.

'I'm sure I can make an appearance,' she said and Mrs Egerton's smile grew warm. 'The Committee will be so pleased,' she said. 'Lucilla, go with Mrs Gaskell now – she'll need help carrying these.'

'Jim will take them,' Elizabeth said, relieving Mrs Egerton's daughter of two of the boxes. The Sunday School was half a mile away – she would be late if she didn't set off soon.

She felt a little discouraged by the response so far, but there were other people she could try.

She hadn't failed, she reminded herself. She just hadn't succeeded yet.

CHAPTER 6

THAT WEEK ELIZABETH wrote to six of her friends about Pasley and to Miss Jopson to request a longer visit, as well as to ask about Pasley's remaining family. She also requested that Pasley should be medically examined before her discharge *to ensure she was fit for employment.* She had to assume that Miss Jopson, familiar with all kinds of girls and their conditions, would understand what she meant. It would hardly do to find a position for her and then discover she was pregnant or ill.

At the Charity Fair she spoke to Mrs Hudson, a small, permanently worried woman whose flamboyant dress sense suggested a different kind of personality altogether.

It wasn't easy to speak to her, partly because of the press of people and partly because Mrs Hudson appeared to be avoiding her. Evidently word had got out, courtesy of Mrs Fairlie and Mrs Kirkby-Wilkes, and she had to pursue Mrs Hudson around the hall before cornering her next to a display of *Hat Trimmings and Essential Accessories.*

'Mrs Hudson,' Elizabeth said, 'what a splendid stall.'

Mrs Hudson looked for an avenue of escape. 'Yes, thank you,' she said. 'We've been so busy – you can't imagine – I've hardly had time for anything . . .'

'Not too busy for a quiet word, I hope?'

'Well—'

'Because you're just the person I was hoping to see. I'm hoping you'll be able to help me.'

'Ah—'

'I need to speak to you about a young girl – a dressmaker by trade, who has been sadly abused. An innocent girl, corrupted by those who should have cared for her and in whom she placed her trust—'

'I don't think—'

'—You and I know, Mrs Hudson, the kind of dangers this industry exposes young girls to by paying so little, forcing them to live in poverty—'

'Mrs Gaskell—'

'It's hardly surprising if some of them fall by the wayside – it's more wonderful that any of them survive. And the ones who do fall, Mrs Hudson, surely they deserve a helping hand?'

Mrs Hudson stared at the floor. But when she did reply it was with a quiet intensity.

'Mrs Fairlie told me you would try to speak to me,' she said, 'to inveigle me into some course of action that could be harmful not only to me but to the girls in my care. Who are trying so hard, Mrs Gaskell, to improve their standing in the community.'

She looked up and Elizabeth saw that colour had flared erratically from her neck to her cheeks. She was taken aback by this unexpected force of feeling in someone so diffident, but managed to say, 'That's not quite fair—'

'It's not *quite fair*, Mrs Gaskell, to expect me to associate my girls with someone who can only add to their burden of disrepute.'

Elizabeth felt colour flaming in her own cheeks. 'What happened to this girl is hardly her fault. The *burden of disrepute*, as you call it, belongs to those whose reputation remains untarnished – because of attitudes such as yours.'

'It's not my attitude, Mrs Gaskell, as you well know. It's an attitude that exists – that they must struggle against every day. How will it look for them if someone from that—' she lowered her voice, 'infamous institution is taken into their midst?'

'It might look as if they were standing by a person in need.'

'I warn my girls every day of the terrible consequences of straying from the path. They know there's no hope for them if they do. So it would hardly be useful to show them that the consequences are not very terrible – if someone can wander and be so easily reclaimed.'

Elizabeth was rendered speechless by this logic and Mrs Hudson took the opportunity to say, 'Now, I have a customer to attend to.'

And she turned away, wrapping some ribbons for a large lady in a fur cloak. Elizabeth could tell she would get no further with her – she had the stubborn quality of the weak person who is easily frightened.

But it was disheartening, and she was further disheartened when she returned home and read her post. Mrs Fletcher-Davies thanked her for thinking of them but they had already found a maid. The Staffords were trying to reduce the number of servants they had now their daughter was married and their son had gone to Oxford. Elizabeth had heard that her relatives, the Hollands, were away, so she wouldn't hear from them immediately. That still left three people who had not responded. She wondered whether they would.

Then there was Miss Jopson's letter. Elizabeth could hear the reproving tone as she read it.

The girl has been examined as requested, although it was much against her liking. She has been found well and in a fit condition to leave.

Presumably not pregnant then or suffering from some dreadful disease.

But how thorough had the examination been?

Miss Jopson said Elizabeth could spend a little longer with the prisoner this time, *although she must be free to attend evening prayers, as I'm sure you, of all people, will appreciate.* Elizabeth felt a prickle of resentment at this assumption, at all the assumptions, in fact, that people made about the wife of a minister.

The Matron included the address of the orphanage in Dublin where Pasley had stayed and said it was her understanding that while Pasley's mother was her nearest relative, there was also an uncle. Neither he nor the mother had visited Pasley in prison. Miss Jopson gave an address for Pasley's uncle but said he was often away. It seemed almost certain that Pasley's mother no longer lived at the address Pasley had for her, so any attempt to contact her would be futile.

She gave Pasley's birthdate as 11th July 1833.

The letter quivered in Elizabeth's hand. She had to hold onto the back of a chair.

On 10th July 1833 she'd given birth to a still-born baby girl.

She'd been so exhausted from her long labour that it had taken her some moments to register the silence in the room.

Then she had.

She remembered saying querulously, *where is it?* As if she were talking about a bag or a book she'd misplaced. She'd insisted on holding her, on seeing the tiny face with its expression of profound concentration, as if she was trying to remember something she'd forgotten.

She'd forgotten to live.

Then they had taken her away, her baby, and the long process of grieving had begun. It had never finished it seemed. The date on the letter pierced her like an arrow.

When Polly was born a year later she'd felt such fear and dread because her living child might suddenly cease to breathe.

'You're all alone,' William said, startling her.

She turned quickly.

'What's the matter?' he asked at once.

'Oh,' she said, her voice not quite steady, 'it's nothing. It's just—' she wouldn't tell him about the date in the letter. He always insisted they should be able to talk about anything, no subject should be forbidden between them. But over the years she'd learned that he would not talk about their lost children, that dangerous grief.

'How can it be,' she said, her voice cracking a little, 'that some people are so alone in the world without anyone to look after them?'

'Lily,' he said, coming closer, but she withdrew from him so he sat down instead on the arm of the chair. He glanced at the prison stamp on the letter and said, 'You mustn't let it distress you.'

This from the man who had wept in her arms over the families he'd visited; the cellar rooms running with rats, the half-naked children, the parents who were too drunk to realise their baby had died.

'How can I not?' she said, wishing she could steady her voice.

'Because you won't be any use otherwise.'

'It seems to me,' she said, 'that the world is full of people who aren't distressed enough by the suffering in it.'

He bowed his head. 'Even so, we have to learn to accept the limitations of what we can do.'

No one did more than William, campaigned harder, gave up his time. Which, he always said, was more valuable than money. But the more he did, the more he was aware of what he couldn't do. It wasn't fair – none of it was fair.

'Why is it that some people are born to suffering and misfortune?'

'We're not Calvinists,' he said gently. 'We don't believe that anyone is born to anything – except to life.'

My baby, she thought, *wasn't born to life*.

'We believe we can make a difference,' William said, 'and therefore we must.'

'But what if we can't?'

'Then we accept our limitations and move on.'

'There are so many limitations.'

'I know.'

How could he stand it? After their son had died they were both ravaged by grief, but he had immersed himself in work whereas she'd been barely able to get out of bed.

Once he'd said to her that at least now he was able to understand what the poor went through, losing so many of their children. Something in the shared experience had given him the strength to go on.

In her secret heart she'd not forgiven him for that.

'But sometimes,' he was saying, 'we do make a difference. Look at Millie Powler.'

Millie Powler came from a family of slum-dwellers, seven of them huddled in one cellar room. The father was dying, the older brother was injured in the brain, beyond employment. But Millie, the oldest girl, now taught classes in their Sunday School.

'But for every single person we help,' she said, 'another ten or fifty spring up in their place.'

What was God doing, the voice inside her demanded querulously, *allowing it all to go on?*

He lifted his hands. 'I can't explain the problem of suffering.'

They had reached the point they had reached before, a kind of wall between them, because he accepted the mystery while she still wanted explanations.

She changed the subject before it got too raw. 'I promised to make a shopping list for Bessie,' she said, moving away. But he caught her hand.

'We do our best,' he said. 'That's all we can do.'

She felt a strange tremor as he said it, a moment of recoil. But she would do her best for the girl, of course she would. It was her duty to help others.

She hadn't spoken to him about Pasley, she'd hardly seen him all week. And she couldn't talk about it now, with the letter and Pasley's birthdate still in her hand. She managed to smile at him. 'Will you eat with us tonight at least?' she said, because for four out of the past five evenings he'd been out, helping to train young workers for the ministry. Free of charge, of course.

'I will,' he said. 'I'm hoping you will be very merry and entertaining.'

'Of course!' Elizabeth said, smiling brilliantly. 'Aren't we always?'

CHAPTER 7

LATER THAT WEEK rain crystallised into tiny whirling flakes that grew fatter and splashed wetly into the windows.

Julia woke everyone up, screaming with excitement, while Florence flattened herself against the windowpane in the bedroom, watching the transformation with quiet delight. Elizabeth dressed as quickly as she could by the fire in her room. Hearn came in bringing an extra flannel petticoat. They exchanged sympathetic looks but didn't speak. Elizabeth thought her teeth might chatter if she tried.

She felt a weight of dread about visiting the prison again.

She hadn't got any further in her efforts to help Pasley. The Greens had arrived unexpectedly from Knutsford. They were passing through Manchester on their way to visit an aunt and had left their two daughters with Elizabeth because Polly and Meta had begged them to. Then William had come home with a Dutch minister and his wife. He'd invited them to dinner without mentioning that they were *vegetarian* - they took no meat or fish of any kind. Elizabeth's cook had looked at her as if she'd said they'd come from the moon, and finally served up a dish of (frankly, terrible) soup made from turnips and grated potato. Afterwards William and the young minister, whose name was Aart, had so much to discuss that it was too late for them to leave. Elizabeth told Bessie to make up the spare room. They didn't have a spare room, of course, so this was accomplished by making all the girls sleep together, and none of them slept at all.

The Greens didn't need a maid themselves but had promised to ask everyone they knew. The Dutch minister's wife looked terrified at the idea of taking on a servant, though Elizabeth hadn't even mentioned the prison. Their servants came with the manse, she'd whispered finally, as if that settled it.

In between guests Elizabeth had written to the orphanage in Dublin, receiving a reply almost immediately from a Mrs Stringer. Mrs Stringer had come to the school after Pasley had left and didn't remember her personally, but believed her to be *of a reasonable intelligence and moderately dutiful, although prone to certain fixed and intemperate passions.*

What did that mean? Was she referring to her attachment to the teaching assistant, Miss Vivienne? Surely the poor girl would become attached to anyone who was kind to her . . .

Miss Vivienne, apparently, had left two years ago to get married.

Elizabeth had hoped to obtain a favourable reference from her for Pasley, something to help her obtain a situation. But since Mrs Stringer hadn't even mentioned Miss Vivienne's surname Elizabeth would have to write again to ask.

As for Pasley's family, Mrs Stringer had no recollection of anyone ever visiting or enquiring about the girl before Mrs Gaskell herself. Which confirmed what Elizabeth had already heard.

It was little enough information to go on. She would have to tell Pasley she was still trying, which was true, and still hopeful, which was less so. But she would have to offer some small crumb of comfort in exchange for making the poor girl talk about things she would doubtless rather not.

The white flakes dissolved into a freezing drizzle as the carriage jogged through the Manchester streets. Jim changed direction twice – to avoid a dray that had capsized, its cargo of barrels spilling into the road and releasing a yeasty odour, and again because a drain had burst, brown water gushing across the street and into the cellars. In which, Elizabeth knew, entire families were packed together with barely enough room to stand. Already their meagre belongings were floating towards the river.

So they were unable to avoid the town centre where the boom

and judder of the factories shook the pavements and the mournful shrieks of sirens followed them like lost souls. Jim said nothing but she sensed tension rising from him as they passed through a maze of narrow streets. There were people watching behind the boarded windows, gangs who lived in the tunnels. If Tommy stumbled or the carriage toppled they would come swarming out like rats from a drain.

She shouldn't think like that, William wouldn't approve. Neither would he approve of her travelling so close to the Deansgate Rookeries, as they were called. Even the police didn't go there.

Now Jim was steering the carriage along a dark passage so full of potholes that it lurched and bounced, flinging her from one side to the other.

'I'm right sorry Ma'am,' he said, 'we'll be through in a jiffy.'

Elizabeth clung to the sides of the carriage until they came to the road where a bitter chemical tang from the river stung her eyes and the back of her throat.

No wonder so many of their friends had left!

She would talk William again about moving to the countryside. She wouldn't be put off any more by his objections about work or the distance he would have to travel. She'd already written to her publisher, Edward Chapman, to enquire about the sales of her novel. She suspected he owed her money and she wanted it before Christmas if possible. It would be sent to William of course, but she would tell him it must go towards the new house. And another carriage if necessary, so he could travel in.

As they lurched onto the bridge over the river Elizabeth could see the shadows of the New Bailey like a silent army on the other side and felt a qualm. She should be thinking about Pasley, not the new house, but her mind was quite blank as though all her thoughts had been jolted out of it. She couldn't imagine what she might say, or how the girl might respond, but it was too late to go back now. Already Jim was pulling the carriage to a halt and getting out of his seat to help her down.

Once more Miss Jamieson led Elizabeth towards the atrium. It was empty this time. Elizabeth could hear the tap-tap-tap of their footsteps echoing and thought of all the girls and women behind the closed doors, listening to them.

The smell had changed to a faintly medical, detergent scent with a tang of lime. But Miss Jamieson hadn't changed, she was silent and impassive as ever. Elizabeth studied her curved shoulders, wondering how to start a conversation. It was hard to tell how old the wardress was; she could be anywhere from twenty to forty, but Elizabeth could hardly ask that.

'Have you worked here long?' she ventured.

No reply. Perhaps she hadn't heard. Elizabeth wondered where the wardress lived. The slums immediately surrounding the prison were hardly fit for any respectable woman.

'Do you live nearby?' she enquired and thought she heard a small grunt. 'I suppose it might be good to walk to work before beginning a shift,' she continued as the wardress opened a door. 'My husband always prefers to walk to chapel – he says it helps him think.'

Miss Jamieson stopped abruptly, unhooking a key from the enormous bunch hanging from her belt. Light streamed behind her from a window at the end of the corridor so Elizabeth couldn't read the expression on her face, but there was no mistaking the hostility of her tone.

'I don't *walk* in Ma'am,' she said. '*This* is where I board.'

Elizabeth should have known that. Many of the female warders had no homes to go to and couldn't afford to lodge elsewhere; the prison was their home.

So Miss Jamieson was as much a prisoner as Pasley, more so even since Pasley's term in prison would end but the wardress had no prospect of ever leaving. That explained the hostility, even the contempt, for those who came and went freely. But it didn't excuse her rudeness, Elizabeth thought. Her glance fell on the wardress' hand, which was chapped, the finger joints inflamed.

'Chilblains are so painful, especially at this time of year,' she said. Miss Jamieson moved her hand quickly out of sight.

'My housekeeper used to suffer from them terribly,' Elizabeth went on, walking through the door, 'but then she invented her own concoction – lavender and mustard.'

Miss Jamieson moved past her without comment or response.

'It sounds horrid but it's really quite effective. I keep telling her she should patent it. I could bring you a small bottle if you like?'

Antagonism rose like smoke from the wardress's shoulders. She muttered something in response.

'I'm sorry?' Elizabeth said.

Miss Jamieson stopped beside one of the doors towards the end of the corridor that was in every respect identical to the others.

'That won't be necessary *Ma'am*,' she said, looking at the door rather than Elizabeth. Then she added, 'This is the prisoner's cell.'

The prisoner, Elizabeth thought, not 'Pasley' or even 'the girl'. It occurred to her that she mustn't make it harder for Pasley – she and Miss Jamieson would have to reach some kind of truce.

'Mrs Gaskell to see you,' the wardress said, pushing the door open and there was a soft, quick sound of movement.

Suddenly self-conscious, Elizabeth entered the cell. Pasley stood beside a table with a pile of yarn on it. A long strand dangled over the side as though she'd just dropped it. Her hands were clasped in front of her apron and she didn't look up. Once again Elizabeth was struck by her thinness, her fragility.

She took in everything about the cell at once: a small window, a plank bed with a thin mattress and a chamber pot beneath, the table with yarn on it, a chair, a shelf with a Bible, a tin mug and bowl. The walls were of whitewashed brick, though in parts the wash had flaked off and the brick showed through. There were signs of damp in one corner, a mottled stain beneath the window and the floorboards were bare.

Elizabeth knew the New Bailey had adopted the system of separate confinement. Prisoners were kept alone all day apart from a single hour for exercise and evening prayers in the chapel. They might be called upon to do a shift in the kitchens or the washhouse but mainly they worked alone in their cells, unravelling thread or picking oakum.

The regime was meant to encourage remorse and reform rather than madness and despair. Elizabeth didn't know if it ever succeeded.

She began to unfasten her bonnet. Rain water dripped from the brim as she shook it. She cleared her throat to break the silence.

'I see you've been busy,' she said, nodding towards the yarn. Pasley didn't respond to this so she asked, 'Do you mind if I sit?' and Pasley's look darted quickly towards the chair. She moved to one side as Elizabeth went to it.

'But where will you sit?' Elizabeth said, arranging her skirts. 'I shouldn't like to keep you standing the whole time.'

Pasley glanced at Miss Jamieson then perched tentatively on the bed.

'I hope we'll have more time to talk today,' Elizabeth said. 'Privately,' she added when Miss Jamieson didn't move.

Pasley looked at her for the first time and for a moment Elizabeth didn't speak. Then she said, 'You've hurt yourself?'

'It's nothing,' Pasley whispered and at the same time Miss Jamieson said, 'She tripped.'

Elizabeth wanted to push Pasley's cap back and take a closer look at the bruise spreading from her forehead to her eye but she suppressed the impulse. 'Has it been looked at?'

When there was no answer she asked, 'Where did you trip?' and again there was a silence until Miss Jamieson said, 'On the kitchen stairs.'

'And you bumped your head?' Elizabeth said, because there seemed to be a cut above Pasley's eye, partially obscured by her cap. Once again Pasley didn't reply. 'Well,' Elizabeth continued, 'we will have to take better care of you.'

She directed this towards Miss Jamieson and the wardress shot her a look. Elizabeth said, 'I'm sure you must be anxious to return to your duties.'

Miss Jamieson started to say something but stopped. Then she said warningly, 'I'll be back to take her to evening prayers.'

'Of course,' Elizabeth said and Miss Jamieson hesitated, then nodded briefly and left. The door clanged softly behind her. Elizabeth was alone with Pasley.

She felt momentarily at a loss. Aware once more of the distance between them.

Well, she could say, *I dare say you're not very used to visitors*. Or, *what have you been doing all day?* Or, *How did you really hurt your head?*

None of these seemed possible. The last in particular might make Pasley retreat into silence.

Elizabeth peeled her gloves off then lifted her hands and dropped them again in a gesture that said, *Well, here we are,* and, *what shall we do next?* She made herself smile.

It was wasted on Pasley since she didn't look up.

Elizabeth's conversational skills seemed to have disappeared. She should be reassuring Pasley, encouraging her to talk. Her gaze flitted around the room to the Bible and the daily schedule pinned to the wall. She remembered that Pasley could read and write which wouldn't help her find employment as a maid. *Makes them uppity*, Mrs Fairlie would say. Perhaps Elizabeth should look into other forms of employment for her.

She glanced towards the window noting how high it was and said, 'You know, if this were my room, I think I would be tempted to put the chair beneath the window and climb up on it to see out.'

She was startled when Pasley spoke. 'There isn't much to see, Ma'am.'

So she had tried.

'You needn't call me Ma'am,' Elizabeth said. 'Mrs Gaskell will do.'

When Pasley made no response to this Elizabeth said, 'There must be something—'

Almost imperceptibly Pasley shook her head.

'What, no – ?' Elizabeth began but at the same time Pasley said, 'There's only the yard and the wall opposite.' She hesitated then said, 'Sometimes there's a moon.'

The moon was rarely seen in Manchester. It was barely possible to see the sun, which was why the street lamps were kept burning all day.

With how sad steps, O Moon, thou climb'st in the skies, Elizabeth thought. She could have recited the poem for Pasley but would that help? Instead she said, 'Do you know why I'm here?'

The girl nodded briefly, fear in the set of her shoulders.

'I'm here because – there are things I need to know – about you.'

Pasley closed her eyes and swallowed.

'I would like you to tell me everything that's happened – to bring you here. Otherwise I may not be able to help you. Do you understand?'

Pasley nodded again, her eyes still closed.

'Good. Because I want to find the perfect situation for you. A real home – where you will be looked after . . .'

Tears came from the girl's closed eyelids. Elizabeth leaned forward and touched Pasley's hand, which lay limply in her lap. She said gently, 'I'm here to help you, not to judge. You can tell me anything – anything at all.'

Pasley brushed a tear away with the heel of her hand. Elizabeth had to blink away her own tears – she never could bear seeing people weep. She said, 'I want you to think of me as – as a friend.'

But that was nonsense. How could she?

Would a friend be interrogating her?

What did she really need to know? Pasley's employers would certainly ask about her background – but did she need to know *everything*?

She tried again.

'Just – tell me everything you can.'

CHAPTER 8

Pasley

'TELL ME EVERYTHING,' she says. But how can I? I can't even look at her.

I look instead at her hands. They are not quite a lady's hands, I think. They are blunt and wrinkled, reddish around the knuckle as though she's been doing the wash. But of course she will not do the wash - she'll have a maid for that. There's an ink stain on her thumb - Miss Jamieson told me she's a writer! I never knew a lady could write books. But *a lady's hands are white and smooth as milk* - Mrs Fenton taught me that. She could tell in an instant which of her customers was a lady and which fabric they would buy. So I look next at the material of her skirt. It's a delaine which is not so fine as cashmere and a dull grey colour but with silvery threads running through. The weave is fine, but just where her little finger lies a small thread has come loose.

I could stitch that for her if I had a needle. Mrs Fenton said I was a marvel with the needle. She would hold my stitching up to the others and say, *there now - would you look at the magic in that!*

Mrs Gaskell is talking to me but I haven't heard a word. She repeats it for me.

'Do you understand why I need to ask you - certain things?'

I understand she needs to provide a good character for me, to say I am meek and biddable and full of sorrow for my misdeeds.

When I don't answer she leans forward so that her hair almost touches my cap.

'Pasley,' she says, very quiet, 'do you understand?'

I don't want her to think me an eejit so I nod without looking at her and she sits back again.

'Good,' she says. 'Then you see that you must tell me everything. Or at least, *something*.'

I look at her then because I think she may be mocking me. And indeed she's trying not to smile. 'I wouldn't like to have to make it up, after all,' she says. 'Even though I do write stories.'

What does she mean? What stories will she make up about me?

She says, 'It's not as though there aren't other things I would rather do. If someone asked me, for instance, whether I would rather go to a tea-party or for a walk in the countryside or even read in my room, I would probably not say, Oh no, I'd much rather visit Manchester's grimmest institution . . .'

Now she's really smiling and I can't help it, I start to smile back, then tuck it quickly away.

I'll knock that smile to the other side of your face, you little whore!

'There are people who might like to know why I would want to visit such a place and what should I tell them? That there was no reason for it and I learned nothing and came away no wiser than before? That would make me seem a little foolish. So, Pasley-whose-first-name-I-do-not-know, perhaps we can make a bargain. You tell me as much as you can and I won't press you for more.'

I always thought I couldn't tell anyone anything about me, the things I've done. And yet – she has a listening face. Pink-cheeked and as if she's always about to smile.

'Anything you do tell me will be our secret, I can promise you that.'

She's looking at me with her bright, bright eyes. She'll know if I'm lying. I mustn't lie.

But I can't tell her the truth.

'Take your time,' she says, and I stare at the floor again. Then, without warning, I start to shake. It happens sometimes. It begins in my knees. I press them down with my hands but they're shaking too.

At once she leaves her chair and sits beside me on my bed. She takes my hands in hers and It's all I can do not to snatch them back, they're so grimy and raw. 'Please don't—' she says.

I can't speak for the chattering of my teeth.

'Pasley,' she says, 'can you look at me?'

I can't. She's too bright, too real.

'Oh, Pasley,' she says, and there's a catch in her voice. I glance at her in surprise and see her eyes are quite pink. She presses my hands to her forehead and I can see her scalp where her hair is parted in an uneven line. There are greyish wisps either side of it.

Then she looks up into my eyes. I want to look away but I can't. Her eyes aren't blue as I thought but grey, with flecks of blue and green.

'I tell you what we'll do,' she murmurs. 'I'll ask you a question, and if you can you will answer me, but if you can't, or don't want to, all you have to do is shake your head and we'll move on. What do you think?'

I manage to nod.

'Good,' she says, squeezing my hands. Then she gets up a little stiffly, and sits on the chair again. She makes a great trouble of arranging her skirts.

She's nervous, I think, but that can't be right. Why would a lady such as she be nervous? Still, it makes me feel a little bolder. I've almost stopped shaking now.

She looks at the window, then the wall, then she says, 'Why don't you begin by telling me about the orphanage? Who took you there? Was it your mother?'

No.

She took me to my uncle, my father's brother. He had steel grey hair like a helmet. And a big nose, that my mother said was a Roman nose, like some old Roman used to own it. He lived in a house by the docks, which he rented because he was too mean to buy it, my mother said. And he never married because he wouldn't keep a wife.

I couldn't imagine anyone buying that house – it was the gloomiest place in the world.

You must be a good girl, she said. The memory causes my ribs to tighten like a great fist around my heart.

Mrs Gaskell is waiting so I whisper, 'She took me to my uncle's house in Dun Laoghaire.'

'And she left you with him?'

I nod.

I heard them talking in the hallway. He said, 'So you will leave her here like luggage?' and she said something, I couldn't hear what. He lowered his voice but I could still hear him. 'How can I take her? I'm not married – I'm rarely in the country. *You* should take her – you and your new husband!'

Take me where? I thought, but my mother started to weep. I crept forward because I couldn't bear her to cry. 'It will only be for a little while – until he gets used to the idea,' she said, 'and the place is said to be very good . . .'

My uncle nodded his head towards me and she stopped. She opened her arms as I ran to her, saying, 'I have to go away for a little while but I'll come back for you, I promise. You'll be a good girl for me, won't you?' And she held me very tight.

'Where?' I asked her. 'Where are you going?' But she was crying again. I would do anything to stop her crying, to make her smile.

I thought she was the prettiest lady in the world.

To Mrs Gaskell I say, 'My uncle took me to the orphanage.'

I didn't cry when he left me there. Only at the last moment I cried for my mother but the matron, Miss Tarleton, held me firmly and Miss Finney said my uncle wasn't to worry, I would settle in time. All the while he was backing away from me and my crying. And then he was gone and Miss Tarleton shook my shoulder hard and said,

Stop that foolishness at once!

Mrs Gaskell says, 'Did you make friends there with the other girls?'

They called me the Watcher.

She's waiting for her ship to come in, aren't you, Pasley?

Maybe she's looking for her husband.

For the devil to ride up in his big black carriage and snatch her away.

But I knew my mother was coming back for me. All I had to do was wait.

Mrs Gaskell says, 'You did well there, I believe, at your lessons. You liked your teacher – Miss Vivienne?'

She was the only one who allowed us to call her by her first name, which I thought very pretty. She was pretty too. She had dark, curling hair that smelled of rosewater. She didn't make fun of me for watching at the window. Once when I stood there past dark, instead of scolding me or sending me to bed she sat with me and lit a lamp and began to read. It was a story about robins, I think – I don't remember it, just the sound of her voice and the shadows made by the lamp and the long pale road outside.

'Ah,' Mrs Gaskell says when I tell her Miss Vivienne used to read to me. 'It's such a comforting thing to be read to! My aunt used to read to me and I always read to my daughters – even the older ones. Sometimes we all sit together and read to one another by the fire.'

As she says this I can see it in my mind – she and her daughters and the fire.

I wonder why her aunt read to her and not her mother? But she's speaking again. 'Did Miss Vivienne teach you to write as well?'

She taught me everything. I would never have learned anything in the classroom there. Miss Murphy was so strict and the girls so sly and the windows too high to see out of. But Miss Vivienne was patient and good to me. And I thought if I could read I would be able to read my mother's letters when they came and write back to her in turn.

She did write once, to tell me about the wedding, and then again to tell me my little brother had been born. But when I asked if I could see him she didn't reply to that.

She didn't tell me I could go home.

But I've forgotten to listen to Mrs Gaskell. I never did listen, they told me that. I was away with the fairies they said.

I try harder to pay attention to what she's saying. She asks how long I was there.

'Nearly eight years.'

'Eight years!' she says. 'I wonder you weren't placed somewhere sooner.'

'My mother was still living,' I tell her, 'so they kept me there.' *In case.*

Some of the girls were adopted, like Sylvie and Jane. Others, like Mattie, who used to creep into my bed at night and out again before the matron came – she was taken to a farm.

'Well,' she says, 'I expect it was useful to have an older girl around.'

I was a good girl, they told me. Helping with the younger children, saying my prayers. Sewing – I was grand at that, they said. Fast and neat. Sometimes I think I was only fast because I hated it so much and when I'd done I could go back to reading my Bible. Only inside it I'd have a different book, from Miss Vivienne.

No one else wanted me to read. There would be no use for readers in the outside world, they said, but plenty for stitchers. And so it seemed.

'But then they did find a place for you, with a dressmaker in Manchester,' Mrs Gaskell says.

Stockport, I think. Mrs Fenton's shop was near Stockport.

I forget to say it aloud and Mrs Gaskell is waiting, her head cocked to one side as though to hear better what I don't say. When I tell her she says she knows Stockport well, she grew up near there. Or at least not very near but not so far either. Her aunt took her more than once to a dressmaker there, although there was a perfectly good dressmaker in Knutsford where she grew up.

Then she asks if I know it and I tell her no. And I wonder again about her mother, why she didn't take her to the dressmaker, but of course I don't ask that.

'So - this lady—'

'Mrs Fenton.'

'Mrs Fenton - chose you from the orphanage?'

'I was the oldest,' I tell her, 'and I could sew.'

I was called out of my class. Miss Vivienne took me to Miss Finney's office where Mrs Fenton was waiting. She was stout, with dark hair piled up on her head and a face that was creamy-pale. I thought her very stately.

'Would you like to come with me, to England?' she said.

I shook my head and stared at my feet until Miss Vivienne took me out of the room. She said, *Surely you don't want to stay here?* I wept and told her I was afraid my mother would never find me in England. She put her arms round me and said she would make sure my mother knew where I was. Did I believe her, she asked, when she said that? I nodded and stopped crying. Then she took me back in again where Mrs Fenton was waiting, and I whispered that I would go and Mrs Fenton smiled and said she was sure we would get along just fine. I could write to my mother whenever I wanted, she said.

Mrs Gaskell says, 'I wonder why Mrs Fenton didn't choose a girl from Manchester rather than going all the way to Dublin?'

I can tell her that because Mrs Fenton told me herself. She'd been brought up in that very same orphanage! And trained to sew, then apprenticed out the same, and then after much hard work she bought her own shop. So she thought she would give the same chance to another orphanage girl.

What would she think if she could see me now? I wonder, and I'm quiet for so long that Mrs Gaskell says,

'And Mrs Fenton brought you to England on a ship?'

I'd never been on a ship before. I tell Mrs Gaskell I was frightened of the sea, although I'd seen it near my uncle's house and in books that told of shipwrecks and pirates. But nothing prepared me for sailing on it. It was like a great beast rolling around.

So many passengers were sick, even Mrs Fenton, but not me.

'You must be a good traveller,' Mrs Gaskell says. 'I'm always a little sick when I go on a ship. And my husband doesn't like it at all!'

I wasn't sick, but I felt a bit giddy that there was nothing solid to be seen – just sky and sea. 'I thought we might sail right off the edge of the earth,' I tell Mrs Gaskell. 'But we didn't. We sailed into the docks at Liverpool.'

'Ah, the Liverpool docks!' says Mrs Gaskell, as though she knows them well.

They were so noisy and smelly – the noisiest, smelliest place I'd ever seen before Manchester. I didn't know England then. I'd no idea about it at all, except it was something to do with the queen. 'Will we see the queen?' I asked Mrs Fenton, but she said if the queen was at Liverpool docks it would be because she was lost.

I wondered what would happen to a queen who got lost.

'Did you take the train to Manchester?'

I'd never been on a train before either. If the sea was like a beast the train was a monster – a roaring thing coming straight at us! The whistle screamed until I thought my ears would burst so I clapped my hands over them and a great gust of wind nearly blew me onto the track. Mrs Fenton had to grab hold of me. She was shouting but I couldn't hear.

I tell Mrs Gaskell that after the train we travelled in a carriage to a place called Longsight. I thought that funny because of the fog which meant you couldn't see very far at all. But there were houses there with gardens and Mrs Fenton's shop.

'I think you said you got on well with Mrs Fenton?'

I nod, then remember to speak. 'She used to say she loved all her girls. That was what she called us – her girls.'

'How many of you were there?'

There was Clara, Irma and Aggie. We slept in the same room, but we each had a bed to ourselves. Clara was thirteen and Aggie, her sister, twelve. Irma was no more than ten – Mrs Fenton had taken her from the workhouse.

'She was good to us,' I say. 'She used to toast cheese for us on the stove. And she had a great cat who sat on the shelf above it, purring like an engine. He was called Calico because of his colour – like unbleached cotton. Mrs Fenton said he'd been left to her by her husband so she kept him always with her. He was a terrible nuisance in the workshop, clawing at threads and sitting on new-ironed shirts, but we all loved him.'

Mrs Gaskell laughs merrily at this and says she has a cat who is a nuisance too – she can't let him in the room when she's sewing because he keeps jumping at the thread.

I tell her that Calico went where he chose like a king. He ate the top of the cream and the tail of the fish and slept on Mrs Fenton's own bed. I used to tug his ears gently until he went to sleep.

Mrs Gaskell is silent for a moment, then says, 'But then, you said Mrs Fenton's business failed?'

'It was the landlord,' I say, 'driving up the rents.' I don't tell her about the men who kept coming for money. Protection money they called it, though they were the ones we needed protecting from. I heard Mrs Fenton crying one night and she told me it was over – she'd have to give up the shop.

She tried to find us new positions. Clara and Aggie were hired by the big shop down the road and Mrs Fenton found a place for Irma in Macclesfield. But they only wanted one small girl they could train – they wouldn't take me.

'But someone did take you in the end?' Mrs Gaskell says.

I don't say anything.

'Mrs Digby, I think you said?'

Mrs Gaskell told me that if I don't want to answer a question, all I have to do is shake my head. So I shake my head but she misunderstands me entirely.

'No?' she says, 'I thought – didn't you say she used to work for Mrs Fenton?' and I pick at the skin at the bottom of my nail until it bleeds.

'She used to do piecework,' I say at last.

'But then she bought the business?'

She will get tired soon, I think. *Surely she will get tired of asking me these questions.*

But she's still waiting. So I tell her that Mrs Digby said she was setting up her own shop to make aprons and shirts for the mill workers and she wanted a good girl who could sew. Mrs Fenton said she wouldn't find a better, and Mrs Digby said she knew it for she'd seen my work before.

'And so you went with her?' Mrs Gaskell asks.

I nod, looking at the grime in the creases of my knuckles.

'So that's when you worked in Manchester?'

I scratch my wrist.

'Where was it exactly?' she asks. When I don't answer she just waits again. She can wait longer than anyone I ever knew.

Mrs Digby said it was just off Oldham Road, which was one of the best streets in Manchester. 'There's a new business setting up every day,' she said.

'Is that the address, then – Oldham Road?' I asked, but she said her business was so new it didn't have an address yet.

I didn't like the idea of my mother not knowing where to find me so I said, 'But what address do you give for correspondence? If – if someone wants to write to me?' and Mrs Digby gave me a look, then laughed and said she could see I was an educated type.

'You just tell them to send it to Mrs Digby's Sewing Parlour off Oldham Road,' she said. 'It'll find me right enough.'

To Mrs Gaskell I say, 'It was at the back of Piccadilly.' It's safe enough to say that since the whole area is stacked with sweatshops.

I can feel Mrs Gaskell watching me. Her waiting is like a heat on my skin, gentle at first, then it burns. But I don't know what else she wants me to say.

After a long time she says, 'And I think you said it was a little different, working there?'

I almost laugh but it comes out like a sob. I say it was very different – so different I could hardly believe two such places existed in the same world.

'What was it like?' she says and I close my eyes. How can I describe that place to Mrs Gaskell?

She is waiting again, always waiting. Her silence is a torment to me. I pick at my nail and hear her shift in her seat. *She'll grow tired of this*, I think. *She'll lose patience.* But all she says is, 'Did you say there were twelve of you?' and I nod. I'm tired suddenly, so tired. I would like to lie down and rest my head on her lap. What would she think if I did?

'And you stayed there all the time?' she says. 'You never went out?'

I shake my head, forgetting to speak up properly.

'Not even to the shops? Or – to chapel?'

As if a woman like Mrs Digby would go to chapel! All I say is, 'We weren't allowed out.'

And I see she doesn't understand.

What's the use of asking all these questions when she doesn't understand?

I shut my eyes again.

'Mrs Digby kept the front door bolted. We only went into the back If we had to throw slops into the yard.'

Or to take the bucket to the privy. But I can't tell Mrs Gaskell about the privy.

'So, you were like prisoners,' Mrs Gaskell says, 'and Mrs Digby was your jailer!'

I feel as though she's talking at me from a great distance, as though she's on the earth and I'm on the moon. Or I'm at the bottom of a well shouting up at her, *Of course we were prisoners!* But she can't hear.

Manchester is full of locked up girls in attics or cellars, but attics are better because of the light – you can't sew without light.

'But didn't you—' she pauses, 'did none of you ever try to escape?'

I used to dream of escaping – strange dreams in which I found the locked doors open and when I went through them I was on a ship like the one I'd sailed in from Dun Laoghaire, lurching about on the open sea.

'There was nowhere to go,' I say. 'Mrs Digby kept saying we didn't know when we were well off. She said that terrible things happened to girls like us in Manchester – bad folk were lurking in wait for us.'

They'd have to be brutal to be worse than her, but I didn't know that then.

Mrs Gaskell isn't looking at me now, she's looking at the window. Then slowly she does look back at me. Her eyes are dark with sorrow and all at once I think she does understand.

So I say to her, 'I would have left if I could but we were always watched. And Mrs Digby said there was no cause for any of us to leave the house. So we worked and ate and slept in the attic on straw pallets running with lice.'

Mrs Gaskell closes her eyes. She's silent so long I think she might have fallen asleep. Then I think she's disgusted by me, by what I've told her, and I start to weep. I'm weeping for myself, for everything I've come to and also because she will leave me.

I didn't know till then that I didn't want her to go.

I hear her move then she puts her arms around me! No one has done that for so long that I sob aloud. 'Please, please, don't,' she says. I press my face into her shoulder. I can smell a bitter smell on her from the streets outside, also lavender water and something musty beneath which is all her own.

After a while I feel her pulling away. She takes my hands gently and looks into my face, which must be very messy and blotchy from all the crying. I want to turn away from her but I can't. I see that her eyes are blue after all, a light clear blue with grey in them.

'Now I want you to be very brave,' she says and my stomach twists so that I think I will be sick all over her. 'I want you to tell me how you managed to leave Mrs Digby's if you were kept prisoner there?'

At this I start to weep again.

'Was it something to do with the doctor?' she asks and I burst into a veritable storm of weeping. 'Oh no, no,' she murmurs, but she doesn't put her arms around me this time. I try my hardest to stop, to tell her what she wants to know although I don't know how to say it. I press my apron to my face and manage to sob a few words through it and she leans close to hear me better. I can smell the powder on her face.

She says, 'Did – did Mrs Digby ask you to leave?'

I nod into my apron.

'And – was this something to do with the doctor?'

Please, please don't ask.

'Was it a – consequence – of what he did?'

I'm terrified that she will make me speak and then I'll lose her, and if I don't speak I will lose her anyway. So my words come out in a rush and tumble.

'She said there were names for girls like me and I had to go. So I went to the river – to throw myself in it!' And I sob into my apron again.

'Oh, you poor girl,' she says and she folds me in her arms once more. 'You poor, poor, girl!'

I tell her I didn't know what else to do for no one ever cared for me in this world. She holds me tighter, rocking me. Like a mother. Like my own mother might have done had she not left me, never looking back.

I wait for her to tell me that what I'd thought to do was the worst sin but she doesn't. She only holds me, murmuring into my hair. When at last I dare to lower my apron and look at her I see her eyes are wet too. I can hardly believe *she* would cry for *me*! She dabs at them with a handkerchief then laughs a little and blows her nose.

'Look at me!' she says shakily. 'I'm no help to you like this!'

Which makes me cry again but just then the bells clang, causing both of us to jump almost out of our skins.

'Suppertime,' I manage, and she says, 'So soon?'

Just as if she hasn't been here for hours! My cell's dark. She looks around as if she's forgotten where she is and what to do, so I remind her. 'After supper it will be evening prayers.'

Already we can hear the trolley rattling along the corridor.

Now she'll go I think and feel a dark pain. But at least it's over, before she's asked me something I can't answer.

'Well—' she says, then the door bursts open so violently we both stare at it but it's only Miss Jamieson. She looks at me then Mrs Gaskell, then back to me. 'Supper,' she says.

Mrs Gaskell stands then and fastens her cloak. I feel another pang of loss and panic that I've said too much or not enough. 'I will come back again, if I may,' she says, and I wonder why she's asking Miss Jamieson who can't give permission, then I realise she's asking me.

I glance quickly at Miss Jamieson then down at the floor. I hardly dare to believe she will come back again after everything I've said, but I remember to nod.

Then she says to Miss Jamieson, 'We will have to hope Pasley suffers no more accidents or injuries before I come again.'

I daren't look up. I can only imagine the look on Miss Jamieson's face.

'I'll come back very soon,' Mrs Gaskell says. I do glance up then and although she doesn't embrace me she smiles tenderly. 'I'll be thinking of you,' she says. Tears well in my eyes again. I would like to say something to keep her just one moment more but the words stick in my throat and she's already leaving and I can't see her face for her bonnet.

Then the trolley arrives and Miss Jamieson has to push past it, shooting me a look as she leaves.

And then I'm alone in my cell.

CHAPTER 9

Elizabeth

ELIZABETH FELT DRAINED as she left the prison. She felt as though the sun, which had gone down while she was inside, would never rise again. She could hear the discordant song of the river, though she couldn't see it without leaning out of the carriage. Even the thought of it gave her a sickening sensation of fall. *I went to the river – to throw myself in it!*

Ah, Pasley!

She had to help her. But how? No one had offered to take her, not one single person she had written to recommending her in every way she could. Most people hadn't answered at all. Others had replied saying they had no need for a maid. Mrs Chisholm had recently taken someone on. The Dukinfield Darbishires had said they would like to help but couldn't just now. Should she write again to ask why, or would that be too pressing?

Mrs Kirkby-Wilkes still hadn't found a maid, but there was the roving husband to consider.

How many women would prefer not to take in a young, pretty girl? Let alone one who'd been in prison. Who might have had a child.

She didn't know that yet; she hadn't been able to bring herself to ask.

She should have tried harder, asked more questions. But Pasley had been so upset . . .

What about Pasley's mother – what was she doing? What kind of mother could be so deaf and blind to her own child?

And there was the uncle. Perhaps she should write to him. He should be made to take some responsibility for what had happened to his niece ...

At the front of the carriage Jim began to sing:

I dreamt I dwelt in marble halls ...

He must have been in the *Nag's Head* again. She shouldn't have left him so long.

She prodded his shoulder. She couldn't be seen riding around with a driver who was in his cups and singing. And he had to take Polly to her French class later.

Jim subsided. The roads were still flooded so they were heading towards Deansgate again where streets on either side led into alleys and alleys into ginnels and courts, like a great warren extending across the city.

This was the Manchester no one wanted to know. A great, raw, heaving machine of human flesh, teeming with wretchedness. Where moneylenders, sharks, gin pedlars and pimps fed off the poor and the poor fed off one another. Where *sweaters* like Mrs Digby or dames in brothels worked their girls like slaves, keeping them penned in so they could never leave.

I would have left if I could, but we were always watched.

The police wouldn't go into the Rookeries but William went with his Domestic Mission. They took tokens for food and blankets to the people who lived in the cellars or tunnels. At one time Elizabeth had gone with them. She'd seen things she could never have imagined, starving babies drugged into a stupor, their limbs broken for begging. One week they'd taken milk and clothing for a new baby, then the next week the baby was gone and the clothes with it, pawned. Eventually Elizabeth had told William she couldn't do it anymore.

'It isn't safe,' she'd said, visiting cellars that were crammed and infested with disease. She might catch something and bring it back to their girls.

'Avoiding it won't make it go away,' he'd said.

'Nothing makes it go away. It's not that I don't *care*,' she went on when he didn't reply. Caring was the problem. Each time she went she felt as though she was sinking into a bottomless pit.

'You aren't required to *sink*,' he replied. 'Our aim is to lift people out, not sink with them.'

'And do we? Do we lift people out?'

There was that look again. 'We've had this conversation before,' he said and they had. Sometimes she thought all their conversations were the same one. There was no point asking why he put himself at such risk going into these warrens that were rife with disease and run by criminal gangs. He would only say simply, 'Because God is there.'

That was what he preached and what he believed, that God was not to be found in the halls of power or the mansions of the rich but in the gutters and hovels, with the destitute and afflicted.

Once the thought had come to her quick as lightning, *not my God*. But she hadn't said it aloud, thankfully, because how could she explain it?

Eventually they'd reached a kind of truce, one of those uncomfortable, unsatisfactory ones that occurred so regularly in their marriage. She'd stopped visiting the poor in their hovels and begun writing about them instead.

Yet here she was again with that same sinking, corrosive feeling. And she was so *tired*. She leaned back and closed her eyes, lulled by the rough motion of the carriage.

But then a fire cart thundered by, siren blaring. Tommy shied and whinnied, the carriage lurched and Elizabeth was flung to the side. Jim leapt from his seat and struggled with Tommy who thankfully didn't bolt. The carriage rocked violently but righted itself. A man ran up to help.

Tommy put one hoof down then stumbled. Jim bent over the pony's leg.

'There, boy, there,' he said.

Elizabeth climbed out of the carriage, heart pounding. 'What on earth?' she said.

'He went right into the road without looking!' the other man said. 'You could've been killed!'

'Yes, thank you,' Elizabeth said, glaring at him.

'I'm just saying, that's all.'

Jim was still bending over the pony.

'Is Tommy all right?' she asked. Jim mumbled something about him needing to be re-shod. 'These cobbles play havoc with pony's hooves.'

'Don't give me that!' she said. 'You've been drinking again! You reek of ale! Do you think I can't smell it? How many times have I told you?'

Slowly Jim drew himself up. His face was flushed but mutinous. She expected him to defy her and then she would have to sack him right there and then. And people were already gathering to watch.

'It won't happen again,' he said.

'No, it won't happen again,' she told him. 'I'll be speaking to Mr Gaskell about this when I get in.'

Then in a different tone she asked, 'Do you think Tommy will get us back?'

Jim bent over the pony once more. His hands were trembling. 'You're all right aren't you, Tommy?' he said, patting the pony's neck. And Tommy did seem to be putting his hoof down now. Jim patted him again then said, 'Looks like the road's blocked ahead. We'll have to go a different way. Will you get in, ma'am? It's a long walk home.'

In fact it wasn't far, but she couldn't walk unaccompanied through these streets. And it would make more of a scene for the spectators who were still gathering. She allowed Jim to help her back into the carriage then he climbed into his seat and looking all around with a deliberate and manifest caution, set off again.

Elizabeth sat stiffly *as though someone had starched her corsets*, Hearn would say. She was furious with Jim, his negligence, his deceit. With herself for threatening to speak to her husband and with William, who would only defend Jim.

CHAPTER 10

HER HUSBAND WAS on all fours in the parlour with Flossie and Julia on his back. Meta was demanding a ride too.

William said he would rather keep what was left of his spine.

'You're so feeble!' Meta said.

William smiled at Elizabeth then said, 'What's wrong?'

Flossie and Julia clambered off his back and ran to her. She cupped Flossie's face in her hands, noting the bluish shadows under her eyes. She'd been awake all night coughing.

'Is everything all right?' William asked her.

No, she wanted to say, *nothing is*. Instead she picked Julia up then looked at her post on the table. A letter from her publisher, Chapman, two more she couldn't identify.

'Not now,' William said as Julia begged for another ride. 'Your mother and I want to talk.' Elizabeth's heart sank. Suddenly she didn't want to talk at all but she left Flossie and Julia with Hearn, promising to read to them later, and followed William into the dining room. His papers were scattered across the table as usual.

'What is it, Lily?' he asked gently.

She wanted to talk about Pasley and about moving house. She wanted to fall on his shoulder and weep. Instead she told him about Jim.

He sat down as she spoke, pushing his papers to one side of the table.

'It's not the first time,' she said. 'He could have caused a serious accident.'

'But he didn't.'

'No—'

'And Tommy's all right?'

'I think so.'

'Then it was just a mishap, nothing more.'

Sometimes she felt her husband was missing the point.

'He's taking Polly out later!'

William frowned. 'I'll speak to him if you like.'

'I've spoken to him before. It doesn't change anything.'

'What would you like me to do?'

'For heaven's sake William,' she said.

They had fallen somehow into this old groove, as if their lines had already been written for them.

William sat back. 'Do you want me to dismiss him?'

'Do you have any better ideas?'

'I can go with him when he takes Polly.'

'Are you going to accompany him everywhere?'

'I'm not convinced that sacking him is the best solution.'

'Well, what is, then?'

William tugged at his collar which was coming loose, she saw. 'I don't know,' he said. 'I'll have to think about it.'

'Can you think of a single reason for keeping him on?'

William hesitated, then said, 'He loves that pony.'

'What?'

'I think without this job he doesn't have very much.'

'Now that's not fair—'

'And I think it's a mistake to take everything away from a man who's battling his own personal demons. Do you want him to go on the streets?'

'Of course not,' she said, thinking of Pasley.

William picked up his spectacles. 'Then perhaps he should be given a warning and another chance.'

'Fine,' she said. 'Put the girls at risk . . .'

He looked at her over his spectacles. 'If you feel so strongly about it then perhaps you should dismiss him. And find another driver who never has an accident on the Manchester streets.'

They had reached this impasse before: William's idealism, her pragmatism as he called it.

William despised pragmatism.

'Very well,' she said, turning away. 'Bury your head.' And she left the room, surprised to feel tears threatening. Why was he not more concerned about her? She could have been killed.

It was a massive strain she sometimes thought, being married to a good man.

Upstairs she went to read to Julia and Flossie but Flossie wouldn't sleep. Elizabeth told her she was too old to be read to sleep, at which Flossie turned her face into her pillow and wept. Stricken, Elizabeth read to her for several more minutes before Hearn came in to relieve her.

Elizabeth kissed Flossie and extricated herself. Then she sat at the small table in her bedroom and opened her post.

There was a letter from the Mothers' Association, asking whether she might speak at one of their meetings. They were teaching working mothers to read so they could read to their children. *It would be such an inspiration, to hear from a real lady authoress*, Mrs Pringle said.

Mrs Pringle had been one of the many ladies who had been forbidden to read *Mary Barton* by their husbands. So Elizabeth would have to be inspirational in general, not particular. She could talk about her book but not in too much detail. And she probably shouldn't take copies to hand out, even as gifts.

Elizabeth sighed. Mrs Pringle wanted her to suggest a date, but there were too many dates to think about. She put the letter to one side and opened the one from her publisher.

Mr Chapman thanked her for her Christmas story which would be out that month and said he looked forward to receiving a second novel from her in the new year.

She'd already promised Travers Madge a new story for his *Penny Magazine*. Christmas, with its usual run of guests, engagements and entertainments was looming. Her friend Tottie was coming to stay, the girls needed new dresses, she had promised to go out distributing packages to the refuges. And visit Pasley of course. But Mr Chapman seemed to think she did nothing but wait for his commissions.

He mentioned that *Mary Barton* was doing very well and had exceeded his expectations. But he didn't say how well or whether any money would be forthcoming, which was what she'd asked.

That was so like him, to avoid answering her questions! Now she would have to write to him again. She would tell him they needed the money in order to move house in the New Year.

Knutsford, she thought longingly. Although William wouldn't move to Knutsford because it was too far away. But there was Timperley or Hale. She would remind him about Flossie's cough which wasn't improving. William worried about Flossie who was always ill in the winter months.

What did Chapman mean by *exceeded his expectations*? Was her novel doing really well or was it just that his expectations were low?

But she knew people were reading it because they wrote to her.

Half the masters are bitterly angry with me, she'd written to Chapman, *half (and the best half) are buying it to give to their work-people's libraries . . . I had no idea it would have proved such a fire brand!*

In fact she had known, but she'd wanted to remind Chapman of its success. He'd held the publication back for nearly a year because of the revolution in Paris, which had triggered a series of disturbances throughout England – marches and demonstrations, chartist rallies. In Manchester factory windows were smashed, there were fires in the streets. And riots against the Irish, who were still flooding into the city after the famine while workers everywhere were being laid off. The Queen had retreated to the Isle of Wight, and more of the Gaskells' friends moved to Didsbury or Wilmslow.

William, of course, would do no such thing. He went into the thick of the riots attempting to calm the men and organise them into peaceful meetings. He provided soup kitchens and parcels of food for the stricken families. And by some miracle he wasn't harmed.

Meanwhile Chapman asked Elizabeth to change the title of her novel from *John Barton*, her main character, to *Mary Barton*, his beautiful daughter, in order to distract from its political content. But there was no disguising the fact that John Barton was a chartist who murdered the son of a mill-owner. She'd published it anonymously but soon everyone was talking about it, trying to guess the author.

She'd been unprepared for the storm when the news broke, the outrage and acclamation and something darker she couldn't name. Quivering, predatory. Everyone wanted to speak to her, to stand with her at parties or sit next to her at dinners. They were interested in what she read, what she wore, even what she ate. She sometimes felt they wanted to tear her to pieces and eat the scraps of her.

In truth she was sick of the fuss. She'd wanted her book to do good – that was the whole purpose of her writing, but as the furore continued she'd felt as though she'd had been snuffed out like a candle and resurrected in a new, monstrous form by her readers.

Still, she was grateful to Chapman for taking on her book when it had been rejected by several publishers. And for supporting her through the reviews which had been mixed at best, accusing her of exaggerating the conflicts and making fiction the vehicle for exposition and propaganda.

Next time, she thought, she would write something completely different and join the ranks of respectable lady writers who never caused any offence to anyone.

The final letter was from Dr Kay, whose book about the conditions of the working class in Manchester she'd used when writing her novel. She'd written to thank him of course, and sent him a copy of *Mary Barton* once the secret of her identity was out. But she didn't know what he thought about it, whether he'd even read it. Probably he thought fiction was for women.

He was asking if he could visit her Sunday School as part of an ongoing project by the Ardwick and Ancoats Dispensary to educate the children of the poor about hygiene.

Elizabeth was inclined to admire Dr Kay's commitment and zeal. Apart from William no one had done more for the poor. They were both involved in almost all the organisations and charities in the city. There was no one Dr Kay didn't know.

The thought came to her then in a cold rush that he might know Dr Billington.

There were so few doctors in Manchester who worked with the poor – surely they all knew each other? Dr Billington might even work at the Dispensary! And Dr Kay had initiated a system of visiting the poor in their homes. Was that how Dr Billington had come to be in Mrs Digby's establishment in the first place?

Tiny pulses hammered in her forehead. Why hadn't she thought of this before?

How many other places might employ him – the workhouses, the refuges and missions? She would have to write to them all.

And say what? That they were employing a monster?

She'd already been accused of libel. One reviewer had called her first novel 'a libel on the masters, merchants and gentlemen of the city.'

She would have to establish what the doctor had done to Pasley before she wrote a word. Had there been a baby or not? If there had, surely there might be some evidence of it somewhere?

And she would have to find out exactly who was employing him.

Dr Kay would know. He could help her – the Boards and trustees would listen to him.

Elizabeth hurried to her desk. She would reply to him immediately, saying he was more than welcome to visit the Sunday School. Then when he came she would make sure he knew what kind of man Dr Billington really was and together they would let other people know.

Death by reputation, her husband often said, was at once the fastest and most protracted, least merciful kind.

CHAPTER 11

Pasley

MY CELL FEELS empty now she's gone.

My food is still here, on the table. I uncover the dish. It's some kind of meat stew, lukewarm and fatty like all the food here. I inspect it carefully as I always do ever since Ella Gibb and Lizzie Clegg made it known what they would put into it. Once I was struck with vomiting and ended up in the hospital, so I knew they meant what they'd said.

I touch the bruise on my face from when Ella tripped me on the stairs.

We will have to hope Pasley suffers no more accidents or injuries, Mrs Gaskell said.

Miss Jamieson wouldn't like that. I hope Ella and Lizzie don't get to hear of it.

The thought makes my stomach churn so I can't bring myself to eat. But Mrs Gaskell said she would help me. She will find me a home – a real home. Like the one she lives in with her daughters.

How lucky her daughters are! I see them sitting around her, the little one on her knee while she reads to them from one of her books.

I wish I could be with them! Not by her knee of course, just somewhere in a corner of the room.

But I push the thought away. As if she would have someone like me in her home!

If I close my eyes, I can still feel her holding me.

I look at my food again. She said I must eat. And they don't like it if I send it back untouched. I break up a potato with my spoon – no cutting knives in here – and stir it into the gravy, thinking about all the questions she asked.

When she comes back she will ask me even more.

The thought of it makes the gravy bitter, the potato loose in my mouth. But I swallow one mouthful then two or three quickly without chewing. Then I push my plate away. I can't eat when I'm not hungry and I'm never hungry. Or I'm always hungry, I don't know how to be not hungry any more.

I shouldn't have told her about the river. She will have been shocked. Although she was so kind to me!

You poor, poor girl, she said. And held me, in her arms!

I can't tell her about the baby. My blood turns cold when I think of it.

How she will hate me if I do!

Maybe it's better if I don't see her again but the thought of this gives me a sad pain in my chest.

When the bell rings I stand outside my cell, waiting to fall in line with the other girls for chapel. I slip in quickly so I'm not near Lizzie or Ella but between Mary Garside and Emma Flowers.

They say Emma Flowers murdered all her children one by one.

Better her than Ella.

In the chapel we sit in wooden boxes to pray, so we can't see one another or talk. Coffins, they call them. I kneel when I have to, mumble my prayers, aware of the other girls in their coffins like mumbling corpses, dead to the outside world. The Reverend says something but I barely hear. I'm thinking about Mrs Gaskell, what she said, and what I didn't say.

Was it a consequence of what he did?

I shut my eyes and pray it will all be over soon, everything, all of it, me.

When I hear the other girls moving I fall in with them. Back to my cell which is so dark now I can barely see the window. The governor will not waste money on candles so we have to do our work in daylight – what daylight there is. It's gone now, along with the dish and the beaker of tea. I can hardly see the basket but I sit at the table and run my fingers through the thread. My memories are tangled the same: my mother, the doctor, Mrs Digby.

I pull the thread so tightly around my finger it almost cuts. Then I push the basket away, get up from the table and lie on my wooden bed looking at the paler shade of the window against the deeper shade of the wall. All my memories come tumbling back like a bag of knives.

When I saw him in the hospital here it was like seeing the devil. It made my heart stop and the blood freeze in my chest.

Good God, he said, *what are you doing here?*

I could have asked him the same question but I couldn't speak – the only sound I made was a howl.

I screw my eyes shut as though I will squeeze from them the things I don't want to see. But when I open them again nothing's changed. I'm still here.

Mrs Gaskell will ask me about him when she comes, about what he did. And I will not be able to say such words to her.

What will I say?

Of course, she won't come again tomorrow. It will be a week at least before I see her.

If I see her.

I shift about on the bed. The mattress is so thin it hurts my bones. Other memories come back to me when I close my eyes, like shards of glass.

Then the strangest thing happens. I sense Mrs Gaskell watching me. She is here with me in my cell! Her face bends over me like an angel. That listening face.

I don't open my eyes in case she disappears.

Tell me everything, she says.

And I know that I can, I can tell her anything, I needn't be afraid.

All my memories settle like tea leaves in a pot. I can see it all so clearly it's like living it all over again. As though I never left Mrs Digby's or Mrs Fenton's where she came for me.

Take good care of this one, Mrs Fenton said, *she's worth her weight in gold.* And Mrs Digby, lying through her yellow teeth said, *I'll be like her own mother.*

Then she stood by watching, with her little wet eyes and a great, false smile on her face while Mrs Fenton kissed me and called me her own sweet girl and said if only things had turned out differently. Which is something I've often thought about since.

What makes things turn out the way they do? Is it God, like I was always told?

At the orphanage they would have said it was man's greed that makes things turn out badly.

Mrs Digby was the equal of any man for greed.

As soon as we were out of sight of the shop she changed. She had taken my arm as though we were friends but as soon as we turned the corner she released it. Her mouth drooped downwards, she had a face on her like a plate of mortal sin. And she spoke to me as though I was no better than the slurry under her feet. I didn't know what to say in return so I said nothing. Anyway she'd never have heard through all the noise.

We walked all the way into Manchester and the closer we got the darker and noisier it was. There was a rattling and pounding that shook the buildings and the ground beneath our feet till I feared it would open up and swallow us. Bells rang, whistles blew and from time to time there was a great hissing noise and a *boom*. There were street sellers screaming out their wares, someone shouting about damnation and what sounded like a fight, but I couldn't see anyone. I kept looking around so I might remember the way but I could hardly see anything for the fog and the cotton tufts and straw blowing around the streets. Once my foot slipped in a pool of mire and I skidded into Mrs Digby. 'Watch it, you lummox!' she said.

No one had ever spoken to me like that before.

There were shapes moving through the fog. I could only make

them out as they drew near. A man with no legs on a little wheeled truck pushing himself over the cobbles with his hands, another limping slowly and muttering to himself. There were lights from shop windows full of drapery and fancy clothes. I hoped that one of them might be Mrs Digby's but we passed them all.

'Stop dawdling, girl!' she said. 'It's like dragging a dollop of stones.'

By this time I knew I'd been lied to and Mrs Fenton as well. I remember thinking, *As soon as we get out of this noise I'll say something*, but then a monstrous face loomed at us out of the fog. A face with no eyes nor nose, only holes and long strands of hair straggling from a bald head. 'Spare us some change,' it croaked, and put a pock-marked claw on Mrs Digby's arm.

She lifted her own hand sharply as though to strike it. 'Get back in the gutter you pox-faced cunt,' she said and the creature fell back just as if it had been struck.

I was afraid of her then because I'd never heard a woman use such language before. Only a man once at the docks and my uncle had chastised him for cursing in front of me.

I could never repeat such words to Mrs Gaskell – I would sooner cut my tongue out!

We went to Piccadilly. I didn't know it was Piccadilly then – I didn't know where I was at all. We turned off a great street choked with carriages and carts into an alley that led to a yard with pigs rooting round in it and a little lad with no clothes on his bottom half. *Where's she taking me?* I wondered but I didn't say anything to her for fear of her foul tongue. And because I was trying not to slip in the brown water running over my shoes or to breathe in the stench coming from it. Which as I learned later, is because it comes straight from the privy.

Just as I was thinking we'd never get there, she stopped. We were in a little, odd-shaped court with soot-smeared washing strung across it. There were piles of crates and barrels in one corner, rotting stuff all over the cobbles and on the far side, a door.

Mrs Digby took a set of keys from her purse and unlocked the door. 'Come on, then,' she said.

When I didn't move she opened her eyes wide. 'What're you waiting for?' she said, 'Prince Albert?'

So I stepped forward, holding my skirts up and brushed past her through the doorway into darkness. Darkness and the smell of boiled cabbage, which I've associated ever since with dread.

There was a little kitchen with a table and a stove. And a stairway leading up from it.

Mrs Digby lit a lamp which threw a feeble, flickering light.

'Up you go,' she said, jerking her head.

The stairs were narrow and angled like Mrs Digby herself. There were two flights. All the way up I could hear the sound of coughing that can be heard everywhere in Manchester. *How can you tell if a worker is from Manchester? If he can breathe he's not.*

The workshop was in the attic. There was no light anywhere else in that building but up there grey light leaked through a window in the roof. There was a bucket underneath it in which raindrops clattered like tiny pebbles. To either side there was a row of straw pallets. The plaster on the walls was scuffed and mouldy where water had run down it. The floor was strewn with cloth and there were girls huddled round it like bundles of cloth themselves. None of them looked up as we arrived.

'This is your new workmate,' Mrs Digby said. A few of them glanced up then.

I looked at Mrs Digby but she only said, 'Go on!' and two of the girls shuffled to make room for me.

This is a mistake! I wanted to say. *I shouldn't be here!*

Instead, I stepped forwards and sat down between them and a great pile of cloth landed in front of me. I looked up and saw a rat-faced girl, her eyes glinting down at me. 'Pinnies,' she said, and someone passed me a needle and thread.

'Work through that lot,' Mrs Digby said, 'and you'll have your tea. The girls'll tell you how it goes.' And she went out, shutting the door behind her.

I wanted to run down the narrow stairs into the streets of Manchester and all the way back to Longsight to beg Mrs Fenton to take me with her, wherever she was going.

But she would have already gone and I didn't know anyone else. And I was afraid of all the people and the noise. So I stayed.

As soon as Mrs Digby went the girls started shuffling and whispering to one another, glancing my way, but none of them spoke to me apart from one who had a broken nose like a fighter. 'What are you gawking at? she said. Then the rat-faced girl, who was known as Squinty Sue, said,

'Get shifting!'

I didn't move. I felt as though I'd stumbled into a bad dream and was only waiting to wake up out of it.

What's she doing, I heard one of the girls whisper and another one said, *hush*. Finally I lifted the needle then pressed it into the cloth and made my first stitch.

I remember the girl with the nose – Fat Alice they called her, which was some kind of joke for she was hardly any fatter than my arm – getting up to use the bucket. Not the one the rain fell into – a different one. There was the sound of her piss then the smell of it filling the room.

She saw me staring. 'Are you looking at my fanny?' she screeched.

I won't be saying that to Mrs Gaskell, either!

Didn't you try to escape? she said.

Did I tell her the door was bolted? I didn't tell her about the privy, which was through a ginnel in a court with high walls all round. The privy was in the corner with a wooden door hanging off its hinges and brown water flowing out from it.

There was a seat inside with a hole in it but I don't know anyone who ever sat on it – the smell was enough to knock a man unconscious.

We just swung the bucket at it. Some of it went inside, some of it spattered against the door or landed in the brown pool beneath.

I couldn't escape then because I was never alone when I went to it. Tucker and Dodds – Mrs Digby's bully-boys – were always there.

Dodds had huge fists and hardly a brain in his head. He had a whining voice like an infant and a swollen jaw from matches – the phosphorus swells your head up so there's no room for your brain.

I once saw him pounding another man halfway to death. I was on kitchen duty with Sal – an older girl, very slow, and Squinty Sue was in the yard with Fat Alice, hanging round Tucker like always. Then some of the other girls came running into the kitchen to watch and cheer Dodds on.

'He's killing him!' I said.

Sal only stared at me, her mouth hanging open.

I wanted to stop him but I didn't know how. Tucker turned to us and lifted his hands. 'It's all right, ladies,' he said. 'This gentleman here was looking to set up shop across the way – take all our custom and drive you out of our jobs. Doddsy here is just persuading him otherwise.'

He grinned up at us.

That was Tucker – always grinning with his little brown teeth. He did all the talking.

Dodds reared up at last with a final kick to the bloodied heap on the cobbles. It didn't even groan. Then he bent over and picked it up and crossed the court with it dangling like a rag doll.

'That's it ladies,' Tucker said, grinning again. 'Show's over. I'll be passing my hat round for a collection later!'

Fat Alice and Squinty Sue both shrieked with laughter, like he was a blast.

If Mrs Fenton'd had two thugs like that in her pay, she wouldn't have been driven out of business.

The first time I was sent to the privy Tucker came with me.

'Put the bucket down,' he said. 'I've got summat to show you.'

I should've just hit him with it and run. But I didn't know what to do so I put it down like a fool, and the next minute he was all over me, pulling my skirts up, his great bristly chin scratching my face.

I didn't have much luck all the time I was in that place, but that day I was still carrying a darning needle. I jabbed it into his hand and tore myself away from him as he yelled.

'You - you are the devil!' I sputtered.

He sucked his hand, then to my surprise he grinned at me.

'Spiky bitch, int'yer?' he said and he made a darting movement with his head like a pouncing snake. 'Gotcher!' he said but I ran for all I was worth, slipping and skidding over the cobbles, leaving the bucket behind.

The next time I was due for the privy I managed to swap with one of the other girls. And the time after. There was always someone who would swap because it got them out of the house. And some of them didn't mind seeing what Tucker had to show them, hard though that is to believe.

Squinty Sue and Fat Alice would come back humming to themselves, wearing ribbons or some such trinkets, the fat from a pig's trotter dribbling down their chins.

I kept watching Tucker and Dodds come and go to see when I might take my chance and run for it. But one of them was always hanging round.

One night I couldn't sleep at all. Water clinking into the bucket, something running over my feet, girls coughing or snoring. And it was cold, as usual. I lay awake thinking about my mother and Miss Vivienne, about Mrs Fenton and how lucky I was then and I didn't even know. Suddenly I sat up in my bed. I thought I would go down and try all the locks, the windows even, to see if there was any way out.

I crept past the other girls, expecting one of them to wake up and ask what I was up to. And then Squinty Sue or Fat Alice would report me. But no one stirred.

I opened the door and crept downstairs in my stockinged feet, holding the clogs I'd been given instead of the good shoes I'd arrived in, in one hand and feeling my way along the wooden rail with the other. Every time those stairs creaked my heart shook. I remember every notch in that rail.

The kitchen was dark as coal. I nearly dropped dead of fright when a voice spoke.

What you up to girl? And I saw her then, a black shadow by the stove.

My mouth was so dry I could hardly speak, but I said, *Nothing – I'm just going back to bed*, and she said, *That's good. I wouldn't want any harm to come to you.*

She lit her lamp and the whites of her eyes gleamed yellow. I could feel them watching me all the way back up the stairs.

I don't know why she was in the kitchen when her own room was upstairs, but that's the way it was. Either Mrs Digby or Tucker slept in the kitchen, keeping watch. I was lucky it wasn't Tucker.

One of the girls told me he was Mrs Digby's nephew. I remember being surprised at them being family – as though they were ordinary folk, not devils. Martha said Mrs Digby had had sons of her own but none of them had lived and when her husband had died too she'd set up this business.

I didn't feel sorry for her though. She was always on at me, finding fault with my work. 'Look at them stitches,' she said. 'Anyone'd think you had hooves, not hands!' Then to the others, 'Pasley now – she thinks she's a cut above. She thinks she belongs somewhere better because we int good enough for her, girls, if you can believe that.' Then she laughed her great cawing laugh and left me to the others, who were sour with spite.

※

It's hard to breathe for my memories choking me. I can't see Mrs Gaskell's face anymore or feel her listening to me. I must have dreamed it, though I'm not asleep. I shift and turn in my bed thinking, *Will this night never end?*

Somewhere in the building a door clangs shut, then it's as quiet as it ever is. It's never completely quiet because of the pipes. You can hear them gurgling and clanking all night long. But all the girls are shut into their cells like hens in coops and there's a hush as though even the walls are holding their breath. So I know it must be the hour before dawn, the dark hour when Miss Hannaway said, *If any of this lot's going to cash in their chips, it'll be now.*

Then there is a *thud* and my eyes fly open. The morning bell clangs and I lie listening to it, feeling dumb and blurred. I must have slept after all. Outside in the corridor the wardress is banging on all the doors, *Get up! Get up!*

Miss Hannaway. My heart sinks a little, even though I've trained it not to care. I rise and dress in the dark, hearing women cursing in the other cells. I roll up my mattress as the door is unlocked.

Breakfast is the usual stiff bread and a mug of tea. The bread tastes like wool in my mouth. I chew it slowly because Mrs Gaskell told me I must eat.

I remember her face bending over me.

But that wasn't real, it was a dream.

After breakfast we walk in single file to the chapel, Miss Hannaway glowering over us as we go. She's short and stout with blunt features, as though someone has taken a ball of clay and moulded it badly with their thumbs. There's a look in her eyes as though sleep hasn't left them and she can't quite believe she's here. When one of the girls coughs she barks at her to be quiet.

I drop my prayer book then bump my head on the pew picking it up. Miss Hannaway's eyes bulge, but because we're in the chapel she doesn't bark at me.

After chapel, we return to our cells, and the usual heap of oakum is handed to me for unpicking. It must be done before the light fades or there'll be no visits for me.

But she will come back, she said so.

She doesn't come that day, nor the day after. On the day after that I think, *She won't come. Why would she, after everything I said?* And I feel a sad pain.

When I finally get to sleep it's by thinking about Mrs Gaskell by the fire, all her daughters gathered at her knee. Then I wake up to that same thudding, thumping sensation in my chest.

But today is Sunday. She won't visit on a Sunday. She'll have other things to do, being a minister's wife.

I feel almost relieved that she won't come. I don't want her to come, asking questions. I don't want her to see me, what she thinks of me. Or for me to see myself that way either – I don't want that at all.

Yet I do want her to find me that home she talked about where I'll be looked after.

She won't help me, why would she?

So my mind goes back and forth like a shuttle, until I'm dizzy with it.

But she won't come on a Sunday – I'm safe for now.

I lie on my bed, wondering she will do on a Sunday.

CHAPTER 12

Elizabeth

THE SUNDAY SCHOOL children, scrofulous, rickety and scratching, were crowded onto eighteen long benches behind eighteen tables. Usually Travers Madge taught the older boys, Elizabeth the older girls, while Susanna Winkworth and Millie Powler looked after the younger children. But today they were all gathered in the big classroom for Dr Kay's visit.

He was late, and the children were shuffling and looking towards the boxes of biscuits. They were hungry of course. Most of them brought something to eat during the lunch break – not much, only bread, sometimes with dripping, sometimes dry. Still it was painful to see the ones who had nothing watching the others which was why Elizabeth had persuaded the ladies at church to bake biscuits for all the children. When Dr Kay still didn't arrive she nodded at Millie and a murmur rose as Millie started to hand them out.

They were excited because of the disruption of their usual routine but Elizabeth wanted Dr Kay to see how well they could behave. So when the noise showed no sign of abating she stood at the front of the room and wrote the words HOPE, JOY, PEACE, LOVE, on the blackboard, then faced the class.

'Who can tell me what I've written?'

A few hands went up. Violet Carnie offered the answer.

'Excellent, Violet. Does anyone know why I've written that?'

Eventually another girl volunteered that it was nearly Christmas.

'Exactly. And what are the Sundays before Christmas called?'

Silence.

'Advent,' Elizabeth told them, 'and Advent is about hope, the hope of Christ coming into the world.'

Some of the children started to write this down, others were busy with their biscuits and there was a small scuffle at the back between Ernie Prior and Peter Clegg, in which Millie intervened.

Elizabeth could feel the energy of the room running away from her.

'Put your pencils down,' she said suddenly. 'I want to tell you a story.'

In the hush that followed she told them about the shepherds and the angels.

'A multitude of the heavenly host came down. Can you imagine that? What do you suppose a heavenly host looks like?'

'Miss, they had wings!'

'And haloes.'

'They'd be shining like gas lamps,' Matthew Parker said and there was some jeering at this but Elizabeth said, 'They were shining – that's what Luke tells us – *the glory of the Lord shone about them*. On that dark hillside with no other lights for miles around. They didn't have gas lamps then – not like us.'

She'd always loved that story – the shepherds on the cold hillside, watchful, bored, a little hungry perhaps. How many times had they kept that same watch, year in year out, with no expectation of better things? Then one night their lives were transformed.

'If it could happen there to those shepherds it could happen anywhere. Even here, in Manchester!' she said.

But Ernie Prior said, 'If it happened here, Miss, no one'd see it for't fog,' and everyone laughed. Then Stanley Clarke wanted to know what a shepherd was. It hadn't occurred to her they wouldn't know. But why would they? Most of them had never seen a field. She started to explain but the bell rang downstairs.

'Our guest has arrived,' she told them, and there was a buzz of anticipation as she left them and hurried downstairs, only to see that Susanna had got there first.

'Ah the famous Miss Winkworth,' Dr Kay was saying, clasping Susanna's hands in his. 'I've heard so much about your translations – I do hope to be able to read them for myself one day.'

Susanna was actually blushing. She started to say that she was hoping to publish them, Mr Gaskell had been very kind and was helping her, when she caught Elizabeth's look and trailed off.

'Dr Kay,' Elizabeth said, stepping forward. 'It's so good of you to come.'

'Not at *all*,' he replied, striding forwards to greet her and removing his hat.

He wasn't, strictly speaking, a handsome man but he did have his admirers. Perhaps because of his air of assurance and conviction. He was only a little taller than Elizabeth but had a dense, compact energy that seemed to add to his stature. Even the air around him seemed more vibrant.

'I've heard great things about the work you do here,' he said, unfastening his cloak. 'This is Nurse Linley,' he added, nodding at the stout woman who'd entered behind him. 'Here to help. Shall we go up?'

Help? Elizabeth thought, but he was already striding up the stairs ahead of her, talking all the way about the Manchester mud, how it had held him up, and all the carriages, how he'd slipped getting out, covering a boot and one leg of his trousers in it. He held his leg out for Elizabeth to see.

Even though he didn't stop talking he was the only one not out of breath by the time they reached the third floor, where the hum of recitation greeted them.

'Prayers,' Elizabeth said shortly. She'd been planning to explain the organisation of the Sunday School to him but had no breath left. 'Shall I introduce you?' she managed.

'I can do that for myself,' he said, striding ahead, followed by

Nurse Linley. He nodded at Travers Madge who stepped to one side, beaming.

The murmur hushed as Dr Kay stood at the front and placed a wooden box like a briefcase on the table. 'Well now,' he said, 'what have we here?' In a single movement, he opened the clasp and swivelled it round to face the children. There was a collective gasp.

'Who can tell me what this is?' he asked holding up a lozenge on a stick. Light from the tall windows glowed through it, turning amber.

Several arms shot up.

'Sir, a lollipop!'

'A lolly!'

'It's a lollipop!'

Dr Kay held his hand up as the voices rose to a clamour.

'There's one for each of you,' he said, 'provided you can form an orderly queue and take your turn – no pushing or shoving!'

'It's just honey and candied peel,' he said to Elizabeth. 'Good for their throats, if not their teeth . . .'

Was he asking whether she minded? He'd already turned back to the queue that was forming in a haphazard way. Susanna and Millie were helping to marshal the children into a line that stretched around the long classroom.

Elizabeth hadn't expected Dr Kay to inspect the children, but Nurse Linley was already checking their hair for nits and lice, their arms for ringworm and examining their fingernails and teeth. Dr Kay opened two more boxes, withdrawing a wooden tube from the smaller one. He listened to their chests, then encouraged them to use the stethoscope on one another which caused some hilarity. Most of them took to it with enthusiasm, only one or two hung back, and for once no squabbles or fights broke out.

Elizabeth was proud of them. Although they all showed the marks of poverty, and gave off its particular smell, most had made an effort; hair was slicked down neatly, clothing patched, feet covered in some kind of footwear. George Phelan had a black eye, Eddie Rimmer's nose perpetually ran, but even he blew it on the handkerchief Susanna gave him rather than wiping it on his sleeve.

The oldest girls were twelve - the age when it became legal for men to prey on them. Elizabeth looked at them and saw Pasley. But these were the *respectable and deserving poor* whose parents somehow found the few pence necessary to send them to Sunday School where they learned to read and write and *do sums* as Millie Powler called it. They worked in factories during the week and had to give up their free time to come. But they were awarded stamps for attendance and once their stamp sheets were full they received a small prize.

Some of the children didn't attend regularly and Elizabeth knew that was because their parents had no money to spare. Edie Dakin hadn't been for some weeks now, nor Albert Buckley. She'd heard that Edie's mother was ill and Albert's father had lost his job. She wanted to tell them they could come anyway but then they would have to say that to all the children. Most of the families were teetering on the brink of that other category like birds clinging to a cliff face.

But she wanted to show Dr Kay that these children weren't in gangs on the street or suffering from some unmentionable disease passed on by their parents. The parents were good, decent people who wanted their children to have different horizons from themselves. The kind of people she'd written about in her book.

The book he'd never acknowledged. Perhaps she should have written it in German, she thought, eyeing Susanna. But he was good with the children, joking with them, producing small cakes of soap from behind their ears.

Each child returned to their seat equipped with a lollipop and a bar of soap. Some of the boys were waving them about, others seemed mystified. A few would be calculating what they could swap them for on the streets.

The inspections came to an end and Dr Kay stood in front of them once more. As the noise died down, he told them he was very impressed by them. They should be proud of themselves - they were the future of Manchester and Manchester, for all its shortcomings and difficulties, was a place of opportunity and hope, where children like themselves could make a difference. He mentioned several famous people who'd lived there: Sir Richard Arkwright, founding father of industry and John Dalton the famous scientist, who had started out poor, like themselves, with little or no education, but who, by dint of hard work, moral rectitude, and above all cleanliness, had become rich, important citizens whose names would be remembered in history.

It was a good speech but rather long and the children were getting restless again. Elizabeth interrupted it by clapping enthusiastically before he'd finished then joining him at the front.

'I'm sure we'll all remember your wise words, won't we children?' she said. 'Now, what do we say to Dr Kay?'

After a chorus of *thank yous*, it was time for the final hymn. Since it was so near Christmas, they had been rehearsing *Hark the Herald Angels Sing*. Susanna banged the keys of the piano, the children sang with more gusto than tune and Dr Kay joined in robustly.

Afterwards, the children filed out in a more or less orderly manner until Robbie Watts nudged Matthew Parker so that he dropped his lollipop and a fight broke out. The two of them had to be pulled apart by Millie. Then Ernie Prior said the kind of word he was definitely not allowed to say in Sunday School and Elizabeth had to intervene. When she looked up again she could see Susanna showing Dr Kay out.

'Dr Kay!' Elizabeth called, hurrying after him. 'I was hoping to speak to you.'

'And here I am,' Dr Kay said, bowing gallantly. She steered him into the office, where he congratulated Elizabeth on such a well-regulated school. Elizabeth thanked him again for his visit, applauded his speech, praised his way with the children, singled out the lollipops for special commendation, and just as his gaze was flickering away, said, 'But I need to consult you.'

His gaze flickered back.

'About a young girl in the New Bailey prison.'

Dr Kay raised his eyebrows. 'I see,' he said.

Briefly she told him the details. 'Do you know Dr Billington?' she asked.

'I may have met him once or twice. At the Dispensary.'

'I thought as much. He shouldn't be working there, or anywhere. He should be arrested!'

Dr Kay shook his head. 'Easier said than done. Are there any witnesses? Is there evidence?'

'The wardress would testify to the girl's distress when she saw him, but—'

'But it's in the nature of the crime that there were no witnesses to what actually happened,' Dr Kay finished for her.

'But we must do something! I thought you might speak to the Board, the trustees—'

'Did you?'

'Well someone has to - since your Dr Billington—'

'He isn't *my* Dr Billington—'

'—ruined this girl! She was put on the streets and now she's in prison. And who knows who else he's abusing—'

He looked at her quizzically. 'You're involving yourself very much in this case,' he said.

'Someone has to - she's so young - she has nothing—'

'Sadly that's not unusual. Poverty breeds crime and abuse, as you know.'

'So - we should do nothing?'

'I will look into it, of course - but—'

'But?'

Dr Kay frowned at the floor.

'Well if you won't speak to the Board I'll have to write to them—'

'I must ask you to do no such thing.'

'Why? Because they might feel it reflects badly on them? It does reflect badly on them—'

And on you, she didn't say.

'Mrs Gaskell, do you know how many people the Dispensary

treats?' he said. 'Thirteen thousand last year alone. Thirteen thousand people who would otherwise have no access to medical care. Do you know what the average life expectancy in the district was before we started? Seventeen years. *Seventeen!* For all you know without Dr Billington the girl would already be dead.'

'He might just as well have killed her! And how many others—'

Dr Kay took her arm, not gently. 'Shall I tell you what will happen if you go to the trustees? Several of the subscribers will withdraw their support. And who will suffer then?'

Elizabeth shook her arm free. 'The subscribers have a right to know what their money is supporting. I can't stand by and let *that man* continue to prey upon young girls!'

Dr Kay was silent for a moment, then he said, 'You ladies and your charitable works.'

'I'm sorry?'

'Sometimes you don't think before rushing in . . . '

'Are you saying I shouldn't try to help her?'

'No, but—'

'But you don't think I should tell the Board. Or the Press? Shouldn't they know what's going on? Doesn't everyone deserve to know?'

Dr Kay closed his eyes briefly.

'There is the truth you can tell and the truth people can hear,' he said. 'They're not the same thing. You of all people should know that.'

What did he mean by that? She started to speak but he said, 'Leave it with me. Do me the kindness of not taking this any further until I get back to you.'

He turned abruptly, and left her.

Elizabeth leaned against the table feeling quite shaken. She hadn't meant to argue with him but she had hoped for a better response.

You ladies and your charitable works.

There was so much she could have said to that! Where would the people of Manchester be without *ladies* and their *charitable works*?

She could have reminded him that many mill owners and

businessmen subscribed to the dispensary. What would they think if they knew about the doctor?

But she didn't want to fall out with him, she wanted him to help her. She couldn't do anything now without going over his head, and risk losing what friendship they had. She would have to wait to see what he did.

She'd meant to ask him if he would come with her to visit Pasley. If he examined her and saw for himself that she'd been with child surely that would make him do *something*? But Miss Jopson might not agree to it. And there was no point asking him now . . .

It wasn't good enough. *She* wasn't good enough. She was failing yet again.

She would have to try to encourage Pasley to talk about the doctor however painful it was for her.

CHAPTER 13

Pasley

THE NEXT MORNING I wake up with a start when the bell rings and don't know where I am. Only as it goes on clanging do I realise I'm still in prison. I get up slowly, tug my dress on and begin rolling up my bed just as the door bursts open. Miss Hannaway stands there with a face on her like a bulldog chewing a bear, as Lizzie Clegg would say.

'Kitchens!' she barks at me.

It's my turn to dole out the tea and bread.

I follow her along the corridor past the sounds of doors opening and women shuffling into line.

'Here,' Miss Hannaway says shoving a cloth at me. I begin wiping the trays. My fingers feel numb, my neck stiff. I must have slept on it crooked.

Of course I spill the tea. Miss Hannaway stands over me shouting while I mop it up. When I finish she thrusts her foot onto the wet patch, leaving the muddy mark of her sole.

'Still dirty,' she says.

Some of the girls would argue with her giving her the excuse to drag them into the corridor by their hair. I mop the patch again.

'You call that clean?' she says.

Ah, God.

As I mop it again she thunders on about the filth of the Irish, living like pigs in their own swill. I don't look at her, even once.

Finally she lets me serve the tea, telling everyone why it's late. The girls shuffle in their places and glower at me.

But it's in the oakum room that the storm blows up. Mary Kelly says she's picked five baskets already, not four, and Jane Morris pipes up the same.

'You've done as many as I say you have!' Hannaway thunders. 'And if I say so you'll do it all again in the refractory! We'll see what the warders there think of your lip.'

'Least they can count you gib-faced bitch,' says Mary.

Everything happens very fast then. Hannaway lands a blow on Mary's head and Mary rears up to her great height and empties her basket all over Hannaway. Jane Morris flings hers at the wall and Lizzie Clegg shouts 'Go!'

Hannaway blows a whistle and more warders come running. Mary and Jane are dragged into the corridor. It takes three warders to haul Mary out, kicking and screeching. The rest of us are herded into the exercise yard to tramp round and round in the sleet.

Even my head feels numb and there's a clawing pain in my stomach. I try to think about Mrs Gaskell and her daughters by the fire but I can't see them properly.

But as we file back Miss Jamieson is waiting. I know at once what she'll say. My stomach turns over and seems to fall.

I follow her back to my cell where Mrs Gaskell is sitting already. She's wearing a blue dress this time.

'Good morning, Pasley,' she says in that voice of hers, so calm and sweet. I can't look at her. My fingers are shaking as I take off my shawl.

'You must be cold,' she says. 'Come and sit near me.'

I glance at Miss Jamieson who nods, so I perch on the edge of my bed.

'If you need me,' Miss Jamieson says to Mrs Gaskell, 'just ring the bell.'

The door clicks shut as she leaves.

'Well, here we are again,' says Mrs Gaskell.

When I manage to look at her, so clean and smiling, I can't speak. My voice seems to have shrivelled up.

She says, 'I'm afraid I asked Miss Jopson for you to be examined. I hope you didn't mind too much. It was necessary unfortunately, to establish the state of your health – before you leave.'

One of the nurses checked my hair, my fingernails and my teeth. Is that's what she means? I don't know what to say about that. I shuffle into a better position, back straight, feet flat on the floor. Like in the classroom at the orphanage. I don't know what to do with my hands. I clasp them together, then rub them along my thighs.

'I need to know – you see – what happened to you.'

My skin tightens and my throat feels funny.

'You do understand that, don't you?'

Tears prick my eyes. I brush them away before they fall on the table.

She touches my shoulder then leans forward and tucks a strand of hair back into my cap. 'I'm so sorry,' she says, softly. Her voice is like feathers. She lifts my face and looks at me long and steady, and my heart and stomach lurch together as though tumbling down a slope.

'I know it's distressing for you,' she says, 'but I need you to tell me what happened with the doctor.'

My face begins to burn. I stop looking at her and stare down at my hands instead, twisting my apron. Because when I tell her she will never look at me kindly again.

She places one of her own hands very gently over mine, my rough red knuckles and bitten nails, until they stop twisting. When she lets go my hands feel cold. She says, 'Why did Mrs Digby send for him?'

It was the cotton-blindness. My eyes grew so sore and swollen from fibres and dust I could hardly see. My chest tightened so I couldn't breathe either but I was most afraid of going blind. I couldn't do my work and I was one of the fastest workers there. Still I never dreamed Mrs Digby would call a doctor, but when more of us were struck down the same she said she would have to though it would ruin her, because a blind stitcher's no use to man nor beast.

I can feel Mrs Gaskell waiting.

So I tell her with many stumbles and starts and she doesn't get impatient with me, she listens and nods, only asking questions when my voice shrivels up completely. When I cry she passes me her own handkerchief!

Only sometimes I see her purse up her mouth into a thin line and then I falter because I must have said something wrong, something to displease her. But she wants me to keep going and I try, I really do. I tell her I went with the others to the parlour where none of us had ever been before. My eyes were so feeble by that time I had to grope my way along the wall. All I could see of him at first was black – a coat so black I thought he'd come to bury me, and a black hat. Then the bitter smell of the drops he brought, like turpentine and cloves.

He dropped them into my eyes and they burned like fire. I cried out, and he made me sit down until they stopped stinging. Then he treated the others the same – all of us crying like cats.

He told Mrs Digby we should bathe our eyes with salt and make sure to boil the water. I expected her to say she had no time for that but she just said, 'Yes, doctor,' meekly enough and he said he would come back with more drops to see how we were doing. And he did come back. And that's when he sent for me on my own.

My words catch up in my throat. I hope she understands what I can't say. I believe she does. No one has ever listened to me so, and yet I can't talk to her. I start to stammer and then I have no words left.

But she touches my hair which has escaped again and says, 'Thank you,' and I look at her, hardly believing she would thank me for such a poor tale as that.

She says, 'You've been through so much,' and I feel tears brimming once more, because no one has ever said that to me.

Then she's silent for so long I fear I must have offended her after all. I see her tongue pass quickly over her lips, darting out and in again. She says, 'Was that – why you had to leave Mrs Digby's?'

I want to tell her, I do, but I'm too choked up. For a second I think she will speak, then she stops herself. She looks almost frightened but how could that be? I try to say something but she puts her hands over mine to stop me.

'No, no,' she says. 'That - it's fine - you've said enough.'

I look at her hardly able to believe it, but she's closed her eyes. Terror strikes me and my words come tumbling out. I'm sorry I tell her, I wouldn't upset her for the world, she must believe me - but she lifts her hand and says, 'You are not to blame for any of this,' and I cry harder then. She doesn't hold me but she takes both my hands in hers.

'You must promise me you won't speak of these things to anyone else,' she says, and I shake my head but I never would have spoken at all if she hadn't pressed me.

She's looking at me so seriously I feel afraid all over again but then she says, 'You're hardly any older than my own daughters,' and her eyes are rimmed pink. My heart speeds up then and the image of that warm hearth flickers and dances in my mind. She presses my hand but looks beyond me and when I look up Miss Jamieson is there, as though she's been standing behind the door all this time.

I bet she has.

Mrs Gaskell stands and I stand with her. She tells me to be a good brave girl and to keep my spirits up.

'I hope to have better news when I return,' she says, and I stare at her dumbly wondering when that will be, but she's already turning away, fastening her cloak.

And once more I'm alone in my cell.

I sit on my bed, going over all the things she said.

You are like my own daughter, she said. Or no, she said I was the same age as her daughters. *And you've been through so much.*

She doesn't know the half of it.

You've said enough, she said, but I didn't say much really, about him.

Take off your dress, he said.

Mrs Gaskell said I wasn't to blame – but I should've said something, I should have asked him *Why?* But I didn't. I didn't say anything at all.

I pick up my pillow and press it to my face to stop the memories coming, but it doesn't stop them. Nothing does. All the things I couldn't say come marching through my head.

The door shut, *click*, and I was alone with him. I could see him properly for the first time. He wore his hat even though he was indoors. He had a pouchy, puffy face.

He sat on the arm of the chair and took his hat off. He had greyish hair, I remember that much, and spectacles. And bad teeth. I remember thinking a doctor should have better teeth.

Do you know why I've sent for you? he said, and I shook my head. Then he said he wanted to examine me properly.

Take off your dress, he said.

After he'd finished he told me to put my clothes on again. My fingers were shaking so I could hardly button them up. I must have been crying because he said, *Dear me, what a fuss.*

Then he wrote something down. *I'll give you something to soothe that cough of yours*, he said. *I'll have it sent over from the dispensary.*

He didn't look at me, he just picked up his bag and left.

I didn't know what to do, I just stood there like an eejit in that room. As if I couldn't even remember where I was.

But I remember the look on Mrs Digby's face. 'Never let it be said I don't take care of my girls,' she said.

I got the shakes that night – I couldn't sleep for them. In the end someone nudged me. I thought at first it was Alice, or Sal. I could only see the shadowy outline of a head bending over me. 'Hush up!' it said. 'You're making a right row.'

It was Martha. I must've been whimpering without knowing it. She said, 'You're mewling like a cat.' Her face tilted over me. 'Shall I get Mrs Digby?'

I shook my head hard as I could.

'You might need the doctor again.'

'*No!*' I said.

'Alright – all right,' Martha said. 'Keep your hair on.' Then she said, 'It wunt so bad were it?'

I stared at her.

'Look,' she said. 'Your sheet's all rucked up – no wonder you can't sleep. Try to smooth it out a bit – what?' Because I'd clutched her wrist.

'Wh – what do you mean?' I asked.

'Lie down,' Martha whispered. 'What d'you think I mean?'

'When – ?'

'When I cut my hand, remember and it all swelled up, and I went into a fever – I were glad enough to see doctor then! What kind of a stitcher has only one hand?'

'But—'

'She has to pay him somehow,' Martha said. She lowered her voice like Mrs Digby's. 'You think I'm made of money? All of you falling like flies and no money to bury you!'

I couldn't speak. Martha said, 'It's that or throw us on streets. Or bury us where we stand and have the rest of us sewing shrouds!'

'I'd rather be on the streets!'

'No you wunt. Streets is hard. Better off here.'

I shook my head.

'Well, you've had your turn now,' she said, thinking to comfort me. 'It won't happen again for a while.'

The thought of it happening again at *all* made me want to be sick on the bed.

'Will you two give over?' Squinty Sue's voice came from the far side of the room. A shape rose from the sheets. 'I'm telling on you if you don't get to sleep.'

'Here – shift up,' Martha said, and she clambered into bed with me. She tucked herself into me, just like Mattie used to at the orphanage, her rump against my stomach. I remember being surprised that she would do such a thing. But my mind was whirling with what she'd told me. I felt sick all over again at the thought of it, that he might send for me again.

I'll write, I thought, *to my mother, and my uncle.* Then I thought, *No one will answer.* Because I'd written before.

'Try to sleep,' Martha said. I could tell from her voice she was already dozing off. 'Shift'll start soon.'

I was still shaking, but with Martha so warm and slumberous beside me, I finally got to sleep.

When I woke up I knew I had to leave.

But I didn't, not right away. Days passed – I don't remember how many. Everything went by in a blur. I couldn't seem to get anything right. My stitches were too big, or I'd sewn the wrong seam. I dropped the pots I was carrying and spilled feathers all over the attic floor.

'What's got into you?' Mrs Digby said. 'Them feathers got in your brain?'

'Look at this mess!' she said. 'Forget your tea – you can clean up.'

'This shirt'll have to be stitched again – you're making more work for everyone!'

I didn't answer her, I didn't even look at her. But then she said, 'Happen the doctor'll have to make another visit.'

'No!' I said, and she laughed at me. 'Oh, you've got a tongue then? I thought the devil had got it.'

She came towards me. 'Come to think of it, you do look a bit peaky!'

I backed away from her. I remember her face, mean and scrunched up, like a picture I once saw of a shrunken head. Only the eyes were glinting like little glass beads. I couldn't help myself, I said, 'You are a wicked woman!'

Her face changed then. 'Wicked, is it?' she said, flicking her filthy cloth at me.

'Don't!' I cried but I was cut short by a blow to the side of my head. I fell backwards over the coal shuttle. I couldn't see but I could hear her shrieking down at me.

'What else are you fit for – you little bitch?' she screamed. 'I take you in and feed you – give you a home – you think all that comes free?'

Spit flew from her mouth, spraying me. When I was too dazed

to answer she grabbed my hair, pulling me upwards and striking me about the face and head till I thought I would pass out.

It was moon-face Sal who stopped her in the end. She dropped the bowl from her hands and stood in front of us crying loudly. And Martha ran up to her saying, 'It's all right, Sal – don't carry on – hush!'

Mrs Digby stopped and straightened up. I lay where I was pressing the back of my hand to my nose which was running with blood.

'What are you lot staring at?' she said. Then she snapped, 'Back to work – the lot of you!'

And they all disappeared. Mrs Digby stood over me, breathing hard.

'As for you – you no-good trollop,' she said, 'get this mess cleaned up!' She made a sudden movement towards me and I flinched expecting a kick or a blow, but she turned and left me.

That's when I saw I'd kicked the coal scuttle over. And Mrs Digby had knocked over a pan full of gruel, chasing me.

I spent the next hour on my hands and knees scrubbing at the mess. My head was still ringing where she'd hit me and my backbone felt like it'd split it in two – I must have hit it as I fell. But I didn't cry. It came to me again on my knees on that filthy floor, that I had to leave even if I didn't know how and I didn't have anywhere to go.

Then I fell sick.

Proper sickness that started early in the morning. By midday I couldn't keep anything down. The first time I managed to avoid throwing up over my stitching by grabbing the pot. Soon I had a bucket of my own.

'Let's hope it int catching,' Squinty Sue said and Martha said it was probably the tea. Water for it came from a big kettle on the stove but it was always brown. 'You'll be better tomorrow,' she said. But the next day I was worse if anything, and the day after, and by the morning of the third day I could only lie on my bed and moan.

Fat Alice said it might be the pox, whatever that was.

Someone, probably Squinty Sue, told Mrs Digby.

Mrs Digby made us all stand in a line while she walked past, the way she did when she was inspecting us for nits and lice. Even before she reached me I could smell the reek of her – gin and something else, sour and sickly. She stopped in front of me, jutting her chin out.

'Well if it int the lost princess,' she said softly, 'She's forgotten where her palace is, girls.'

I stared over her head.

Then her face changed. She stood back and looked at me.

'That int no pox,' she said. 'You're up the duff, or I'm a mermaid!'

Squinty Sue had said her sister had been *up the duff* three times and never known the father. So I knew what it meant but I couldn't believe it.

'I can't be—' I said.

'Half the mothers in Manchester have said that.'

I stared at the other girls. All of them were looking solemn or sly. Sal's mouth hung open as usual, Squinty Sue was smirking, but Martha looked pale and sick herself. The truth tolled inside me like a bell.

'What'll I do?' I stammered.

Mrs Digby said. 'You can clear out of here – that's what!'

And I surprised myself by bursting into tears.

She pushed her face into mine, breathing her foul stench. 'Skriking, is it?' she said. 'I can tell you this much – skrikers don't even know what suffering is. You'll find that out.'

And I stopped crying then, because there was so much menace in her I could hardly breathe. And because it was true. It was years since I'd cried for my mother.

'I've nowhere to go,' I said.

'There's places for trollops like you,' she said, and she carried on so I can hardly bear to think of it now, about how she'd taken me in, put a roof over my head, she could hardly be expected to look after my bastard as well – she ran a respectable establishment.

She said all that to me – and I just stood there and let her without once speaking back!

I was so ignorant then. I didn't even know it had anything to do with what had happened – with *him*. I didn't know how babies were made!

Mrs Digby told me to pack my things and go.

What things? I might've said to her, but I picked up the shawl and the clogs she'd given me for when I took the slops out instead of the good coat and shoes I'd arrived in. All the time she was ranting on at me, but I hardly heard. It was as if I'd gone deaf and blind with this new thing that had happened to me.

And then I asked for my wages.

Ah, you should have heard her! You'd've thought I'd asked for the moon.

'Wages?' she said, and before I could move her filthy cloth shot out, stinging the side of my face. '*You* talk to *me* of *wages?*' She flicked the cloth towards me again and I backed away. All the girls were clustered behind her.

'She's not paid any of you!' I cried to them. Mrs Digby lashed out, sending pots tumbling to the floor but just in time I dodged her. She was shrieking at me like a harpy from hell, how it was *she* who was owed money for keeping me, and about ingratitude and shame. I kept backing away from her but soon she had me trapped by the broom cupboard. She raised her fist to me but I caught the cloth, and twisted it from her grasp. All the girls gasped at once as though the air had been sucked from the room.

'No!' I said, staring straight into her beady eyes.

Then I shoved her to one side and ran to the door!

Dodds was there, staring at me with his mouth hanging open. There was no sign of Tucker for once, which was a mercy for I'd never have got past both of them. Dodds made a move towards me but Mrs Digby was screaming after me to get out and never come back, and so he let me go.

I ran right past him, out of that house and the yard. I'd never been further than the privy all the time I'd been at Mrs Digby's but now I saw there was another ginnel behind – so narrow I had to squeeze through sideways. I hurried on, slipping on something foul and turning my ankle. I could hardly see but I followed the sounds from the road.

Then suddenly I was on it.

Noise hit me like a steam engine, clanging and banging and roaring. The smell stung my eyes and I couldn't see much in any case because of the smoke. Easy to believe I'd missed my way and gone to hell. I shrank back and pressed myself up against the wall. I wanted to shut my eyes and clamp my hands over my ears. I even wanted to run back to Mrs Digby's.

But I couldn't do that so I stood like an eejit, staring at all the wagons and carriages and people.

One cart clattered past on iron wheels spattering me with mud and filth. I fell back into the alley, breathing hard.

I couldn't think for all the noise and I couldn't see the other side of the street for the fog. I was free at last on the streets of Manchester, I could go where I liked, but I hardly dared move.

I didn't tell Mrs Gaskell any of that.

Or about the baby.

She didn't ask.

I thought she would ask me, I thought that's what she wanted to know.

I'm glad she didn't, I don't know what I'd have said. But still I wonder why.

You've said enough, she said. I must have offended her. I wish I could take it all back! She said I mustn't speak of such things to anyone – and I never would have, but she asked me! And now I've driven her away.

CHAPTER 14

Elizabeth

RAIN DRIPPED FROM the rim of Elizabeth's bonnet, down the collar of her cape. She sat in her carriage forgetting to open the umbrella.

How could she have been so foolish?

She'd so wanted to get some evidence against the doctor she'd nearly asked Pasley something she shouldn't. Because if Pasley had been pregnant and got rid of the baby she could be imprisoned for life.

Or hung.

Nausea swam in her stomach. She pressed her hands to her face. A moan escaped her.

She remembered something Dr Kay had said, about his patients from the Deansgate brothels. Young women who'd suffered a certain *procedure*, often performed by their dames who would take care of *unwanted conditions*.

Then he'd stopped as if he'd said too much. Obviously it was not the kind of conversation any gentleman would have with a lady, but Elizabeth had four daughters after all. *I'm not entirely unfamiliar with female biology*, she'd said. And then he'd told her, in more detail than she could possibly want, that a caustic fluid such as lye was injected into the womb.

'They get it from the wash houses, or make it themselves by soaking wood-ash in water and mixing it with lime,' he'd said. 'Ingenious really. Generally, the patient goes into shock because of the burning, and the liquefaction of flesh and fat which precipitates a miscarriage.'

Elizabeth had felt sick although she would never have let him know, not while he was watching her, probably hoping she'd faint. 'Potentially lethal of course,' he went on when she didn't. 'Although good for trade. Those girls who survive the process never conceive again.'

Even now remembering it a bitter fluid filled her mouth. Because of her own children and the ones she'd lost. She could feel a low cramp in her stomach as though her womb remembered them, an ache beneath her ribs. Sometimes she felt as though they'd never left her, they were humming through her blood like a lost tune.

Could Pasley have had an abortion or been in a brothel like the ones in the Deansgate Rookeries which they were passing now?

Jim was trying to avoid a fight between gangs of youths. Missiles of various kinds flew across the road and Elizabeth finally remembered the umbrella as slutch spattered the carriage. Younger children ran after them crying for money and food. Then a tiny child toddled into the road. Jim pulled up sharply shouting, 'Hoy!' and the little boy turned and grinned at Elizabeth, a great, cock-eyed grin, revealing only one tooth in a smeared face.

A woman dived between the child and the carriage like a scrawny pigeon. 'What have I telled you – you black-faced bastard,' she screeched either at the child or Jim, it was difficult to say. But she pulled the child's arm until he was lifted quite off his feet. The cock-eyed grin turned square and he started to howl as she dragged him back to the pavement.

'Sorry, ma'am,' Jim said bitterly, over his shoulder.

Elizabeth couldn't breathe. She felt a pain like a stitch in her side.

That little boy, his smile!

Her own baby son had grinned at her in that same lop-sided way. That morning, when she'd found him in his cot . . .

For months afterwards nothing had made sense. She'd started taking laudanum to keep herself in a state of oblivion - just a few drops more each time.

She hadn't thought of it as killing herself of course, she'd thought of it as *being with him*.

Only when she'd actually started to see him in his cot in the room she'd left untouched, had she frightened herself into trying to stop. She'd gone in talking to him and Hearn was there.

She could still see the look on Hearn's face.

Then she'd been carrying Julia which meant she had to stop taking the drops. The withdrawal had been terrible. She'd thought she would go mad.

Four years had passed since her baby son had died and still it was too raw, too near, to think about.

That little boy! How rough his mother was!

And all the abandoned babies, the tiny bundles dropped into the river . . . surely even abortion was better than that?

Still, she couldn't bear to think that Pasley might have got rid of her own baby in some obscene procedure. Or that she'd been in a brothel.

Her image of Pasley slipped into something at once coarser and more coy. A suggestive tilt of her chin, a lewd smile like the street girls she'd seen walking past groups of men.

But that wasn't Pasley - she shouldn't think such things of her!

But the baby - or the abortion - she could never ask about it again. Elizabeth moaned aloud once more.

'Is something wrong, Ma'am?' Jim said.

'No,' she answered in a choking voice. 'Keep going!'

This place, she could have said. It was this place that was wrong. The children born here, what chance did they have? The slums were like a sinkhole from which no one escaped.

Pasley had tried to escape and ended up in prison. Elizabeth didn't know how or what had happened to her after leaving Mrs Digby's. And now she was afraid to ask.

You ladies and your charitable works, Dr Kay had said. And she'd been so annoyed with him! But she'd virtually proved him right. She would have to try harder to prove him wrong.

CHAPTER 15

Pasley

ALL NIGHT A woman cries and screams for her lost cheating love. I hear her being dragged along the corridor to the poky, I expect, unless Mary and Jane are still there. I lie awake thinking about Mrs Gaskell. She's a writer, Miss Jamieson said. What's that like? To tell a story to the whole world.

I can't tell mine.

I think of all the things I will never tell her.

About leaving Mrs Digby's – how I'd no idea where I was going, I only knew I had to get away.

Every time someone loomed towards me through the fog I thought it was Tucker coming for me.

Three times I tried to cross that road and three times I fell back. On the fourth go I managed it, slithering over the muddy cobbles. Then I felt my way along a wall until I came to the window of a paraffin shop with lamps glimmering in it. Further along there was a man shouting some tale on the corner – 'Read it here first!' I dodged past him and turned off that road, desperate to escape the crowds and the smoke and cotton dust that was blowing into my eyes and mouth.

I was on a long street with houses either side. Some half built or crumbling away and many with signs in the windows: *good logins 4d/night*. I hurried past them because the people seemed so rough. Grim looking women with their arms folded across their pinnies, scabby dogs nosing through the muck and little children crawling after them.

I must have been near the Rochdale Road because the smell from the gasworks was thick as rotten eggs and the fog had turned brown.

I followed the sound of factory bells and joined a long queue for stitchers and dyers. I got almost all the way to the front before I was turned away and the girl in front of me said, 'There'll be nothing now till Monday.'

But I had to find work before Monday! I screwed up my courage and tried inns and taverns and gin shops with no success.

I tramped many hard and weary miles that day, past boys wheeling barrows and ragged children stealing from them. At last I found myself on Piccadilly where everybody was selling something, from flowers to string. I was so hungry and so many stalls sold food! I passed one heaped with apples where an old woman stood warbling a song: *how well they may bloom, how well they may bear, that we may have apples and cider next year.*

The smell of the apples made me dizzy but they cost a farthing each and I had no money. The old woman didn't falter when I walked up to her and I saw she was quite blind. I thought I could take an apple without her knowing, but then she turned her blind gaze on me as if she could see my soul.

I backed away for shame but there was another stall selling salted eels. The smell went straight to my stomach. I wondered what I could do for food with no money, and where I could go for a bed if it cost fourpence? I had to have a bed for the night or what would I do?

There's places for trollops like you, Mrs Digby said.

But I couldn't think about her or about the baby – I couldn't think about that at all. I told myself I'd escaped and survived so far on the streets with nothing but my clogs and shawl.

Then I thought I could try to sell the shawl.

The weather was warm enough, I didn't need it. And if, God forbid, Mrs Digby was looking for me, she'd recognise it right away.

I found a shop with a clutter of objects in the window. *Ma's Odds and Ends* it was called. Two elderly ladies came out and a rough-looking man. I dithered outside for a moment then slipped in.

There was a big table heaped with all kinds of things: an oil lamp burning, a stuffed bird in a cage, a set of weights and measures. And behind it, a tiny woman in a big shawl.

She stood up as I approached, hardly any taller than when she was sitting, and shuffled round the table. She took a long stick with a hook at the end and tugged at a blind over the window but only succeeded in rattling it. 'I thought you'd fixed this!' she called to someone in the back room, then she sighed and propped the stick up on a hat stand.

'Now,' she said, 'what can I do for you?'

I held out the shawl to her. 'I was hoping—'

'Sell, or pawn?' she said fingering the material. 'Pawn's better - you can always come back for it later, when the chill sets in.'

'How much?' I asked.

She shuffled back to the other side of the table. 'Int much call for shawls - most folk make their own.'

My heart sank. 'It's a good shawl,' I said.

'Might run to a penny.'

'A penny?'

'Or you could swap it for any of these fine objects here,' she said, nodding at a tray piled with ribbons and combs.

'I need money.'

'Don't we all, dearie?'

'I need lodgings.'

'Well now, that depends on how particular you are,' she said. 'There's places down by the river'll only charge tuppence.'

'Then I need tuppence,' I said. Her gaze flickered over me. 'Them's not a bad pair of clogs.'

I couldn't imagine tramping the streets of Manchester in my stockinged feet and said so.

'Stockings?' she said. 'Not silk by any chance?'

I looked at her. How likely was it I'd have silk stockings?

'Knit them yourself did you?' she said.

In fact I had. I'd knitted them at Mrs Fenton's and hadn't taken them off the whole time I was at Mrs Digby's since my feet were often cold.

'How much?'

'Throw in the shawl and I'll call it tuppence.'

'What?' she said, as I glared at her. 'You're welcome to try another shop but you won't make a better bargain. I'm shutting early, so make your mind up. I want to catch the market.'

I hadn't even the strength to haggle. And in any case I knew I wouldn't win. So right there in the shop I peeled off my stockings and passed them to her with the shawl.

'You won't miss them,' she said, handing me tuppence. 'Weather's lovely and warm.'

I said nothing. I felt like weeping but I wouldn't in front of her.

As I left she said, 'Try the *Fox and Goose* by the river. Tell them Ma sent you – they'll set you up nicely, you'll see.'

It felt strange, walking without stockings or shawl. I could feel every draft, and the spatter of mud on my shins.

Another great clanging of bells told me the factories were closing and the day's work was done. Soon the streets were heaving with women in striped skirts and shawls, men in caps and boots. I never knew there were so many people in the world! And all of them shouting and jostling. I was carried along with them to a market square where there were yet more stalls selling pots and geese. Then a group of lads came wearing brass-tipped clogs and carrying iron bars. People scattered before them so I ran too into a side street. Already I could hear the sound of glass smashing, howling and screaming.

I kept going and found myself on streets even more soot-blackened and tumble-down than before. Many of the windows were boarded up or smashed. A sign in one read NINA but I didn't know what that meant then.

I'd no idea where the river was but I thought it might be downhill so I walked down a sloping street. But it came to an end, the streetlamps disappeared and the fog grew dense and dark. I had to cut through an alley where the stench sickened me and step over a man lying on the muddy cobbles.

I could see no sign of the *Fox and Goose* and began to wander in a higgledy-piggledy fashion, forward and back. At last I came to a row of houses that looked as if they were crumbling into the river, but there was a sign on one saying *2d a bed*. I knocked on the door and when a barrel-shaped woman answered I asked her for lodgings.

'Sixpence up front,' she said.

I looked at the sign.

'Price has gone up,' she said. And then, 'We don't want your sort here,' pointing to another sign, NO IRISH NEED APPLY. Then she slammed the door. I felt as though I'd been punched in the stomach, but what could I do?

There were more signs, the same, in each window along the row.

I couldn't believe these rough folk thought themselves so superior! That because I was Irish all doors would be closed to me.

At last I began to weep hopelessly, remembering how my mother had deserted me, what the doctor had done to me and how I had not a friend in the world.

I wondered what my mother would think if she could see me?

Nothing, I thought. *She would think nothing at all.*

I made my way out of that street into another and at the corner of what I now know as Toad Lane I saw a pump. I bent over it, drinking from my cupped hands and splashing my face. I straightened slowly, thinking I'd found no work and had nowhere to go, I'd lost even my stockings and I was fit to drop.

Then at last I thought about the baby, a tiny grub eating away at me. I bent over double and was sick on the cobbles like a common tink! The nothing that was in my stomach spattered on the ground.

That's when I knew I wasn't fit to have a baby. I couldn't even take care of myself.

Slowly I straightened and looked around as well as I could through the fog. I realised I'd accomplished part of my aim at least for I could hear the rush and slap of the river, the sounds of boats passing.

And I thought there might be an end to my troubles after all.

I made my way there and stopped on the first bridge I came to. I leaned over it, seeing the slow churn of its waters, the brown foam. But just then, a voice spoke from nowhere, startling me.

'Problem is,' it said, 'it's nigh on impossible to sink. Water's too thick. Worst that can happen is you'll float around for a bit – then you'll have to climb out again, considerably damper than before.'

※

Morning comes at long last, bleak and drear. After breakfast, I put on my bonnet and cape again and fall into line between Annie and Mary this time. We trudge around the yard in the freezing rain, for exercise they tell us.

I keep step with the rest, eyes lowered, hands clasped. They're chapped, the knuckles red. I can't remember when they weren't like that.

Someone in front of me stumbles and Miss Hannaway shouts at them. She's miserable from hating us. Her nose is red in the cold air but she's holding a mug of hot tea and steam rises from it.

I match my steps to Mary's. If we fall out of step there'll be trouble. I can hear the ragged breathing of Annie behind me, Mary's hacking cough.

After an hour of tramping round we go inside and remove our bonnets and capes. Then we stand in line for inspection. Some of the women mutter and groan, and Miss Hannaway calls order. We will all have points taken from us she says.

No points, no privileges. No visits.

I stand very still, eyes lowered as Miss Hannaway walks along the line. I'm a model prisoner, that's what Miss Jopson says. I heard her say it to Miss Jamieson.

One of the girls has a stain on her apron, another's hair has fallen from her cap giving Miss Hannaway a reason to bellow at her. I make sure not to look up as she stops in front of me, pushing her great red face close to mine. She sniffs at me like a dog.

'What have you been up to, Irish?' she says. That's what she calls me, *Irish*. Does she think I don't know Hannaway is an Irish name?

'You're a sly one, aren't you?' she says. My heart is pounding so I think she must surely hear it and I feel the urge to laugh like a demon. I have to bite my cheeks.

'Butter wouldn't melt,' she says.

Of course I don't answer. She'll get tired soon of baiting me. And she does, she moves on quickly for once. I return to my cell taking a basket of oakum with me.

There must be enough yarn in here to wind around the world and tie one end to the moon.

Soon, they tell you, you'll grow calluses on the ends of your fingers. Not soon enough – mine still bleed. I've tried winding strips of cloth around them but then I can't pick out the fibres. So my fingers hurt but it takes my mind off other pains.

Sometimes I pull the thread hard to make them bleed. Today instead I think about Mrs Gaskell, her face bending over me.

I see the fire, the books, her daughters at her knee.

You're just like my own daughter, she said.

Then my heart begins to beat like a savage on a drum. She must need help sometimes with the house and all those books?

I put the yarn down and walk about my cell. I tell myself not to be foolish, but there is a new feeling in me like a candle or a hot potato that you hold to warm your hands.

The day passes like any other apart from this new feeling of hope. I unpick three more baskets of yarn, wondering when she will come to me next, and what she will say, and what I will say to her. I mustn't seem too eager when she asks.

I wonder what else she will ask me. It's hard to remember what I've said already and what I haven't said.

Then a new, terrible thought comes to me. Did I say the word 'bladdered' to her, like a common tink? I did say 'eejit' – I'm almost sure of it. My face burns – she will think me so low! I rub my arms as they start to itch and scratch, though I know it will make it worse. As though I will tear my skin off in shreds.

I press my hands together to stop them scratching. There is a kind of grease on them that I never had before even on the streets, a prison grime. It comes to me suddenly that I must smell, that she will smell it on me. I can smell myself, rank and rancid as old meat. It's not the kind of smell you can ever get rid of even after scouring yourself. It's the foul stink of sin.

I could never take that smell into her home.

All my hope drains away like dirty water down a sluice. I have a bad feeling as though beetles are crawling around inside me. If I open my mouth they will crawl out of it.

I remember looking down at the water, clinging to the rail to stop my fingers trembling.

I must try to sleep, to stop the thoughts from coming. I pick up my blanket to shake it for lice, but just then the door to my cell opens very quietly. I stare at it; no one is there. Then I hear Miss Hannaway's voice saying, 'There you are ladies, she's all yours.'

And they enter silently, Ella Gibb, and Lizzie Clegg, with other girls behind.

CHAPTER 16

Elizabeth

ELIZABETH WAS STILL worried about Pasley and the horrible mistake she'd nearly made but she was too busy to return to the prison. The next day, the writer Geraldine Jewsbury came to lunch and despite Elizabeth's best efforts stayed for tea. This when she was trying to prepare her talk for the Mothers' Association. Then Elizabeth and William were invited to the Behrens' for Hanukkah, and William went from there to the Sun Inn to meet with a group of writers who were campaigning with him for the Free Library. These 'labouring poets' as they called themselves, had produced ballads about it on leaflets. Elizabeth said she would give them to the Sunday School children for their parents and put them in the food parcels she was helping to prepare for the recently unemployed.

She just managed to complete the story she'd promised to Travers Madge for his *Penny Magazine* before Tottie arrived. Tottie, whose real name was Eliza Fox, was an artist. She was much younger than Elizabeth but as soon as they'd met a spark had kindled between them. Elizabeth had talked to her about writing, about never finding the time. And then when she had the time, her courage failed her and she would do almost anything else to distract herself. She'd even told Tottie her guilty secret – that she sometimes imagined living alone in the country or by the sea, writing freely without interruption. Tottie had understood immediately. And now they would be together for three whole weeks and there would be so much to talk about! But extra food had to be ordered, the bedrooms rearranged, the sheets washed and a chimney sweep found since the bedroom fire wouldn't light without discharging quantities of smoke and soot into the room.

They were barely ready when Tottie arrived in a flurry of laughter and talk. She'd brought sweets and drawing materials for the girls and spent most of the afternoon showing Julia how to draw a cat, and Flossie a cow, then arranging Polly into various poses while Meta sketched her.

All the girls loved Tottie. It was hard to persuade them to go to bed but at last Elizabeth was alone with her since William was out teaching one of his classes.

Tottie told Elizabeth about her plans to coach girls for the Royal Academy Schools. Her father was using his considerable political influence to persuade them to take on female students at last. And in the New Year she would be travelling to France and Italy with two of her favourite models to study there.

Elizabeth listened wistfully. They would be spending the winter in Manchester, although she might persuade William to venture as far as Silverdale in the spring.

'And,' Tottie said, leaning forward conspiratorially, 'what do you think?'

Elizabeth, thinking about Silverdale or possibly Grasmere, had lost the thread of the conversation.

'My dear, lovely, generous father, has offered his library to me and my friends for *life* drawing!'

Elizabeth looked blank.

'So we can draw undraped models!'

'Ah!' said Elizabeth, adding, 'Wonderful,' a little uncertainly, although she and Tottie had frequently deplored the prohibition against female artists drawing from life.

'My good friend Francis who paints at the Academy has said he will speak to some of the models there to see if they will come – and we may have men as well as women!'

Elizabeth grappled with this notion. 'Will that be quite – safe?'

'Safe?'

'I mean – might there not be gossip – from your neighbours?'

'No one will know!' said Tottie. 'That's the beauty of it. There's a high wall around my father's house and tall trees in the garden. If anyone notices people arriving they'll think it's just a regular soirée!'

Elizabeth couldn't help thinking that if she held that kind of soirée in her house her neighbours would soon find out. The news would spread like fire. There was something still a little village-like about Manchester when it came to gossip. Perhaps they should go to London rather than Arnside or the Lake District, she thought.

Paris or Rome, of course, would be preferable . . .

'And, you know,' Tottie was saying, 'Meta is such a talented painter – if you wanted to send her to stay some time – it would be a marvellous introduction for her—'

'Oh – !'

But she was saved from responding by the arrival of Hearn who told them that Julia had just been sick and they were out of sheets, but might she perhaps wrap her in a quilt? Should she stay in the same room as the others? Elizabeth hurried upstairs to comfort Julia, but having determined that she'd eaten all the sweets Tottie had brought, helped Hearn to take the sheets from Julia's bed then tucked her in with Flossie.

Tottie was contrite and had to be reassured that it was no trouble at all, moving the girls around. Then William came home and they all played cards together in the dining room.

So many thoughts whirred around Elizabeth's mind as she sank finally into bed, about Paris and Rome and Christmas shopping with Tottie and the letters she still had to write. With a pang of guilt she remembered Pasley. Could she fit in a visit to the prison in the few days before Christmas? Perhaps she could send a parcel instead? But she would have to write to the governor first as well as the Matron and then put the parcel together and post it.

There was so little time before Pasley's release and still nowhere for her to go.

CHAPTER 17

'CAN'T SHE STAY here with you?' Tottie asked.
'Oh, no - I don't think so,' Elizabeth replied quickly. 'There's so little room.' She thought guiltily of Pasley's tiny cell, 'And we're looking for a new house - that would be unsettling for her . . .'

How feeble she sounded! 'William wouldn't like it,' she said, knowing that William would have half the homeless of Manchester in their house if she let him. And then it would be her job because he would be out.

'Have you asked him?' Tottie said.

In fact, she hadn't and in that moment she knew why. She felt a rush of heat in her cheeks.

'He's so busy,' she said. *When was he not busy?* He was chairman of the Portico and professor at the New College as well as teaching classes at the Mechanics Institute and training working men for the ministry. And there was the Lit and Phil, and the Domestic Mission, and the library campaign . . .

'It would hardly be fair to him.'

Tottie looked doubtful. 'Well, if I wasn't going abroad in the New Year she could come to me.'

'But you are,' Elizabeth said, unaccountably irritated.

'But if there's really nowhere else for her to stay—'

'Who's coming to stay?' said Meta, entering the room.

'No one,' said Elizabeth with a warning look at Tottie. 'I was just saying we've had quite enough visitors as it is. Not you, of course!' she added hastily to Tottie. 'You're family.'

'I like having people to stay,' Meta said. Crouching by Tottie's chair she went on, 'Aunt Tottie – you said you would show me how to draw Polly again.'

Tottie laughed. 'I don't remember that.'

'You did, you know you did! I want to draw her while she's at the piano! Do come with me!'

Tottie allowed herself to be pulled out of the room. Elizabeth started to clear papers from the table, shaking them aggressively into place.

Can't she stay here with you?

Why was it all up to her?

It wasn't fair! No one else had done anything to help Pasley.

What was Parliament doing for girls like her?

It was alright for Tottie who had never been married or had children, to suggest Elizabeth should take Pasley into her home. Obviously she thought it would be nothing, no extra effort, just one more mouth to feed.

She was cross with Tottie – furious, even!

All the talks they'd had about how women were forced to surrender their artistic talents to domesticity. How a talented woman would subordinate herself to her more important husband, managing his affairs, promoting him, acting as secretary. Yet now it appeared Tottie saw Elizabeth in the same wifely, motherly role!

She was a wife and mother, of course, and proud of it. Why was she so offended?

Would it really be so bad to have Pasley?

Elizabeth sat down again, pushing the paper to one side.

How would the girls react?

She could tell Pasley not to speak about her past but they would want to know. Meta would have it out of her. And then something would be lost or tainted, just hearing about such things. Nothing would ever be the same.

Elizabeth would be responsible for her education, her physical and moral welfare, her marriage. Or if she didn't marry, given her history there was the prospect of her living with them as their maiden foster-daughter. Of providing for her in their will.

Unthinkable. Were there no limits to what she was supposed to do?

That's what comes of having a God who sacrificed himself for mankind, Charles Behrens had said to her. Although Charles himself was a great philanthropist, using his considerable wealth to fund schools, asylums, infirmaries, and countless other charitable causes.

Nothing equalled the vast machinery of philanthropy in the city! The churches, the charities, the refuges, the missions, the institutes, associations and schools. Virtually everyone in Manchester was engaged in the industry of charity, but to what effect? *It's an interesting truth*, Dr Kay had said when she was researching her book, *that no matter how much effort is expended on the misfortunate, their numbers do not reduce, but are steadily, even rapidly, increasing. That's a statistical fact.*

The image of Pasley rose in Elizabeth's mind, her wounded face, her jutting wrists. She did want to help her, of course she did. But she couldn't take her in as an extra unwanted daughter. Or as a replacement for her lost daughter, who would have been the same age as Pasley now. Elizabeth didn't want to replace her.

She'd longed for another child after losing her baby boy. Another son if she was entirely honest, but Julia had been born just over a year later and now she was three years old. Elizabeth didn't want to try again, even for a son.

She felt a vertiginous sensation, as though the dimensions of the room she was in had suddenly changed. *She didn't want to be a mother again.*

Something else was calling her, something shadowy and ungraspable. She didn't want to know what it was. She didn't need to know.

All she knew was that she wasn't going to take Pasley into her home.

Surely she hadn't given her the impression that she might?

She went back through the conversations they'd had, what she'd said. She didn't think she had . . .

But perhaps she shouldn't see her so often in case it gave her the wrong idea.

A wave of relief tinged with shame passed through her. She needn't try so hard to visit Pasley before Christmas.

But she wasn't abandoning her like everyone else – she would help her in any other way she could. She would send that parcel and a letter, to let her know she wasn't forgotten. *You are in my thoughts*, she would say. *Constantly.*

You are constantly in my thoughts.

CHAPTER 18

Pasley

WHITE OBLONG, BLURRED. Orange when I close my eyes. Shifting and bobbing when I open them.
Think you'll talk to your lady-friend do you?

Bile pumps from my stomach out of my mouth.
For God's sake!
I've changed these sheets already!

※

White oblong, blurred at the edges.
Window.
Not my window.

※

Can you open your eyes for me please?
Open your eyes. That's right.
Blurred light, shadow.
Open your mouth.
Stuff this in her mouth!
Open your mouth for me, please.
Grey-black curls and a yellow face. Pouches under the eyes, dragging down. Bloodshot whites, rimmed red.

Can you lift your arm?
Pain like knives in my ribs.
Soon have you back on your feet.
Doctor.
I don't want a doctor.
Something presses against my lips. Sore.
Some kind of drink.
It tastes bitter and hurts like gravel going down.

I sink back. Orange against my eyelids. *Window. Not my cell window.*

I've been here before. When *he* came. The other doctor.
I don't want to be here. But it hurts to move.
I turn my face away.
Sleep.

※

'Pasley?'
'Pasley, can you hear me?'
Slowly I open my eyes. Blink in the light.
'That's it, girl – that's better.'
Miss Jamieson. I close my eyes again.
'Doctor says you're getting better.'
Doctor.
'He says you can stay here tonight, but in the morning we've got to move you back to your cell.'
I feel her weight on the end of the bed.
'I know you can hear me.'
'Miss Hannaway won't be there – she'll be on a different wing . . .'
Slowly I turn my face to her and open my eyes. I see her wince. It's her turn to look away.
'I can send for a chair, if you like . . .'
A chair? I think of one of the sedans that rich ladies are carried around in. Then I realise she means a wheeled chair.

I think of being pushed along corridors, everyone knowing what they did to me. I turn my head away, no.

'But you can't walk.'

Can't I? For the first time I wonder what they've done and a memory comes like a lightning flash, of not being able to breathe.

Irish cunt.

I move my legs in the bed. Pain shoots from my knees to the top of my skull.

'Can you sit up?'

I don't even try.

'Well,' she says, gruffly, 'not long, now . . .'

She means till my release. I look at her again and see her registering what that might mean. That I won't survive on the streets, I'll be dead within weeks. Or worse . . .

She blinks as I look at her. Suddenly I wonder what they've done to my face.

Is there a mirror here?

But she's pushing herself up from my bed.

'I'll be back for you tomorrow.'

When she's gone I try to sit up but it makes blood pump in my ears. Pain twists from my ribs down through my guts, my hips.

What have they done to me?

The nurse comes, a runty, bow-legged creature. It takes all I have not to cry aloud as she shifts my pillows and props me up against them.

When I can speak again I ask her for a mirror.

'Int no boudoir,' she says.

I stare at her and she leaves. I touch my face. It seems swollen, bruised, but I can't feel scars or burns. My nose isn't broken. There's a patch of dry skin on my chin but that was there before.

The nurse comes back with a mirror.

My hand trembles as I hold it out. She passes it to me but I drop it on the bed, so she holds it up and I almost cry out. All

I can see is brown splotches. Then I realise it's the mirror that's freckled not my face.

I peer into it.

My eyelids are swollen and pink, my face blue-black apart from the red bit near my chin, a cold sore on my lower lip.

My teeth are yellow, but still there.

I turn my head from side to side in case they burned my hair off.

'Good enough for you?' the nurse says, and I sink back.

They've not cut my face.

I once saw Silas split a girl's lips open from ear to ear but they've not cut me.

What does that mean?

Does it mean he wants me back – to work for him?

For the first time I turn my face into the pillow and weep.

※

Mrs Gaskell bends over me, sweet and merciful, like an angel. And then I realise it is an angel, a stone angel in the cemetery. It's the angel from my mother's grave. She was dead all this time, and I didn't know it.

I wake myself up crying.

It hurts to cry. And when I try to shift myself in the bed.

Does Mrs Gaskell know I'm here? Has she visited me?

They wouldn't let her see me.

Still, I would like to know if she came.

※

The doctor comes again but I won't look at him. If he asks me to take my clothes off I'll scream. He pokes and prods about and listens to my chest. But all he says is, 'Well, I think you're ready to go back now. No lifting and carrying though.'

Then he says, 'You'll have to be more careful in future.'

I don't say anything.

'Stay in your cell for now,' he says. 'That's the safest bet.'

I don't say anything to this either. How stupid would you have to be to think me safe in my cell? Wasn't that where they came for me?

He harrumphs about and gives some medicine to the nurse, then there's a knock on the door. Miss Jamieson with the chair. It has a wicker seat and three wheels.

I won't go in it.

But as she and the nurse lift me from the bed I cry out. My knees buckle when I try to stand. She's right, I can't walk.

They lift me into the chair and cover me with a blanket. A porter helps Miss Jamieson carry me down two flights of stairs, then she bumps me over the cobbles in the yard.

I shrink back as we approach the cells.

'What?' she says. Then she says. 'You needn't worry – Lizzie and Ella are in the refractory.'

The poky. So small you have to stand. No window, no air.

I don't ask how they knew it was them, or about the others, at least six of them. I say nothing all the way to my cell.

Another warder helps Miss Jamieson up the last flight of stairs then she wheels me along the corridor.

So many locked doors, so many women behind them listening.

The door to my cell is already open. I blink as Miss Jamieson wheels me in, then blink again. The smell of lime stings my eyes, my nose.

It takes me a moment to realise they've scrubbed away the blood.

Just for a moment I want to weep and beg Miss Jamieson not to leave me here, but I don't.

I watch as she turns the blanket back and plumps the thin pillow as far as she's able.

'Come on, girl,' she says.

I try not to gasp as she helps me into the bed telling me to get some rest, she'll come back with my medication soon. Only as she's leaving do I say, 'Has Mrs Gaskell been?'

She stiffens but all she says is, 'We've not heard from her.'

I nod to hide my disappointment.

'How long was I . . . ?'

'Just over a week.'

A *week?* I heard they don't keep anyone more than two nights in the hospital. Even the ones who try to off themselves they patch up and send back again fast as they can.

'What day is it?'

'Monday. Just over a week off Christmas.'

Christmas.

'We'll have you right again by then.'

'She hasn't written or – or left a message?'

'Don't go bothering your head about her,' Miss Jamieson says and because she means it kindly tears prick my eyes. 'Folk like her start off well but they all fall off in the end . . .'

I will not cry.

'Try to get some sleep,' she says. 'I'll bring some crutches later so you can practice walking.'

I turn my face away. After a moment I hear the door clang shut. Then I'm alone.

Mrs Gaskell didn't come or leave a message.

Perhaps I won't see her again.

I can't talk to her in any case – Ella and Lizzie have seen to that.

Think you'll talk to your lady-friend do you?

They needn't have worried – I've told her nothing. Nothing of any note.

This is for Ginnie.

I could never tell Mrs Gaskell about Ginnie.

When I try to summon her face to comfort me it's Ginnie I see. Then Silas and Ida and Buzz.

Too many faces.

I can hear my breathing rough in my chest. Hurting my ribs.

I think about the water, lapping and sucking at the bridge. And I realise there is still that. I can finish the job I started on that bridge.

Mrs Gaskell was so shocked when I told her about it.

I shift about my bed as far as I can without hurting myself. After a long time, it seems, I fall asleep.

But when I wake again in the night it's all I can think about. The bridge and the man on it. The shock of him being there when I'd thought I was alone.

He was a little man, even smaller than me. His legs were too short for the rest of him and his back was crooked. But he had thick, curling brown hair, and his face was almost beautiful. He looked like one of the statues of angels in churchyards, come to life.

'Nothing worse than wet clothes,' he said, 'this time of year.'

I clung to the rail to stop my fingers trembling.

'Filthy an'all,' he said. 'I wouldn't want to swallow any of that.'

I felt a prickle of vexation. 'Leave me alone,' I muttered, not looking at him.

'Could do,' he said, 'or you could tell me why a nice girl like you is hanging over a bridge.'

I retreated from him but he followed me. He extended his hand, which of course I didn't take. 'The name's Stanford,' he said, 'Stanford Busby, though you can call me Buzz.'

I glanced back at the water and he said, 'Now don't say you're going to make a little chap like me jump in after you? In these fine clothes?'

He was wearing mustard-coloured trousers and a purple waistcoat. He held a walking stick with a horsehead for a handle. I thought he looked ridiculous.

'That'd be half a year's savings gone – just like that,' he said, clicking his fingers. 'And then I'd have the expense of getting myself togged up again. A gentleman in my line of work has to look the part, you know.'

I wouldn't ask what his line of work was. I sidled away from him again as he took a step towards me. Not too close. He seemed anxious not to frighten me. And oddly enough I wasn't frightened. Maybe I was too far gone for that.

'Please – just go,' I said.

'So you can get on with drowning yourself?'

When I didn't reply he said, 'You know what? You don't have to tell me anything – I'll tell you. Let's see. Pretty girl like you, dress torn, dirt on her face – seems like someone's done you a bad turn.'

I touched my face.

'Some chap or other I shouldn't be surprised. It's a common enough tale. Young girl comes to the city with hope in her heart but things don't turn out the way she planned. City int kind. It chews folk up and spits them out again. Before she knows it she's lost her way and can't find it again.'

All the time he was talking he was edging closer to me. He was small but stocky. I didn't fancy my chances of fighting him off but I was reluctant to leave the bridge, having summoned up my purpose. I moved away from him once more. He stopped and nodded towards the water.

'Powerful wet down there,' he said.

Go away, I thought.

'I don't suppose you've a job of any kind?' he said.

I pushed a strand of hair from my face then said I was a trained seamstress.

'A seamstress!' he exclaimed. 'Well you can't be short of work in Cotton City! There are jobs everywhere for those skilled with the needle.'

'Not for me,' I told him.

'You can't have looked very far – I'll bet there's twenty jobs going on this street!' he waved his hand at the row of houses teetering on the banks. 'Of course it's after-hours now, but you come here tomorrow and count all the boards in the windows!'

All of them saying No Irish, I thought. When I didn't answer, he said, 'Do you have anywhere to go?'

I shook my head.

'Anyone to go to?'

I shook my head again.

'Then it's settled,' he said. 'You can come with me. I know a place you can stay and get a bit of food down you as well.'

I backed away from him. 'I'm not staying with you,' I said.

To my surprise he burst out laughing. 'With me?' he said, 'I shouldn't think so!' Then at the look on my face he said, 'I was thinking of another place. It int what you'd call grand but young ladies like yourself might lodge there awhile and work for their keep.'

'I've no money,' I told him.

'And there's me thinking you were rich.'

I said nothing so he went on, 'My sister works there.'

I looked at him suspiciously, 'Where is it?'

'Well, if you come with me, you'll find out.'

I started to reject his offer but he said, 'I tell you what — In the morning, if you're still in the same frame of mind, I'll come back here with you and help. You'll not stay under on your own,' he said, when I stared at him. 'But see — I've got this,' he brandished his walking stick at me. 'Hold anything under, this will.'

I took another step back and looked around in the hope of finding someone who would help me, but could see nothing through the mist.

'I'm terribly difficult to get rid of,' he said. 'That's what my mother always told me, anyway. *Tolly,* she said, *I've had six children, and lost most of 'em, but I seem to be stuck with you.*'

'I thought your name was Buzz,' I said despite myself. He shrugged.

'Stanford, Tolly, Buzz — what's in a name? You haven't told me your name yet, by the way.'

When I didn't answer he said, 'I think it must be Lily. Or Rose. You look like a flower, drooping and forlorn.'

'Please,' I said quietly, 'I just want to be left alone.'

'That's what my mother used to say!' he exclaimed. 'Well, listen, this is my last offer. Come with me, and if you don't like it, I swear I'll let you go on your way. Or my name's not Stanford Bartholomew Busby.'

I glanced down at the turgid water and felt a wave of sickness at the thought of sinking into it. How long did it take to drown?

'It's better than there,' Buzz said, nodding towards the river. 'Cleaner and not so wet. What should I call you, by the way? You can make a name up if you like,' he said, when I didn't answer, 'but I should like to call you something.'

I bit my lip then said, 'Pasley.' I wouldn't give him my first name. In any case I was hardly used to it by now.

'Pasley?' he said, screwing up his face. 'I'd rather call you Rose.'

'It's Irish,' I said, expecting him to recoil. But he said, 'Ah – the land of the thousand welcomes!' in a reasonable accent. 'Didn't I guess that from the sound of your voice? The fair fields of Erin! I've travelled them all!'

'Have you?' I asked, surprised.

'A marvellous country,' he said. 'A thousand welcomes to you, Irish rose.'

Well, it made a change from No Irish Need Apply.

When I still didn't take his arm he sighed, rolled his eyes and began to walk away. I looked once more at the water but my urge to jump into it had gone. It seemed I couldn't even drown myself in peace.

If I'd known then what I know now I would have jumped and taken my chances on damnation! But as it was I followed him over the bridge and down some steps.

Straightaway we were in darkness, as though all the light had been snuffed out. I'd followed him like a fool into a ginnel, where anything might happen.

'Where are you taking me?' I asked and at the same time he said, 'Watch your step – the things people throw!'

The alley was ankle deep in filth. I saw him disappear into the next ginnel. 'Where are we *going*?' I asked, but all he would say was, 'Not far now!'

I was already lost – I couldn't have found my way back in that murk. So I went on with him through what I now know as the Rookeries.

The houses leaned to one side as if propping one another up. Gates hung off and people sprawled in the yards. One man's legs stuck out across a ginnel and we had to step over him. In another yard a tiny girl sat in a pool of muddy water holding a baby. It was blue-white and still as death. The little girl didn't even move as we stepped past.

I stumbled after Buzz, cursing myself for a fool.

At last we came to a road. Buzz took my arm and steered me round some broken glass on the pavement. I was too shaken by then to object.

'Where are we?' I asked and for answer Buzz looked across the street to where a massive shape loomed through the fog. It looked like several buildings stuck together with a great chimney to one end. The sign above the doorway read *Manchester and District Union Workhouse*.

'What – ?' I said then, 'No!'

'This is where my sister Ida works,' said Buzz. 'Where are you going?'

I'd turned away from him. Yet I balked at the thought of making my way back through those dreadful slums alone. I stood twisting the fabric of my dress and a great sob burst from me.

'Now then,' Buzz said, placing his hand on my shoulder. I was too wretched to shake it off. 'There's no need for that!'

I couldn't speak for sobbing.

He searched his pockets and produced a handkerchief. 'Don't cry,' he said. 'I can't bear it. There's no need for it! Look – you'll have food and a bed. My sister'll look after you and you won't have to stay long because she'll find you a proper job – see if she won't.'

He held out his arm again and this time I took it.

CHAPTER 19

IN THE ORDINARY way of things Buzz said I would need a ticket for the workhouse but because his sister worked there he could get me in. And true enough I was signed in that same evening.

The next part I found mortifying in the extreme. I was taken to a room with two tin baths and ordered to strip. I couldn't believe I had to take all my clothes off in front of the nurse and stood unmoving until she asked if I wanted her to undress me. Then I removed them and climbed into the bath and hot water was poured over me so that I cried out, getting soap in my mouth for my pains. I'd not had a bath all the time I was at Mrs Digby's so my skin shrank from it and felt sore. Afterwards I was given different clothes, a calico shift and an overdress in a tough gingham. There were stains on it near the neck and hem but it smelled clean enough.

And who was I to be particular?

I was given bread and tea, then admitted to the Female Casual Ward for the Able Bodied. It was noisy with women snoring and crying out, but even so I slept like the dead that night. In the morning I put the dress on and after breakfast, a thin gruel eaten in silence, a sour woman with eyes like pale wood and a bitter, downturned mouth gave me an apron which I tied over my dress. She told me her name was Miss Mullen and I wasn't to speak unless spoken to. Then she took me to the wash house, a long, low room, full of clutter and steam. I couldn't make anything out at first and the smell stung my eyes. Then I could see a great wooden tub, a stove with a copper pot on it, a tin bath and a basket full of linen. There were rails suspended from the ceiling with cloths draped over them.

Miss Mullen said, 'This is where you'll work. We wash and bleach, starch and iron. All stains removed apart from sin.'

'Sin don't wash,' a voice piped up from the corner. 'If it did, you'd be out of business!'

'Hold your tongue!' said Miss Mullen. 'Haven't you finished them sheets yet?'

'Give us a chance!'

'If you pounded that posser as hard as you flapped that tongue you'd be done by now,' Miss Mullen said. Then to me, 'This is Ginnie, our general help.'

'Your maid-of-all-work, you mean,' said the voice.

I peered through the steam but could only make out a short figure with a bright cloth tied around her head. She leaned on the dolly stick in another tub and said, 'What's your name, then?'

'This is Pasley,' Miss Mullen said. 'She'll work with you, for now.'

'Pagley?' said the girl. 'What kind of a name's that?'

'*Pasley*,' I said but either she didn't hear or took no notice. She pulled a face at me through the steam and I saw she had a tooth missing. 'Welcome on board, Pags,' she said and I didn't correct her. I was Pags from then on.

Miss Mullen left and Ginnie pointed to the tin bath. 'Roll your sleeves up,' she said.

It was hard work. The sheets had to be soaked in the tin bath first, lye poured over them then scrubbed with black soap on a wash board and pounded in the dolly tub. Then they were rinsed again in a second tub, pulled out with big wooden pincers, passed through a mangle, and hung on the airers to dry.

There were two dyeing tubs, one full of madder and the other for the stinking substance called Sheele's Green which was what caused the smell. I had an apron and a cap but nothing for my hands. I soon found the smart of the soap unbearable, as though it would take the skin off, so then I took a turn at the mangle instead.

I was sick twice but managed to get myself into the outhouse. Then Ginnie gave me a bucket. 'Must be the smell,' she said. 'You'll soon get used to it – we all do.' She passed me a chunk of bread from her pinnie. 'Settles the stomach,' she said with a wink.

I hardly knew what I was doing but Ginnie helped me through. When I dropped a bucket of dirty water she threw a cloth over it quick and pushed her mop through the spreading pool. And when I ripped an apron string she put it in the basket with the other mending and fished out another one.

I had no idea why she was looking out for me. I was poor enough company and barely spoke.

By the time we finished our shift my back and arms ached as though I'd been on the devil's own rack and my feet were sore in their clogs. I hobbled after Ginnie to the kitchen where there were long tables set with plates. The food there was better than Mrs Digby's – there was a slice of meat at least and bread to mop up the gravy.

We ate in silence as before, then filed out. I followed Ginnie since I'd already forgotten the way and saw the ward clearly for the first time. It was a long room with brick walls washed white. I couldn't remember which bed I'd slept in, but Ginnie took me to one where there was a sheet and blanket rolled up near the pillow.

I picked up the sheet but someone stepped in front of me. A big girl with bulging eyes and a thrusting chin. 'Who're you?' she said.

'This is our new roommate,' said Ginnie. 'Pags – meet Pegs. Peggy Doyle. She's one of the long-timers here.'

'I dint ask you,' Peggy said, and to my alarm other girls began to gather round.

'Now, Peggy,' Ginnie said, but Peggy just stared at me with her great eyes. I looked down and spoke my name.

'Irish int'yer?' Peggy said. 'I int sleeping next to no Irish.'

'Where's she supposed to go then?' said Ginnie.

'In with the pigs like the other Irish,' said Peggy, and there was laughter as though she'd said something clever. Peggy grinned round, showing her yellow teeth.

I kept my eyes down but inside I felt the first stirrings of something I hardly even recognised.

Ginnie said. 'Move over, Peggy. She's staying here.'

'Who says?'

'I says.' Ginnie took hold of the sheet but Peggy snatched it off her. 'I'll take that,' she said. 'Irish dunt need sheets.'

'Give it back,' I said.

'Hark at her!' said Peggy. 'What'll you give us for it then, Irish?'

She flicked the sheet at me and I grabbed it. There was a flare in her eyes and one of the other girls shouted. 'Do her Peggy!'

Peggy yanked the sheet so hard I almost fell over. Then, surprising myself, I wrenched it back. I wasn't used to fighting – we would get in trouble for any misbehaviour of that sort at the orphanage – but even so my fist shot out. The blow missed her face and struck her shoulder. I heard Ginnie gasp and the girls shouted, 'Fight!'

Peggy reared up with a face like a Lurgan spade. I knew I was no match for her, but I hardly even cared. She lunged towards me but I stepped back quick. Things might've gone ill with me but then one voice sounded above the others.

'That's enough, now.'

It was a flat voice, not loud, yet all the girls fell back. Peggy looked like a balloon that had been pricked.

The source of the voice was a little bent woman with a pockmarked face, one drooping eyelid and only three teeth in her mouth. She looked at me with her good eye and something in me recoiled. When she spoke a reek came from her mouth.

'Pipe down now,' she said in the same flat tone.

'Tell them Ida,' Ginnie said, and I realised this must be Buzz' sister. There was nothing similar about them other than the fact they were so short.

'Come now,' she said to me.

I looked at Ginnie who nodded, so I followed Ida through the door and across the landing to a smaller room with only four beds in it, two of them empty.

Ida stood by one of the empty beds. In the next bed there was a very ancient woman lying like a rail beneath the sheet. The only way you could tell she was alive was by the suck and rattle of her breath pumping the sheet up and down. Ginnie whispered to me that she was called Old Mary. In the bed next to her was her friend Dorothy, who had milky eyes and a face that seemed to have collapsed in on itself. She had no teeth, though her mouth moved in a chewing motion and from time to time she spat on the floor.

Ida left then and Ginnie said, 'You'll be all right now,' and I understood the bed was to be mine.

That night I lay listening to the rattle of Old Mary's breathing and Dorothy's cough and restless moan. The air grew stale, then foul. Already I could feel the first waves of sickness that came at morning light. I could imagine the thing within me starting to squirm.

I took a long, shuddering breath and turned on my side.

And saw Ida gazing at me with her one good eye. A pang of terror went through me but all she said was, 'When's it due?'

I began to weep. Ida said, 'It can be fixed.'

I stared at her, 'How?' I asked.

Ida winked. 'I'll sort it.'

'What – ?' I asked, but she only patted the tip of her nose.

'Sleep now,' she said.

I wanted to ask what she meant, but she'd already turned away and in the morning she'd gone. Ginnie came in.

'Feeling better?' she said. 'Breakfast!'

'Wh – ?' I said, but she pressed a finger to her lips because we weren't supposed to speak. After breakfast I followed her into the yard where we were met by Buzz. 'How are you doing, Irish rose?' he asked.

I was so surprised to see him I didn't answer. 'I hear you've met my sister,' he said, as I stared at him. 'Ida says you've been poorly.'

I wondered what else she'd said but of course I would not mention my condition to him. I mumbled something about the substances we used in the washhouse.

'The washhouse?' Buzz said to Ginnie. 'Didn't I tell you this girl's a seamstress?'

'Don't look at me,' Ginnie said. 'I don't decide who works where!'

'Ida'll sort it,' Buzz said. 'She'll look after you.'

'Go on, take her!' he said. Ginnie rolled her eyes but took me to the stitching room as it was called, around the side of the main block. Ida was already there waiting. She said nothing but winked at me with her single eye.

I felt as though nothing made sense. I was as far from understanding as from the moon. But I understood the work here at least. I sat on a stool in the corner and sewed old sheets together to make new ones and hemmed aprons and repaired any uniforms that had been damaged. I worked alone, separate from the other girls, which suited me, and without the smells of the washhouse I coped better with my sickness. Ida left me to it while she went about her other business whatever that was. I didn't like to ask.

As I bent over my sewing however I did wonder what she meant by *sorting it*, and *fixed*. I resolved to ask her as soon as I saw her again.

But I didn't see her the rest of that day or Ginnie either.

That evening we were told we could write to our families or loved ones. I wrote a long letter to my mother. Would she come for me, I asked her? I told her where the workhouse was and said I would wait for her. I didn't tell her about the baby for fear she wouldn't come. She would be ashamed of the workhouse but she would have to come here to get me out. I was desperate to leave before anyone else knew of my condition. If Ida knew then surely it would not be long before everyone did and I couldn't bear it. I would rather have jumped from the bridge.

I waited for my mother to reply, working in the sewing room where I saw no sign of Ginnie, who was in the laundry I supposed. Sometimes I saw Ida's little bent figure in the distance with its bobbing, ducking walk but after that first night the bed next to mine was empty. When I plucked up courage to ask about Ginnie I was told she'd gone. I felt a pang of terror at being left. What would become of me?

That night I was shaking in my bed because I'd had no word from my mother. I didn't know how long I could stay in the workhouse and I had nowhere to go. Late in the night Ida took the bed next to mine again.

'I thought you'd gone!' I said and she said she was going soon.

'Will I go with you?' I asked. 'Will there be work for me?'

'Don't worry about that,' she said, tapping her nose.

'What will I say?' I asked her, meaning to Matron, if I was going to leave.

'Don't you worry,' she said again, adding, 'Ginnie'll be there.'

She said nothing else but my heart lifted foolishly at the thought of seeing Ginnie. There was still no word from my mother so I became reconciled to the idea of leaving with Ida. I grasped it indeed as my only hope.

The next day Ida brought a dress for me and a shawl. They weren't the ones I'd arrived in but I'd learned she didn't answer questions so I didn't ask. I took off my uniform and pulled on the dress which was a brown work-day smock, too large for me, but the shawl covered it. And so we left without anyone hindering us at all. We went back through the same dark ginnels and courts I'd been through with Buzz. There were pigs in one and a cow poking its matted, knobbly head over the gate of another and a stream of muddy water running over the cobbles. I couldn't help thinking of my mother, that perhaps she would turn up for me after all at the workhouse gate and miss me. But I couldn't bring myself to go back.

Finally we came to a house with soot-black walls and boarded-up windows. Ida unlocked a door that led to steps going down. There were two rooms in the cellar, one locked. When she opened it I saw there was a bed in the corner and a window with bars across it. I looked at her.

'Keeps the riffraff out,' she said, and winked.

The other cellar room was so dark I could hardly see. But I could tell it was part flooded. There was a strong smell of damp and mould.

'Charlotte?' Ida said, and something stirred. 'Come and show the new girl your face.'

A small figure moved out of the shadows. A timid, hunched creature. As she drew closer I could see the skin on one half of her face was tight and puckered, her features pulled out of shape. She had no hair on that side of her head and only one eyebrow.

'Weren't no need for that,' Ida said, 'if she hadn't tried to leave.'

※

The sky is paling already and I've hardly slept. It's so cold I feel as though I'll never be warm again. In the next cell someone is coughing hard enough to break a rib. I shift onto my side pulling my blanket up, though it hurts to move.

My memories hurt more. And Mrs Gaskell not coming – that hurts worst of all.

Despite everything, despite Lizzie and Ella, I wish she would come.

I wonder where she is now, and what she's doing? In her bedroom, I think, tucked up in her bed. There will be a fire in the hearth to keep her warm.

CHAPTER 20

Elizabeth

EVEN UNDER THE quilt Elizabeth could feel how cold the bedroom was. The fire had died down and through the gap in the curtains she could see frost on the inside of the window. The tip of her nose felt frozen.

She'd dreamed she'd had a letter from beyond the grave. It was from her mother, and she was desperate to read it but she couldn't decipher the writing. She managed to make out the first sentence: *I never meant to leave you . . .* but try as she might she couldn't read the rest. She'd woken from the effort, her cheeks wet.

Instinctively she turned towards William before remembering he was in London with his brother.

The chink of sky through the curtains was pale. She was usually dressed by now but she'd stayed up past midnight with Tottie, discussing the nature of goodness of all things. Tottie had said only the human race strove towards goodness and only the human race was so destructive – surely the two things were linked? Elizabeth had agreed but thought there were circumstances in which it was impossible to be good, poverty being one of them. Like the man who had killed his wife and their three children rather than watch them starve. Or Pasley – but she wouldn't bring the subject of Pasley up again with Tottie. She didn't want to think about Pasley at all just now. She had to get up and get on with her day.

Bracing herself she pushed the bedclothes back. It took two goes to fasten the smaller buttons on her blouse and she kept dropping the pins for her hair because her fingers were numb. She'd barely finished when she heard shouting downstairs.

Throwing a shawl around her shoulders Elizabeth hurried onto the landing where she smelled smoke and heard Bessie shrieking. Tottie and the girls were peering from the doors of their rooms but she motioned them back.

The kitchen was a mess of smoke and feathers. A bird was butting itself into the cupboards, there was milk all over the floor and more shouting could be heard from outside.

'Whatever is it?' she said to Hearn, who was attempting to soothe Bessie. 'What's going on?'

She flung the door and windows open while Hearn explained that a man had jumped the queue at the back door, and when Bessie had spoken to him sharply he'd unleashed a tirade of abuse.

'That's why we shut the door,' Bessie sobbed. Although a bird had flapped into the kitchen and in the commotion Bessie had burned the milk and set a pan on fire.

They could hear the man roaring from the other side of the street, 'I hope you clem to death, you fat bitch!'

Two women were shouting at him to get back in line and a man seemed to be arguing with him. Elizabeth shrugged William's coat on over her shawl and slipped on her overshoes.

'Meta - no!' she said as Meta attempted to push past. 'Polly - take the little ones!' She signalled to Tottie and Hearn to usher the girls into the front room, then marched out of the house. Unexpectedly the man cowered away from her. He was filthy, his face sunken and wrinkled, his teeth blackened stumps.

'What kind of behaviour is this?' she said in her Sunday School voice. 'There are others here just as hungry as you!'

Then watched disbelieving as he spat at her, a green gobbet shot through with brown landing at her feet. 'Don't you dare!' she said, too late.

'That's for your charity!' he said. 'What's the matter? Int I grateful enough for you?'

'You bad bugger!' one woman called. 'Get away!'

Elizabeth thought of saying *you're lucky we're feeding you at all!* But that might provoke him further and offend the rest of them, two of whom were now attempting to manhandle him out of the queue.

'Leave him,' she said as he cursed them. 'Bessie!'

Bessie came running, holding the end of a loaf. She passed it to Elizabeth then hurried back inside without even looking at the man. Elizabeth handed it to him. His knuckles were knotted with arthritis, his nails lined with grime.

'Where's meat?' he said and she had to suppress an impulse to laugh. But she stared him down until he backed away, still muttering curses at her. He wasn't dangerous after all – only hungry, heart-sick and furious.

'What about us?' someone cried but she couldn't send him away without food. *He might be John*, she thought, her brother John, begging for food in a foreign country.

The thought trembled inside her as she turned back to the kitchen. If it was John begging in a strange land she hoped someone would give him food.

In the kitchen there was another crisis. Someone had taken the beef from the kitchen table while Bessie had run out with the bread. Bessie was inconsolable. 'Three pounds of topside!' she wailed. 'Whatever will we do for dinner?'

Elizabeth hurriedly doled out the rest of the bread and porridge then bolted the door against the grumbling queue.

'You'll have to come back tomorrow!' she called through the window. Although it could have been a cat, or the bird. But what kind of bird could carry three pounds of beef in its beak?

'Stop it Bessie!' she said as Bessie's lamentations grew. 'It's no one's fault.' But she did wonder what they could have for the evening meal – there was no money in the house, and William wouldn't be back until tomorrow.

'I'll take the girls to the fish market,' Tottie said, hurrying downstairs.

'Oh no, you can't!'

'Of course I can – you've been so generous to me! And Hearn will come to show me the way – we'll do some Christmas shopping!'

She kissed Elizabeth swiftly, whispering, 'And you can have some time to yourself!' She ushered the girls away as they tried to follow her into the kitchen. 'No breakfast today!' Elizabeth heard her saying. 'We're going to have tea and cakes.'

There was a flurry of putting on cloaks and boots while Elizabeth helped Bessie to clear up in the kitchen. Bessie, ashamed of herself, offered to bring Elizabeth a pot of tea in her room and set the fire. Elizabeth daubed some jam on the last crust of bread for her breakfast and carried it upstairs.

Finally the house was quiet.

Soberly, Elizabeth put the plate on her dressing table, thinking about the man, how gaunt he was.

I hope you clem to death, you fat bitch!

She remembered another man, suspected of violent activities against mill-owners: fire-setting, machine smashing, personal attacks. He'd said to her with tears in his eyes, 'Aye ma'am, but have you ever seen a child clemmed to death?'

Her own son had recently died, but not of starvation. Elizabeth could hardly imagine such a thing. The question had haunted her, finding its way into her novel. It was the question John Barton put to his friend – do the rich ever see their children starve?

She went to the window, looking at the frayed edge of the curtain she'd meant to mend, thinking now about her brother John who had sailed to India and never returned. He was the oldest of her mother's children and the only other one who'd lived, although he must be dead by now. But she'd never given up hope that she might hear from him one day, see him on a street somewhere or on a beach.

He'd brought back a button for her button necklace from every country he'd sailed to, and if she guessed which hand it was in he would tell her a story.

He would draw a face on each of his fingertips and tell her they were the Waggle family. Mr Waggle with his stern moustache, Mrs Waggle with lorgnette and curls, Peter Waggle the eldest son, and Pinky Waggle the baby. His thumb was Grandpa Waggle, an old sailor who had lost a tooth in every country in the world.

Ho, ho! said Papa Waggle in his big, deep voice. So you think you've been good enough for a story?

I have, I have, I've been very good! cried Pinky Waggle in her little squeaky voice.

'I don't sound like that!' she'd cried.

She had to choose which member of the Waggle family would tell the story. Papa Waggle would tell her a parable and Mama Waggle some moral tale, so she always chose Grandpa Waggle with his seafaring adventures, or Peter Waggle's stories of naughtiness and derring-do.

John had a gift for stories. He'd written a book she'd never had chance to read. Then because no one would publish it he'd gone to sea.

What would he think of her now, an author?

She could remember going with her father to see John sail for the first time. She'd been ten years old. To this day when she thought of her brother she thought of sunlight and heat, the smell of spices and the bright silks of the markets that he wrote about in his letters . . .

What a day this was already, Elizabeth thought, dabbing her eyes.

She should try to get something done or at least make a plan. Tottie, out of the goodness of her heart, had taken the girls off her hands. She would want to know what Elizabeth had done with the morning so generously donated to her. And what would Elizabeth say? *Well, I sat around moping . . .*

It wouldn't do. Elizabeth knelt down beside her bed feeling for the small chest she kept beneath it. She owed a story to *Sartain's Magazine* and wanted to read through her old notes. After rummaging through the chest and getting distracted by an early diary she found the notebook she wanted. Then she realised that the notes were all about a young woman caring for her invalid brother.

She closed the chest and rested her head on the bed.

Did other writers have this problem? Did Geraldine Jewsbury, who had written two novels already as well as numerous articles and reviews? Or Miss Bronte, whose first book had come out shortly before *Mary Barton* and who had already brought out another? *Shirley* was also about the disputes between mill workers and owners and the controversy around it threatened to eclipse *Mary Barton* entirely. Only one critic seemed to remember that Elizabeth's novel had come first.

Both Geraldine Jewsbury and Charlotte Bronte were younger than Elizabeth. Neither of them were married or had children. But there was Charles Dickens who, despite his large family, editing work, reading tours, prolific correspondence and twenty-mile walks around London produced a substantial book a year.

It was said he knew every writer in England, that he cultivated them assiduously. Soon after *Mary Barton* had come out Elizabeth had been invited to his house. He'd greeted her like an old friend, she'd breakfasted with his wife and attended a party to celebrate the publication of his latest book. Yet he'd never once mentioned her novel or acknowledged that it had been sent to him.

So many people had acknowledged it, but not him.

It doesn't matter, she'd said to her editor who had been hoping to get a quote from him for the press.

Privately, she'd determined she would never ask Mr Dickens for anything again but it was hard to avoid the glare of publicity surrounding him. When he'd sailed to America it was reported that the dock nearly sank beneath the weight of people waiting for him. He'd practically been mobbed. And now there was another novel, another tour – the press was full of it.

Why was she thinking about Charles Dickens?

Did she want that kind of fame herself? It was hardly likely, since she couldn't seem to bring herself to write . . .

The problem wasn't Dickens, but her inability to concentrate when she had so many other things to do. She hadn't finished her

Christmas shopping, there was yet another charity fair to organise at church, William's relatives were threatening to visit and she still hadn't sent that parcel to Pasley.

She hadn't done anything for Pasley...

Stiffly, because of her knees, she pushed herself off the floor. The tea hadn't appeared and the fire was still out. Presumably Bessie too was still unsettled by the morning's events. Should she go downstairs to remind her?

That would be another distraction.

Instead she went to the bureau looking for paper. Then she sat down, her mind a jumble of unusable thoughts. Finally she remembered the little gathering she'd planned for the New Year before Tottie returned to London. She had to write some invitations for that, to the Winkworths and Henry Burnett.

Mr Burnett was the brother-in-law of Charles Dickens, but that wasn't why she was inviting him. She felt sorry for him because his wife had died of consumption a little more than a year ago and his older son had died shortly after. He lived nearby with his younger son and Elizabeth thought he might like to meet with Tottie or Susanna. Mr Burnett taught music, Susanna taught piano, and they both had a lively interest in art.

She wasn't trying to match-make, of course. William had often scolded her for that. She just couldn't resist the possibilities of new acquaintance. Her mood brightened even as she wrote the invitations. If she was quick she could post them before Tottie returned with the girls.

※

'Well if you aren't a sight for sore eyes!' Thomas Wright said.

'Thomas!' Elizabeth exclaimed, guiltily aware that she hadn't told him about her prison visits when he was the one who'd suggested she should go.

'Always a pleasure,' he said, removing his hat and performing an odd, stiff little dance. Then he sighed. 'My knees won't do it any more.'

'You work them too hard,' she said and he replied as always, 'Aye, well – where there's life there's work.'

His cheeks looked even more sunken than usual, his eyes more prominent. He worked in the iron foundry from five in the morning until six at night, preached in the congregational chapel on Sundays and somehow fitted in prison visits between.

She'd told him he should retire but then he would have no income. She and William had come up with a scheme to get him a pension which involved canvassing likely patrons for subscriptions, but it was possible, given his pride, that he wouldn't accept it. And in any case she remembered they'd done nothing about it, consigning it to the great list of things *yet to be done* . . .

'I hope you'll come back with me for a cup of tea,' he said.

'Oh, no!'

'But you must! I never see you these days!'

Now she felt doubly guilty. She could see him calculating whether he would be able to offer her anything more substantial than tea. If he did she would have to refuse since he couldn't afford it.

'I think Mary might have baked some biscuits,' he said.

Mary was the only one of his nineteen children still at home. They inhabited a crumbling terrace on Sidney St close by. Elizabeth used to visit him regularly after his wife died, trying not to notice the smell of damp, the peeling wallpaper. She'd proposed hiring a maid for him but he wouldn't consider it. He didn't believe in servitude, it was an evil. Why should the able-bodied not wait upon themselves? The lord hadn't set the Israelites free without reason.

She knew most of his speeches by heart. He knew she employed servants but didn't say this directly, while Elizabeth didn't mention the fact that his daughter worked harder than any maid. The last time she'd seen Mary she seemed to have turned the same yellowish colour as the wallpaper, looking much older than her sixteen years.

'No I really can't,' she said. 'I have a friend staying and she'll be back soon with my daughters – they're all out together.'

Before he could try to persuade her she told him she'd been visiting the prison.

'So you've seen her then,' he said eagerly.

'I have indeed.'

'And you've taken to her – don't say you haven't – of course you have!'

'I believe you knew I would when you sent me,' she chided.

'Well now, there'd hardly be any point sending someone who didn't care. How was she?'

'Much as you described her – an unfortunate innocent.'

'Isn't she just! It's a mystery to me why some infants come into this world to be so sorely used. I'll not ask my Maker much when I finally meet Him, but by jingo I will ask Him that!'

Elizabeth sighed and shook her head, thinking she'd only intended to pop out for a moment.

'But can you do anything for her?' Thomas asked. She told him about the letters she'd written, the response from their congregation. He shook his head. 'You should let me preach to 'em,' he said.' I'll melt their stony hearts.'

He had preached in their chapel before in his thundering style. There had been complaints. Elizabeth steered him away from the subject.

'I'm running out of people to ask in Manchester,' she said.

His face was a mask of horror. 'Oh not Manchester – never Manchester!' he cried.

Elizabeth looked at him in surprise. She'd thought of asking whether he might take Pasley on to help Mary, although she knew what his response was likely to be.

And she didn't want him to put the same question to *her*.

'She'll be in mortal danger,' he said.

'Whatever do you mean?'

'These gangs – she'll not escape their clutches here!'

'We don't know that there *is* a gang—' Elizabeth began.

'Oh there'll be a gang,' he said. 'There's always a gang.'

He went on before she could stop him, 'Dragsmen, cadgers, flashmen, bully-boys, moonshiners, fences – you name it – they don't let go of their own. Soon as one of theirs is taken into a respectable house, they're all over it like flies on a cow pat if you'll excuse my language. They'll strip it bare. And she'll be the one to be arrested again. Or hung . . .'

Mrs Fetherington took in a prison girl out of the softness of her heart, and the next thing you know she'd let in her accomplices . . . Mrs Fairlie had said.

'I've written to my friends in London as well,' she said, interrupting a grisly tale about a maid, a housekeeper and bodies in the cellar.

'London's worse!' he protested. 'These gangs all know one another. Half of them are related! Poke one of them in Salford and someone in London'll strike back.'

She suspected him of showing off his superior worldliness. He thought she lived a sheltered life but she knew the dreadful suction of poverty as well as anyone else.

However, since she needed his advice, she sighed. 'What should I do, then?'

'Send her to the country,' came the prompt reply. 'Not,' he added, 'that there aren't gangs there . . .'

She hadn't written to her relations in Knutsford yet – although perhaps that was too close. But there were her friends in the Lake District or Whitby. And the country air would surely be better for Pasley than the city . . .

'That's an excellent idea,' she said, and he preened. 'I don't know why I didn't think of it before! If I hurry, I'll just have time to draft a few letters before the girls come back . . .'

He protested, but she told him Pasley's release date was imminent, so she would have to act on his brilliant suggestion right away. She promised to tell him as soon as she had any news, finally escaping just as the first drops of oily rain spattered the pavements. She quickened her pace feeling a sensation of lightness, reprieve. She was justified after all in not taking Pasley in. She could say as much to Tottie and even William.

Later that day she wrote to everyone she could think of in the Lake District: the Fletchers, the Roberds, the Wedgwoods – even the Wordsworths in Grasmere and Harriet Martineau in Ambleside, although she was sure they wouldn't want Pasley. She included Christmas greetings with each letter and was up late, writing until her wrist was painful and her fingers stiff. The next morning she posted all the letters, along with her responses to various invitations and engagements.

Finally they could think about Christmas. But then William returned from London full of cold and illness descended upon them, a heavy, flu-like pestilence that poured into the sinuses like glue with a cough that racked them through the nights. Elizabeth felt so bad about Tottie who'd come to them for a holiday but Tottie said there were always contagions going round London and she might as well suffer in company as on her own.

Polly and Meta helped Hearn, who was also suffering, to make mustard poultices and pots of tea from dried herbs. William, who would never acknowledge illness, set off in the fog and rain for his meetings looking grey and grim. The Statistical Society were preparing a report on infant mortality in the slums for the government and they needed his contribution.

Elizabeth sat by the fire with Tottie, torn between feeling she should make an effort like William and a dragging inertia. Outside, the weather persisted in dreariness, a grey-black fog clung to everything seeming to penetrate her brain so she could hardly think. Inside the clock ticked, the brasses gleamed and the fire crackled and spat.

Guiltily she remembered Pasley. How was she? What would Christmas be like in prison?

She'd had no replies from anyone in the Lake District or her friends in London, although according to Thomas that might be a good thing. Of course everyone would be caught up in the Christmas season, but Pasley would soon be discharged onto the Manchester streets and Elizabeth had nothing arranged.

Miss Jopson had replied to her saying the girls were not usually allowed gifts or extra reading material in their cells, but in the circumstances she could make an exception.

Elizabeth had wondered about this briefly, but concluded it was because it was Christmas and so near Pasley's release date. When Tottie excused herself and went to bed in the afternoon Elizabeth went to find Hearn.

Together they prepared a parcel. Hearn altered one of Polly's old nightgowns and edged a shawl. Elizabeth, remembering that Pasley liked to read, found some copies of a magazine for her. Then she sat by the fire composing a note that said nothing about her imminent freedom or Elizabeth's failure to find a situation for her, but promising to visit very soon.

The magazines contained one of her own stories under a different name. She thought about telling Pasley this but changed her mind, because then she might feel obliged to say she liked it.

She stared into the fire for a moment, remembering it.

'I think I should like,' she said hesitantly to Hearn, 'to write about girls like Pasley. To change people's minds about them.'

Hearn said, 'It's their hearts you have to change.'

'Those too.' That was surely the purpose of fiction.

'They'll not change,' said Hearn.

'People can be educated. They can be made to see things differently. That's what books do.'

'There are a lot of books, and a lot of poor folk.'

'But not all the books are about poverty.'

Hearn was silent for a moment, then she said, 'Folk will always want other folk to look down on.'

Surely she wasn't referring to herself? Hearn was more like a friend than a servant.

'Well I don't suppose I can make everything equal,' Elizabeth said. 'But I can try to speak out at least.'

Hearn said nothing and Elizabeth felt obscurely wrong-footed. She thought of asking Hearn whether she was dissatisfied in some way but her housekeeper had pins clamped between her lips and couldn't reply. Elizabeth thought of all the years Hearn had been with them. She had no husband or children of her own. She'd helped bring Elizabeth's daughters into the world and looked after them and they all loved her, but they weren't hers.

She'd once said nothing would stand between her and God because she owned nothing apart from the clothes she stood up in. And a spare apron.

But Hearn was indispensable to them, like soil or air. If Hearn died, Elizabeth would grieve more for her than almost anyone.

She could hardly say *that* to her . . .

She looked at Hearn's bent head, the cap with one of its ribbons caught in her collar, the small crease on her chin that only appeared when her lips were pressed together. Hearn was mother, sister, friend to her. They had grieved together over her baby boy, sat up through the night worrying when one of the girls was ill. She felt she should say something, but nothing seemed adequate.

So she told Hearn about meeting Thomas Wright and what he'd said about sending Pasley away.

Hearn looked up then, a wistful expression on her face. She glanced towards the globe that stood on a small table in a corner of the room. 'If I could go anywhere, I wouldn't choose England,' she said, 'not when there's all the rest of the world . . .'

'Really?' Elizabeth said. She hadn't known Hearn wanted to travel. 'Where?' she asked and there was a catch in her voice. *Hearn would go*, she thought. She would leave her just as her brother had.

'Oh, anywhere,' Hearn said, gazing towards the window. She had a broad lovely face, although her skin was a little pockmarked from a childhood illness. Why had she never married? Elizabeth had asked her once and Hearn had joked that if she wanted to take on more washing, ironing and shopping she could have found a bigger family to work for.

Which had ended that conversation.

'Italy might be nice,' she said, 'or Africa.'

'Africa!'

Hearn coloured a little. 'I used to read stories about it in the Sunday School magazine,' she said.

'Perhaps we could go together,' Elizabeth said, 'to Italy, I mean...'

Hearn smiled her downward smile. But why shouldn't they, Elizabeth thought? Tottie was already going to Italy. Maybe they could all go together! Many a gentlewoman travelled with their maid.

Hearn wasn't a maid.

Companion then. Yes, she would be Elizabeth's companion. She thought of saying so but Hearn excused herself and went to check on Flossie who'd had stomach-ache after tea. Leaving Elizabeth to think about all the things she hadn't said and couldn't say, and about Hearn's mysterious inner life and about sending Pasley abroad.

Where would she be accepted apart from the penal colonies? There were increasing protests against transportation in this country as well as Australia and Canada. William had written about the conditions on the ships...

A huge yawn nearly dislocated her jaw. It was no good, the cold had taken too much out of her. She would wrap the parcel tomorrow and send it to Pasley. With any luck it would get to her before Christmas.

CHAPTER 21

Pasley

WHEN A PARCEL arrives for me I can hardly believe it. I stare at Miss Jamieson as though I've lost my wits.

It's soft as though there's cloth inside. Something crackles when I press it.

'You should keep it for Christmas,' Miss Jamieson says, but I open it right away while she watches. It's been opened already of course, so it's no task to open it again.

First there's a shawl in plain blue wool but finely knit, with a crocheted border in darker blue.

'Very fancy,' Miss Jamieson says as I wrap it round my shoulders. It's not *fancy* exactly but it's not either what the factory girls wear.

I blink tears away, remembering the shawl I pawned, then pass it to Miss Jamieson who takes it without comment. I suppose she will give it back to me when I leave.

There's a nightgown as well, very prettily made over with a pleated front and ruffled neck. The sleeves are gathered with a tiny edge of lace around the cuffs.

I won't try that on with Miss Jamieson watching. I pass it to her the same.

I wonder whether Mrs Gaskell knew I wouldn't be allowed to wear such things here?

But there's more! As well as the shawl and nightgown there are three magazines and a small card. The card is edged in gilt with a border of flowers and Mrs Gaskell has written on it! Her writing is fine and flowing.

My dear Pasley, she writes, and although I know it's the usual way to start a letter my heart skips a little. *I feel so wretched that I haven't visited you. It is the usual excuse that time has run away with me – which is no excuse at all! I hope this small gift will be some recompense until we meet again, and trust you will believe me when I say it will be very soon.*

You are constantly in my thoughts,

And then she signs herself,

E. C. Gaskell

P.S. (she writes to me extra!) *I hope you find the stories of interest – there is one in each issue. It is the –* here the writing is cramped to the edge of the card and there's a tiny smudge. But I think she's telling me the story is in three parts.

I told her I liked to read so she's sent me these magazines! I've seen such things in shop windows but never owned one or expected to, and now I have three!

And she says I am constantly in her thoughts! And she will visit very soon . . .

'Don't go getting your hopes up,' Miss Jamieson says. I'd almost forgotten she was there. I turn away from her a little so she can't see me press the card to my lips.

I wonder what the 'E' and 'C' stand for. *Emmeline* perhaps, or *Eliza*. And *Christobelle*. All of them very pretty names.

The magazines all have the same plain cover, with HOWITT'S JOURNAL printed at the top, and LITERATURE AND POPULAR PROGRESS beneath.

I pick the first one up.

The smell of it takes me right back to the orphanage and the books I was given by Miss Vivienne. It's the smell of stories and other worlds. I can't resist opening it even though I know I won't be allowed to read it here.

Miss Jamieson coughs and I look at her guiltily.

'Well,' she says, 'I'd best be going.'

Reluctantly I hold the journal out but she says, 'Don't bother.'

I stare at her, not understanding.

'I'll take these,' she says, (meaning the nightgown and shawl) 'You can keep them.'

I feel myself blush to the roots of my hair so surprised am I by this good fortune! She makes a small, exasperated noise and says, 'Make the most of it – you'll be back on rota soon.'

As soon as she leaves I flick through the magazines, expecting to find half the pages torn out or scribbled through, but no one has tampered with them at all! I sit at my table with the first one.

There's a great list of contents and many pages of fine print. Each page is divided into two columns. The stories have titles like *The Gypsy Mother*, or *Labour's Muse*. Then there's *Life in Manchester – Libbie Marsh's Three Eras*, by Cotton Mather Mills Esq. which is a strange name . . .

I scan through the other magazines and find the same name and title in each, but a different date: St Valentine's Day 1847, Whitsuntide 1847 and Michaelmas 1847.

I was with Mrs Fenton then, and then Mrs Digby.

This must be the story Mrs Gaskell means me to read!

It's a long story and all of it in Manchester. I've never heard of such a thing! I thought stories came from distant places like in the Bible or the book of Arabian Nights Miss Vivienne read to me.

I'm desperate to read it before Mrs Gaskell comes – which will be soon she said! But we're not allowed candles in our cells for fear of mischief and the light's already fading. I stare as hard as I can at the print but soon I can't see a thing. I will have to wait until tomorrow.

I slip it under my pillow so it's there beneath my cheek while I sleep but I can't sleep for thinking about it. Will she ask me about it? I'm afraid I will sound foolish to her.

When the bell clangs I wake with the same sick, thudding sensation as usual. I feel stunned and stupid until I remember my magazines, then I scrub my cell as fast as I can before inspection.

The trolley comes and I sit with my breakfast tin and start to read. I read the whole story by Mr Cotton Mather Mills in one go. It's the story of a young seamstress who has no one. Her mother, father and brother are dead, her friends have moved away and she has no prospect of marriage. She lodges with a family called Dixon who are spinners. Even so, they can afford cream in their tea.

I see why Mrs Gaskell wanted me to read this tale. I feel almost that I *am* Libbie! I never thought stories could be written about people like me.

As I read on though, I learn that Libbie was good and kind. She didn't steal, or work in a whorehouse. Such things I suppose can't be written.

In some ways it's a sad story. Libbie gives a canary in a cage to a crippled boy and becomes friendly with his mother who is a widow. But the little crippled boy dies and his mother is overcome by grief. She says it will kill her to come home from work to find his place empty. 'No one will ever call me mother again!' she says and my heart goes out to her. Then I think of my own mother who didn't want to be called mother by me.

The end of the story is that Libbie goes to live with the little boy's mother and becomes like a daughter to her. She is 'no longer a desolate, lonely orphan, a stranger on the earth.'

I read this bit twice, moving my lips over the words.

It seems to me a fine ending. Libbie no longer has to live with the Dixons where she doesn't belong, and whose daughter, Annie, is set on marrying a drunkard. Libbie speaks her mind to Annie, saying that her own father killed her baby brother in a drunken fit – such a terrible thing! But the only response she gets from Annie is that Libbie is a 'born old maid'. Then Libbie says that there is 'plenty of work for old maids to do and the blessing of God on them as does it.'

Fair play to her! Libbie is just like me – I don't want to marry either.

I read it again, noting all the places Libbie goes. The Dixons live in a 'narrow Manchester court,' where each of the houses look the same. I've seen many such. In this story though the people are friendly, the boys play marbles together and the women who don't work look after the children of those who do. That does happen sometimes, although the women are often senseless with gin and the babies drugged to a stupor.

At one part, Libbie takes the little boy to a beautiful woodland. From there they can see a 'motionless cloud of smoke' hanging over 'ugly, smoky Manchester'. Mr Mills must know it well to write about it so.

'Dear, busy, earnest, noble-working Manchester,' he calls it. I stand on my stool and try to see out of my window the Manchester he saw with its friendly courts and noble working people, but I can only see fog. Somewhere out there is Mrs Digby's shop and Ida Quayle's house.

Libbie wouldn't know such places. She never stood on a bridge thinking to throw herself off it. She is a good, kind, charitable girl, who never did anything to be ashamed of. Not like me. I have been eaten away by shame until there's hardly anything left.

One day, you catch sight of yourself in a window, or a glass, and think *who is that?* And for the life of you, you can't answer.

That's the difference between me and Libbie Marsh.

Such thoughts make me feel queasy and fearful, like a hunted thing. I want to crouch in the corner of my cell but I don't of course. I get ready for bed where I lie restless, my mind swarming with memories: Mrs Digby, Libbie, Ida Quayle.

The next day I'm all set to read again when a new wardress arrives. She's short and skinny with a pockmarked face. 'You're for the washhouse,' she says.

It's the first time I've been out of my cell since *it* happened. I keep my eyes down for fear of seeing one of them – for they will surely not still be in the poky. Then I think they might be in the washhouse and I stop dead before the door, but it's only Fanny Wardle who opens it with Ellen Atkin behind.

I work all day in silence as we must, though more than once I hear Fanny and Ellen whispering and catch them glancing my way. Soon my back hurts and my hands are sore but at least I don't see anyone else other than the new wardress. I realise that some of the whispering is because Fanny and Ellen are smuggling soap in their clothes. They'll be after trading it because some of the girls want it for their hair. Either the new wardress is blind or she doesn't know what to do about it, because she seems not to notice. I stay out of it because I don't want to lose my visiting rights. It's all I can think about, that Mrs Gaskell will visit me again.

When I get back to my cell it's too dark to read even though I hold the magazine up to the window, and I feel very peevish about it. I lie one way then another on my bed thinking about Libbie's story. Then I pace about my cell telling it to myself.

But a parade of faces gets in the way: Ida, Buzz, Silas, and Ginnie.

I can't tell Mrs Gaskell about Ginnie. Or the baby.

She'll ask about it – I know she will.

Such a thing would never have happened to Libbie.

The last of the light drains out of my cell and my hope with it. But when I lie on the bed and close my eyes I seem to see Mrs Gaskell's face again, bending towards me. Waiting for me to talk to her.

Then I see, plain as day, the house where Ida took me.

There were more rooms than you'd think from the outside, which was poky and black. Inside there was a kitchen and a separate room for the washing. Upstairs was Ida's room and a back room, then an attic, where the other girls slept.

Downstairs was the cellar room with the barred window.

I felt a damp terror as Ida took me into it.

There was a brownish carpet worn bare by the tread of many feet and a smell of cheap scent as well as damp. There was a rope attached to the bed head. I didn't understand why and dared not ask.

The bed itself was full of stains, but Ida told me to get on it.

'Wait here,' she said, and left me.

Soon I heard a small noise. It was Charlotte holding a bag of greyish liquid and a tube. She kept her face turned to one side.

Ida came in after.

I started to get up, but Ida said, 'Lie down.'

Then she pushed the tube into me while I shifted and writhed making wet patches on the bed. She cursed and I wept for all the toil and mess and shame.

When the pain came it was terrible. My sweat soaked the sheets and I couldn't breathe. I shut my eyes so tight I could see sparks of colour behind the lids. I felt as though I was flying up into darkness, like a spark from a fire flying up an enormous chimney. I heard a rushing noise becoming louder and nearer. I thought it must be God I was rushing towards and that God was a blind, roaring thing, like a train. I think I passed out, but even in my stupor I could feel pain like knives shooting through me. I wept in a high voice like a child who cannot believe there is such pain in the world. At one point I heard Ida's voice.

'Birthing's worse,' it said.

I remember thinking if it was why would any woman do it?

'Has it – gone?' I managed to ask and she said, 'Burned it, with the rubbish.'

I retched then and Ida held a bowl, though there was nothing left in me but a stinking bile. She gave me something to make me sleep which didn't work the first time so she gave me more. The same potion she gave all her girls to keep them senseless and dazed. Uncle Godfrey she called it, as though it was some kind gentleman come to visit.

I don't know how long I stayed in that room. Charlotte came from time to time to press more of the potion on me. I drank and sank into merciful unconsciousness and wept when I woke. At last I saw Ginnie bending over me whispering, 'Told you Ida'd help!' She'd brought soup, 'To keep your strength up,' she said. I turned away.

'Pags!' she said. 'How you going to get better if you don't eat?'

I wanted only to die and said so.

'Guff!' she said. 'You're alive int'yer? You've got a roof over your head and food!'

She tried to tug the stained sheet from under me. 'Here!' she said, as I rolled off the bed and onto my knees. 'Just take a spoonful, for me.'

But as soon as I did I began to heave and she called for Charlotte who came again with the sleeping potion.

I drank it all, everything she gave me, even though it might have been poison. I hoped it was.

CHAPTER 22

My memories are all jumbled like rags in a tatting basket and I'm trying to sort them - going through them over and over.

There were other girls in that house. Ella and Lizzie, and Charlotte of course who never spoke but kept her twisted face bent down. And a very little girl called Elsie who couldn't have been more than eight or nine. One time I caught her coming from the locked room. She was sniffing and I thought she must be crying, but when I put my hand out to comfort her she said *fuck off you minge-eating twat*.

I left her alone after that.

I saw little of the other girls. It was Ginnie who came to me, fetching cups of tea and soup. Ginnie who coaxed and bullied me into sitting up, then walking. She told me I had to move out of the locked room but said I could share her bed which was in the washroom, made up on the floor.

I was glad enough to stay with her rather than the other girls because by that time I'd heard the men tramping up and down the stairs. Once a man hammered on the door of the cellar while I was in it. I'd begun to suspect what kind of place I'd come to.

So I slept on the floor in the washroom with Ginnie tucked into me. She had a little whistling snore and she muttered as she slept. In the morning she got up early, to go to the workhouse she said. She told me to keep the door shut and get some sleep, but I couldn't sleep for the pain and for the footsteps pounding up and down the stairs. It seemed a long time until Ginnie came back carrying a sack.

When she opened it a great quantity of clothing and frills and fancies fell out.

'Look at me,' she said, fastening a ribbon under her chin. It was bright pink with a yellow feather.

'Here – put this on,' she said, passing me a lacy one with a red jewel dangling from it.

I was quite sure I wasn't supposed to wear it but I felt too dull and stupid to argue. 'Whose is it?' I asked.

'Who knows,' Ginnie said, tying a purple cloak around her shoulders.

'Won't it be missed?'

'Nah,' she said. 'Clothes get mixed up in a washhouse.'

Then she said she would take me out when I could walk as far as the door.

'Where to?' I asked.

'Deliveries,' she said, and went to the kitchen to get me some broth.

A few days later she said I was ready and passed me a sack of clothes.

I hardly felt strong enough to walk, but Ginnie said it wasn't far and found me a bonnet. I followed her out of that house into a narrow alley where the air smelled even worse than it in did indoors. The alley was almost too narrow for the bag I carried and the smell made me feel ill.

I've asked myself many times why I didn't try to escape then. But I was still weak and besides, where would I go? I'd seen where running got me. Also I had a strange feeling, as though I'd already died with my baby. Or I'd really jumped off that bridge. Nothing felt real any more.

And there was Charlotte with her ruined face. So I did nothing, just stumbled after Ginnie trying not to slip until we stood outside an inn.

There was a green lantern above the door and a sign with a thin moon on it and *The Crescent Moon* painted beneath.

I hung back as Ginnie went towards it. I'd never been in such a place.

A cat streaked past silently as she opened the door. We went in to a dark, reeking passage with matting on the floor and a sign above the stairwell with a naked lady on it.

'I'm not going up there!' I said.

'Suit yourself,' said Ginnie and she began to climb the stairs, disappearing quickly into shadow.

The thought came to me then that I'd been tricked. I would be pounced on at any moment and dragged into a room. I couldn't even scream for help since I was afraid of who might come.

Then I heard Ginnie's voice from the stairs calling, 'Lulu? Pearl?'

A light flared and I saw a bald head with rouged cheeks and lips poking over the banister.

'Is that Ginnie-come-lately, making all that racket?' it said.

'Cora!' cried Ginnie, running up.

Cora kissed Ginnie on both cheeks and held her at arm's length. 'You're like a breath of fresh air – straight from the sewage works!'

'Cheeky mare!' said Ginnie and Cora said, 'Just a minute – I'll get my wig.'

And the head disappeared, then returned, wearing long, golden ringlets.

I'd never seen a she-man before. I wanted to turn and run but instead I followed Ginnie up the stairs, holding the bundle of clothes. My heart was knocking in my chest. When Cora said, 'Who's your friend?' I stopped. More she-men were gathering on the landing wearing hoops and pantalettes, all exclaiming over Ginnie and eyeing me up. I could hardly look at them, yet at the same time, I couldn't stop looking at their big hands in lace gloves, their feet bulging out of their slippers. And their voices were strange to me, not like men's voices or women's either.

Ginnie said, 'Come on – they won't bite, you know.'

'Well, Bella might,' said Cora, 'but I'll put her muzzle on for you!'

What else could I do? I could hardly run back the way I'd come, still carrying the sack of clothes. At the top of the stairs was a room full of mirrors and lamps and dressing tables. It was the untidiest place I'd ever seen with clothing scattered over every item of furniture and the floor. And such clothing! Silks and satins in all colours, frills and ribbons and shawls.

The she-men pulled the clothing from Ginnie's sack, exclaiming at each item.

'What do you think of this sash?'

'Yellow's your colour, Lulu - goes with your cheeks.'

'How about this bustle?'

Cora said, 'What's your name darling?'

'Pags,' said Ginnie when I didn't reply.

'I can't call you Pags - what kind of a name's that for such a pretty one? Int she pretty, girls?'

'Wants a bit of styling, said one.

'Looks a bit pale, poor love,' said another.

'A touch of rouge'd set that right.'

My cheeks burned. Ginnie stood by looking sour. She didn't like me getting so much attention but that made two of us.

'Never mind the girls,' Cora said. 'They're just jealous of your natural beauty - they get theirs from a bottle!'

'It'd take more than a bottle to help you, Cora, unless it had a genie in it!'

Cora shook her fan. 'Where's your manners, girls?' she said. 'Introductions first. This is Bella Donna, this is Gardenia and this is Pearly White.'

Each of them bobbed a curtsey and feeling foolish I did the same, which delighted them greatly. Pearly White was the darkest colour I'd ever seen. Her eyes were nearly black and she had a big, gleaming smile. Gardenia was dressed in white lace with silk flowers in her hair. 'What've you brought for us?' she asked.

'Frills and fancies,' said Ginnie, opening my sack, 'feathers and furbelows.' Out came a heap of chemisettes and pantalettes, a camisole and satin slippers. And a lace mantilla so fine you could see right through it.

Each item was greeted with squeals of delight from Cora and the rest.

'Ooh are they for me?' said Lulu, grabbing the pantalettes. 'I'll just nip into my boudoir and try them on.'

'You can try them on here,' said Cora. 'We've all seen what you've got.'

'Well, *she* might not have,' said Lulu, giving me a wink at which I blushed even more, and Gardenia said, 'Oh bless her – she's gone as pink as a rose!'

'We could call you Rosy Cheeks!' said Lulu, touching my chin.

'Put her down Lu,' said Pearly. 'You don't know where she's been. More to the point, *she* dunt know where *you've* been!'

'I was only thinking of a dab of powder,' Lulu said, turning my face this way and that. 'Or a touch of *crème celeste.*'

'She dunt need it – that complexion's pretty enough as it is,'

'A spot of rouge on her lips, maybe.'

'You could do wonders with the curling tongs on that hair.'

And they were off again, saying how fine my nose was and the colour of my eyes. I squirmed away from them but that only made them laugh and try harder to make me blush.

'I'll have to do you up!' Lulu said, and Ginnie cried, 'What about me?' but just then there was a disturbance downstairs. 'Ladies, ladies! What's all this palaver? This hullaballoo? They can hear you in Kendal Milnes!'

There was a flutter, then.

'Silas!'

'It's Silas!'

'That's his scarf, Lu – take it off!'

'Hide it in the bottom drawer!'

'He can rummage in my bottom drawer any time!'

The door opened and a man came into the room. He stood looking around in the sudden hush.

Everything about him was long. He had long, slanting eyes, a long chin and a shaved head with ginger stubble.

Behind him came Buzz, wearing the same mustard-coloured trousers and purple waistcoat as he'd worn that day on the bridge. I was so shocked to see him there in that room I shrank back, feeling a sudden dread of him seeing me.

'Ladies,' he said, 'Look at you in your frills 'n twills!'

Lulu twirled towards him and all the she-men screamed with laughter like so many peacocks.

Silas' gaze settled on me. I looked down quickly. There was something disturbing about those eyes, but I couldn't look closer while he was staring at me.

'Who's this then?' he asked.

'Pags,' said Buzz. 'She's our newest recruit.'

'Pags?'

'That's what Ginnie calls her. She's a seamstress, aren't you my lovely? A real treasure - pure gold. She can do any alterations you like.'

'Can she now,' said Silas. I could feel his gaze on me. When I glanced up he smiled. It wasn't pleasant. I blushed and looked down again.

'A shy one, int'yer?' he said. 'Where'd they find you?'

'By the river,' said Buzz. 'All sad and forlorn. Thinking of doing herself a mischief.'

There were cries of dismay.

'Was she now,' Silas said, giving me his unnerving stare. I noticed then what was odd about his eyes. They were two different colours, one almost black and the other green, but with a large freckle in the iris.

He walked all the way around me.

'Not bad,' he said.

'Not bad?' said Buzz 'She's special!'

I said nothing, wishing myself a thousand miles away.

'She could be our honey-trap,' Silas said.

'That's just what I was thinking!' said Buzz.

'That's my job!' said Ginnie.

I'd no idea what they meant.

'Smarten you up a bit,' Silas said, walking round me again. 'Bit of lace here, a feather there..'

'*I'm* your honey trap!' Ginnie said.

'Well, now you'll be a pair,' Silas said. 'Like Beauty and the Beast!' And he laughed, because he hadn't said who was which.

'How d'you like that, Pretty?' he said to me. 'I'd be your new boss.'

I stared at the floor.

'There's money in it,' he said, and my heart beat faster then. I'd had no pay since Mrs Fenton's.

'There you are!' said Buzz. 'What did I say? I told you I'd find you a job, didn't I?'

'You'll have to pay me extra,' said Ginnie.

'Will I now?'

'For training.'

'Training?' said Silas. 'Is that what you call it?'

'Someone'll have to show her the ropes.'

I looked from one to the other, desperate to ask what they meant.

Silas slipped his hand into his coat. 'What've we got here?' he said, bringing out a silver shilling and holding it up. 'Now – who shall I give this to?' he asked. 'Pretty, or you?'

'I brung her here!' cried Ginnie, and she tried to grab the coin, but he moved it out of reach. 'Sixpence each – that's only fair!'

'I int got sixpence. You'll just have to see if you can talk Pretty here into spending some of it on you.' And he passed me the coin which I took and stood foolishly looking at it. I hadn't had money of my own for so long I hardly knew what to do with it.

Ginnie scowled. 'Tint fair!' she said.

Silas chucked her under the chin. 'You'll be in charge,' he said, 'you can keep her company when she brings in the goods. You're still our go-to girl, int'yer?'

He looked directly at me. 'You'll like that wont'yer?' he said. 'Bit of company?'

I still didn't know what he meant but I was thinking that I

could save any money I earned and maybe find a different job.

Or my mother.

Pearly White held out a silk pouch towards me. 'Keep silver in silk, it turns to gold,' she said, with her big smile.

For the first time I smiled back and everyone cheered. Cora said she hadn't known I had a smile in me.

'That's settled then,' said Silas. 'Girls – get to work!'

There was an immediate flurry. The 'girls' stood around me facing outwards while Ginnie helped me into a dress of yellow lace which was quite bare at the shoulders.

Then they turned round to inspect me.

'Could do with another frill.'

'Some beauty spots on her shoulders,' this was Lulu. 'And just here at the throat.'

'Feathers on her wrists.'

'She'll look like a canary,' said Bella. 'Do you sing, love?'

I shook my head but it hardly seemed to matter, for they were applying rouge and lipstick, powder and some kind of shiny cream to my hair.

'Now then,' said Silas as they finished. 'That's more like it.'

'Told you,' Buzz said. 'I knew it as soon as I saw her.'

I stared at myself in a mirror. It was like looking at a stranger or a poster I'd once seen of a clown. All I could think was, *is this the same girl who sailed across the sea with Mrs Fenton and was worked like a slave by Mrs Digby?*

'Go and show Ida,' Silas said to Ginnie. 'Tell her she int for her – not yet anyway!'

He winked at me and I looked down, furious at myself for blushing. I still couldn't bring myself to ask what he meant.

Reluctantly Ginnie got down from her high stool and I followed her downstairs while the she-men called after us telling us to come back soon.

'All right, all right,' I heard Silas say. 'Settle down ladies – they'll be back soon enough!'

As soon as we were outside I asked, 'What kind of place is that?'

'A Molly house int it?' she said indifferently. She was short with me because of all the attention I'd been given but I hurried after her.

'What's that?'

'They put on shows and stuff.'

'What shows?'

She sighed at my ignorance. 'You know - like the Penny Gaff.'

I didn't. I'd never been to any kind of show. 'You mean like a theatre?' I knew what a theatre was - I'd seen posters for them in Dublin.

'That's it - dancing and stuff. Silas runs it.'

'With Buzz?'

'Buzz'd like to be his partner but he int. It's Silas' place. Monks' Mollies they call it, because he's Silas Monks.'

'What do they do there?'

'I told you - dancing and stuff.'

'What *stuff*?' I asked.

Ginnie groaned aloud, then, seeing the look on my face, 'It's a Molly House int it? That's what all the rooms are for above - where all our washing and mending comes from.'

I still didn't understand. And I felt very conscious of myself on these back streets in my fancy clothes. We seemed to be taking a long time to get back to Ida's house. I was out of breath already, I had a cramping pain in my stomach and my legs felt weak but I said,

'What about Ida - what did he mean when he said I'm not for her?'

Ginnie rolled her eyes, 'You won't be working for Ida - you'll work for Silas. And me.'

I started to say no one had said I'd be working for Ginnie but she was going at a pace and I found it difficult to keep up. I thought we must have passed Ida's place by now. When I asked Ginnie where we were going, she said,

'Watch this,' and ducked into an alley pulling me after her. At the end of it we were behind a row of tall houses and in one yard a maid was unpegging clothes from a line.

I looked at her mystified, but she said 'Wait.' As soon as the maid went back into the house Ginnie nipped over the gate, nimble as a monkey.

'Here you are,' she said, flinging the clothes over the top of the gate. Like a fool I caught them.

She clambered down and took the clothes from me, wrapping them in her shawl, then ran off.

I hurried after her as well as I could. 'We'll be arrested!' I panted, clutching the stitch in my side.

'Run faster then,' she said.

All I wanted was to get back indoors, where people couldn't see me in my ridiculous finery, but I hung back. 'It's wrong!'

'*That's* wrong,' she said, jerking her head towards an old woman huddled in a filthy doorway.

I had nothing to say to that. Catching up with her again I asked, 'Is this why you don't sleep in the attic with the other girls?'

'*Them*,' she said scornfully. 'they're just hens in a coop. I don't work for Ida - I work for Silas. And so do you now.'

'What work?' I demanded. 'Why have they got me up like this?'

Ginnie rolled her eyes again, then explained.

My job was to walk along the streets dressed in my finery, with my head and shoulders uncovered until a gentleman followed. Then I had to lead him into an alley where someone called Doll would hit him with a crowbar and rob him blind.

'Who?' I managed.

'Doll. You int met him yet. He int bad, so long as you don't get on the wrong side of him.'

She went on to tell me a terrible story about someone who tried to cheat Doll of money and thought he'd got away with it. Then he came to the show as usual and Doll invited him on stage. Next thing was, Doll had carved his face right off - peeled it like a fruit in front of everyone - like it was part of the show!

'And he – will go with us?' I asked faintly.

'If he dunt, someone will,' Ginnie said. 'But most of the time it's Doll. Cheer up, Pags! At least you'll be working on your feet, not your back! You won't have to do owt if you're quick – just lead'em on and Doll'll do the rest!'

She tucked her arm in mine. 'Stop worrying!' she said. 'You'll go out with me first, wont'yer? I'll show you what's what.' Then she said, 'Here we are,' and I realised we were back at Ida's door at last.

CHAPTER 23

THE CHIEF WORK of the house was whoring of course, but there was also sewing and repairing the clothes the Mollies used in their show which they put on every Friday and Saturday evening. It took place in the inn where the main room had been gutted and a platform built as a stage, with oil lamps all around.

At the top of the stairs there was a landing that ended in a doorway with no door in it but a rail across. Noise rose from the room below, laughter and song. Half-fearful, I joined Ginnie at the rail and looked down.

I could see a piano and a woman playing a kind of musical box and a bar, with another woman serving at it.

Ginnie said, 'Look at the singer.'

On stage there was a tall woman in a green, glittering dress. She sang in a low, husky voice:

Kiss me in the lamplight, Where it's too dark to be seen. Kiss me in the lamplight, And I won't ask where you've been . . .

Ginnie was looking at me curiously, but I could hardly take my eyes from the performer who was so graceful, moving like silk as she sang.

She wore long gloves and a black lace mantilla.

It was the mantilla I recognised first. I'd recently taken it to Silas. No!

It couldn't be – I looked at Ginnie and she grinned at me. I looked back down.

The woman with the musical box was Buzz! Doll was serving drinks in a lace cap and crinoline! And it was Silas on stage – *Silas Monks!*

Ginnie looked at me in glee. I shook my head, speechless. Downstairs the music became livelier. Someone else was singing to the side of the stage:

There's nothing so pleasant as getting a present
From a lover ardent and sincere
But the present that Rose got from one of her beaux
Takes the cake – go on, show them my dear.
Then the dear little flirt coyly lifted her skirt . . .

With each verse Silas took something off, a glove or the black mantilla, and threw them into the audience.

And all the men in the audience, for it was only men, roared the chorus – *Naughty! Naughty! Naughty! Naughty!*

They were pressing forward, their faces red and shiny.

I'd seen enough then. I turned and hurried back to the stairs.

'What?' cried Ginnie, running after me. 'What's up with you?'

'It's a house of sin!'

She gawped at me. 'Who are you – the Temperance Brigade? It's just blokes having a bit of fun. No one's up to any harm. What's wrong with having a laugh?'

I couldn't answer that. It hardly seemed worse than the things that went on in Ida's house. It was just that I'd had no idea about such places before.

The show was the reason there was so much work to do. The sheets from the inn needed washing and mending and the clothes Ginnie stole needed 'prettifying' as she said. Because I was skilled at stitching I was put to work regularly, making a waist bigger, adding a lace frill around a hem or extending a satin slipper to fit a man's foot.

This part of my work I was happy to do. I spent more time with the Mollies in The Crescent Moon than at Ida's – I even got to like being there. Whatever troubles they had the Molls always seemed happy. Only joking and laughter were allowed in that dingy pub. It was a bright spot of warmth and life in the squalor and mirk of the Rookeries.

Every day we took bundles of clean washing and altered garments to the pub and exchanged them for bundles of dirty washing and mending, together with any special requests from the Molls.

'A few more frills, please, round the neckline.'

'Feathers on the tops of my shoes.'

'You could put some lace on your own dress, sweetheart,' this was Lulu. 'Brighten yourself up.'

'She dunt need it,' Silas would say. 'She's pretty enough as is.'

Then he would wink at me and I would look down, furious at myself for blushing.

Ginnie took me with her when she went out looking for things the Molls wanted. She showed me how to dress to *look the part*, meaning respectable, so no one would suspect us of thieving.

'Here,' she said. 'Take this bonnet and shawl. Streets get chilly.'

It was a dark blue bonnet, with a broad ribbon. And the shawl was a matching blue. I'd never worn anything so grand.

'But—'

'You can't go out like that,' Ginnie said, 'Not unless you're on the cadge.'

'Begging,' she said, when I didn't understand her. 'Don't you know owt?'

I looked at the bonnet and shawl. 'Whose are they?' I asked.

'Who cares? said Ginnie. She put on an enormous hat with feathers and we giggled at one another as we tied the ribbons beneath our chins.

Then we walked out together, two young ladies arm-in-arm, on Deansgate with its grand buildings, Kendal Milne, the Empire Hotel, and on to the rest of the town. We passed queues of people outside pawn shops, cripples begging on carts, and a blind man sitting outside the Corn Exchange with a plaque that read *God Sees All* around his neck.

So much building work was going on that the air was choked with dust. On every corner there was scaffolding, or people digging up the road. Ginnie showed me many short cuts through Manchester, including the tunnels which ran beneath the city. She took me down into them, but I never liked them, the echoes and the smell. 'Useful if you want to disappear though,' she said, 'and come up again in a different part of town'.

That's how I got to know Manchester, with Ginnie, all the markets and corner shops, gin shops, pawn shops and inns. And the people who used them, the whores and cadgers, tippers and fly men and fences, guttersnipes, mudlarks, quacks, organ grinders, sweepers, bullies and cracksmen. And rich people passing them by in carriages just as if they didn't exist! It was a different world from Mrs Digby's, or the workhouse – and not just one world but many.

Ginnie was happy as a lark on the streets, sparring and joking with a man on the black pudding stall or slapping a beggar girl clutching at her skirts. One time she got us a parcel of whelks by looking after the stall while the woman nipped off to relieve herself. Another time she haggled down the price of salt fish and got a slab of batter thrown in. We stood munching it around a brazier. Ginnie's cheeks and nose were red from the cold and the damp mist made her hair cling to her face in wet strings.

'This is the life,' she said. 'Who'd work in one of them slave-ships?'

She meant the factories that reared above us, great slabs of blackened brick belching noise and smoke onto the streets.

'Poor sods,' Ginnie said, 'you wouldn't catch me in there.'

'What choice have they got?' I asked.

'Well, Buzz int doing it, is he?' she said, through a full mouth. 'Or Silas. Come on – let's see if we can get some ribbons.'

I was never as quick as her at lifting, as she called it. More often I kept the stall owner busy while Ginnie nicked the goods or carried the stuff she stole as we ran through the streets. One time she put a thick coating of soap on my arm and poured vinegar on it to make it look blistered. All that day I was her injured sister who needed money for the doctor. And much to my surprise people gave it.

I was a fast learner she said. And though I shouldn't like to say this to Mrs Gaskell, it was true. I soon forgot my scruples and learned new skills as Libbie never did.

I've thought about this often since reading Libbie's story. Libbie doesn't change from the start to the end of it, she's always good. That's a difference between her and me. Sometimes I think I must be more than one person or that I am one person, but not solid and fixed, more like jelly poured into different moulds. I've been one kind of person in one place, and quite another elsewhere. I was a vicar's daughter once, and then on the streets with Ginnie.

I told myself I would need to know the city if I was ever to make my way around it on my own when I started earning. Truth was, I liked dressing up and going out. There was always something new to see, something going on. The crackle of braziers, the shouts and cries from the stalls. The man who walked up and down with a live goose under his arm, charging a penny to feed it by hand. And slices of plum duff to eat, or a hot potato.

I learned a bit more about the Molly House as well. And about Ida. Ginnie told me Ida's name was Quayle, not Busby, because she'd been married a long time ago and had a half-wit son called Noah. He helped in the inn or sometimes took Doll's place, following the girls and beating the punters. So Ida was tied to the Molly House through her brother and her son, as well as running her own business and working in the workhouse. Though that didn't bring in enough money to keep a cat Ginnie said.

Ida took all the clothes and sheets from the Inn to the workhouse for washing and brought back girls with her who had nowhere else to go. So the three businesses, workhouse, whorehouse and Molly House were really one.

Ginnie said Ida had taken her from the workhouse when she was hardly more than a nipper, but she'd soon started picking the pockets of the men who came to her. The first time she met Buzz she picked his wallet and he'd been so impressed he'd offered her a different job, stealing anything that was wanted from washing lines, market stalls, shops and even people in the streets – lace handkerchiefs, silk purses, shawls.

'Best go-to girl they ever had – that's what Silas says!' she said. She was always 'tarted up right' and she knew exactly who to pick and what to say and do. You couldn't be too careful, she said. Time was, you could be hanged for running a Molly House. These days you were more likely to be locked up or transported. But the Crescent Moon was safe enough, she said, while there were so many councillors in the audience. And judges and even an MP.

So that was the Manchester I came to know. It was not like Libbie's Manchester, or Mrs Gaskell's either, I should think. I would never have gone out in it without Ginnie. For one thing I still feared running into Mrs Digby or Tucker, although it seemed unlikely in the crowds of people appearing and disappearing in the murky air like motes of dust, or drops of rain on the river. For another there was always some fighting going on, some gang at war over their pitch, a thief handy with his knife, or some bully-boy treating his girl to his fists. I was only safe so long as I stuck with Ginnie, kept my shawl over my head and remembered the way back to the inn.

CHAPTER 24

ONE DAY GINNIE told me I was ready. I didn't have to ask what she meant. My stomach turned over and seemed to fall. I'd foolishly hoped the other work Silas mentioned had been forgotten. But now Ginnie said she would *do me up* herself.

I put on the dress of yellow lace and a band with a feather in my hair. Ginnie brushed powder on my face and rubbed my lips with rouge until I told her to stop - I would look like Punch in the puppet show.

'Better than looking like a ghost,' she said. Then she said we had to be quick because Doll was waiting.

I was struck by terror at this.

'What if he isn't?' I asked.

'Int what?'

'What if he isn't there?'

'He will be,' Ginnie said.

There seemed to me to be many cracks in this plan but Ginnie said Doll knew what he was doing. 'He dunt get paid else. And besides,' she added, 'you don't want to spend the day in there.' She nodded towards the locked room which I now knew was kept for *rollovers* - men who rolled up one after the other to have their sport with the girl trapped inside.

So I went out with Ginnie. I was horribly aware of going without my bonnet as no lady would. I could feel the air on my neck. We turned onto a street that sloped downwards. There were sounds of fighting coming from the courts, shouting and glass smashing. When a man approached us walking unsteadily, I shrank away from him.

'Looking for company, love?' he asked me.

'No, she int,' said Ginnie, 'but you can have the two of us together at a special rate.'

The man stumbled off muttering. I gripped Ginnie's arm, digging my nails in. 'Ow!' she said, shaking me off. Then, 'You don't want the likes of him, he int got two farthings to rub together!'

I wondered how she knew, and how I would ever know who to choose.

We passed an inn called The Cloggers, where a number of men slouched on a bench outside, and one or two of them called out half-heartedly as we passed.

'Come over here and I'll show you a good time!'

'Like you'd know how,' said Ginnie.

At the back of The Cloggers the path was a mire and we had to pick our way through to a little court that opened onto a square.

'This is where you bring 'em,' she told me. 'Doll'll wait here.'

'Bring *who*?' I asked, feeling desperate now.

'Toffs,' was all she said.

What if no one follows me? I wanted to ask. But she was already leading the way again, uphill.

We were walking up Hardman Street now, off Hardman Square, where some of the houses seemed quite respectable with flowers in boxes beneath their windows.

The nearer we got to Deansgate the more people there were. I clung to Ginnie's arm, ashamed to be dressed as I was, but no one seemed to notice. However I soon saw that two men were following us.

One of them wore a pale grey frock coat and a waistcoat with a silver stripe. He had a very substantial beard.

'This is where we split up,' Ginnie told me, and I clutched her even more tightly. 'Bear up, Pags,' she said. 'Remember what I told you about where to go? Now let's see who follows who . . .' And with that she shook me off and set off across the street without me.

I was alone.

Immediately I was struck with terror, sure I would not remember the way, or that no one would be there waiting and the man who followed me would have his way with me and cut my throat. I wanted to run after Ginnie but she had disappeared.

I had nowhere to go so I carried on, fearing that every step might be my last.

It was the man with the beard and the striped waistcoat who followed me back to Hardman Square, and then to the little court where my worst fears were realised, for there was no one waiting, or no one that I could see, and the man who'd followed me all that way without saying a word took my arm and said, 'Right then . . .'

Bile filled my mouth as he pushed me towards the wall. My hand slapped the bricks as he tugged my skirts up. I wanted to cry out but my voice stuck in my throat.

Then there was a *crack*, and a thudding noise, and the man hit the wall beside me with a wet grunt.

I twisted myself away.

Someone who could only be Doll stood over the bearded man with an iron bar in his fist as he slid down the wall leaving a trail of blood. He barely glanced at me but I saw he had a long, curving face and a mournful expression that barely changed even as he was beating the life out of the man who had followed me.

I took all this in like lightning, for I didn't stop to watch but ran as fast as I could. I thought of screaming for help, but just as I was nearing Deansgate Ginnie came flying out of an alley and caught my arm, steering me back towards Ida's house.

I was babbling like a madwoman, making no sense but she kept saying, 'Look you're all right, int'yer?' and 'No harm done,' whenever I tried to protest.

Later she laughed at me for running off without so much as a coin, for that, I learned, was how we were 'paid' - by lifting the wallets of our 'gentlemen' before handing them over to Doll or Silas a little lighter. Not too much, of course, or they would take the iron bar to us, but Ginnie undid the neck of her gown and showed me where she had a small pouch for money stitched inside.

She swore she'd told me already but I had no memory of it. In any case I hardly cared. I could still hear the grunt of the man as he hit the wall and the crack of the iron bar against his skull. I seemed to feel his hands on me and kept running my own hands down my dress as if they were stained with blood.

'Never mind,' Ginnie said. 'You'll know what to do next time.'

I told her there would not be a next time, but of course there was. That was how I was to earn my keep.

It kept me apart from the other girls in Ida's house. They worked at nights and were often asleep by day. Or else locked into that room which had a particular horror for me. Some of them, especially Ella and Lizzie, seemed to resent me having different work but Ginnie stood up for me saying I was with her and it was no one else's business what I did. You could never tell what mood Ginnie would be in from one moment to the next, bossy or spiteful or kind, but she looked out for me all the time I was there. She was the nearest to a friend I ever had.

I had little to do with Ida at that time, or even Silas or Buzz. But once when I was taking a bag of clothing to the Mollies, I heard them talking in the room they used as an office, which was up the stairs to the left.

'The council int going to *shut us down*,' Silas' voice said, 'not while we've got friends on it.'

'I'm just telling you what I've heard,' Buzz said. He sounded almost panicky. 'The police have warrants to search any premises selling alcohol.'

'Chrissakes – it's an inn innit?'

'Well, but—'

'You worry too much.'

I glanced through the pane of glass in the door. Buzz had his back to me. He was unlocking a drawer in the bureau and when he moved to one side I saw it was full of money! Banknotes of different shapes and sizes – I'd never seen so much in all my life. I ducked down as he turned, slipping the key into his waistcoat. I was in a hurry to get away as soon as I could, so of course I tripped and almost fell.

Out spilled all the clothing from the sack. I started picking it up again, heart in my mouth, but to my amazement no one seemed to have heard, or at any rate no one came, and I could still hear their voices behind the door. Silas' voice fell to a murmur and there was a low laugh. Through the glass panel in the door I could see Silas looming over Buzz.

He tilted his face from side to side provokingly as he lowered it towards Buzz. Then their mouths met in a long kiss.

I hurried away to a downstairs room where I sat sewing a long seam on a ripped sheet. For the first time I wondered how it had ripped, and an image flashed through my mind of Buzz and Silas tangled in it but I suppressed it quick. And soon the thought of the money overcame all else. There must be hundreds of pounds in that bureau!

I didn't do anything with this knowledge at that time but tucked it away in my mind.

While the show was on I could stop my work as 'honey trap' – there were too many other things to do. But as soon as it finished I had to go back to it. Each time was terrible to me, although I learned how to select the men and smile at them and walk a certain way. I got better at running off, so I didn't have to see Doll bludgeoning a man to a bloody pulp, but I never did get the knack of relieving him of his wallet in the short time between him grasping hold of me and Doll delivering the first blow. So I was earning my keep but no more, just like at Mrs Digby's, and was even less satisfied with the arrangement now. Whenever Ginnie told me I had to go out I came up with excuses but all she said was, 'Get yourself tarted up.'

I told myself I knew my way through the alleys by now, and would run back to the Mollies if need be. So I put on my silk dress and left my hair uncovered and let her paint my face.

Then the time came when my worst fears were realised. I went out and very soon someone followed me. I looked round once or twice but he didn't even try to hide it. Where was Doll? I was always fearful that he wouldn't be where he should and I would be trapped. Still I did 'the walk' through the alley into the little court.

The man had a whiskery face, the hair striped in different hues, grey and black and tobacco yellow. He was very stout. I felt sick to my stomach but I told myself as soon as I got to the court I would run. A man so fat could surely not catch up with me – and hopefully Doll would deal with him.

But before I reached the court he grabbed me and lifted me clean off my feet. One fat, sweating hand was clamped over my face, the other pulled up my clothes from behind. I twisted like a fish on a hook and tried to squeal so that Doll would come for me, but then I felt a violent pain as he thrust himself into me.

Moments later he was done. He left me there, his filth dribbling down my legs. Then Noah came out of the shadows.

'Where were you?' I cried.

Noah only grinned at me with his jutting teeth, tiny eyes darting everywhere like flies in his great thick skull. I ran all the way back to Ida's, where Ginnie was at the door.

'What's up?' she said when she saw me. I clutched her and couldn't speak. Her face changed.

'Sit down,' she said. But when I finally gasped out my sorry tale, all she said 'Is that it? I thought you'd been hurt!'

'But he—' I said, 'Noah—' I couldn't stammer it out.

'Probably owed him a favour or summat,' she said. 'That's the way it goes.'

No one had told me! But all Ginnie said as I sobbed was, 'Count yourself lucky – I've known girls get themselves cut up!'

I didn't feel lucky. I couldn't rid myself of the feel of that man inside me or the look on Noah's face – the thought of him watching made me want to curl up and die.

'Anyway,' said Ginnie. 'I've brung you a bit of good news. Tomorrow we're working the inn!'

I stared at her.

'There's some celebration on streets, and peelers'll be out in the crowds so Silas wants us inside.'

After the show the Mollies would entertain their 'guests'. There would be so many of them that Silas would need our help lightening their pockets.

'Beauty of it is, they don't complain because they shunt be there in the first place. Some of them even tip! And best part is, Silas dunt know who's got what – so long as he gets a share – and what he dunt know dunt hurt him!'

I could feel the shaking starting again in my stomach. My jaw seemed to have clenched.

'Tell you what,' she said kindly. 'Stay here. I'll fetch the mending to you.'

She saw to it that I was left alone all the rest of that afternoon, but I felt no better. I couldn't bear the thought of such a thing ever happening to me again.

So I came up with a plan.

Next evening, the show was livelier than usual. There was a great deal of shouting and laughter and drunken singing. This, together with the noise from the streets meant it was hardly possible to hear yourself think.

I didn't have to think. My plan was not difficult or clever. It was simply that I would take what I found in guests' pockets and run away with it, seeing how far it would get me. I didn't think any further than this – I just wanted to end the terrible dream I was trapped in.

Everything was chaos backstage, the Molls all screaming at one another and Buzz running round in circles. The punters left their clothes in what the Mollies called their 'boudoir' – a small dressing room to one side of the bedrooms. While they were about their business we slipped in and helped ourselves, not to money – most were too canny to leave their wallets – but to watches and watch chains, scarf pins, cuff-links, snuff boxes – even a silk cravat or handkerchief. We hid it all inside the washing sacks.

Then, as I passed the office I noticed something gleaming on the back of a chair.

Buzz' waistcoat!

Greatly daring, I pressed the door handle, not expecting it to open. When it did, I couldn't breathe.

I slipped inside, past a coat stand which I hoped would hide me. I ran my hands through the waistcoat pockets and feeling a small lump in one, drew out a key!

I sank to my knees. There was hardly any light in the room except for the flicker that came from the theatre below so it took some fumbling to find the lock, especially since my hands were shaking. First the key wouldn't turn, then I couldn't find what I was looking for – the desk was no longer stuffed with money. But I groped around until my fingers found a tin. Of course it was locked, but I shook it and thought there was money inside.

There was no time to try to open it. I stuffed it hastily into my sack and rose, feeling as though all the blood had rushed to my head.

But it drained away again as I saw Silas in the doorway. He was dressed in his glittering green like a snake, his face was powdered and rouged, and he was smiling a wide, curved smile.

'Hello Pags,' he said. 'What are you up to?'

※

Somewhere in the prison someone starts to sing. It's not a sound we often hear in this place. It sounds as if it's coming, not from the cell next to mine but the one after that. Emma Flowers, she who murdered all her children and never speaks! Yet now she's singing *The First Noel*, all the verses, and when she gets to the end she starts again. It's not beautiful or even tuneful, yet it plucks at me painfully.

No one shouts or comes to stop her. We all lie listening in our cells.

I remember that tomorrow will be Christmas Eve.

All over Manchester, the factories will be closed, the churches decorated and lit. In the slums and gin houses and sweatshops, people will be waiting for Christmas morn. Factory hands, brickmakers, railway workers, glass blowers, iron turners, chimney sweeps, weavers, rag sorters, dyers, brush makers, flower sellers, bleachers, bone boilers, match sellers, night soil men, bone-grubbers, rag men, knocker uppers, mudlarks, cobblers, cracksmen, tramps, landlords, picklocks, beggars, shoe-blackers, postmen, all waiting for their day of rest.

Even whores will have a day off.

Not servants though. In the big houses they will be preparing for their hardest day, while the children dream about their presents.

I wonder if my mother will have bought presents for her children.

I wonder what presents Mrs Gaskell's daughters will have.

Will she read to them after their Christmas dinner?

Will they play games?

Here it is a long day with nothing to do. I clean my cell as usual and wait to be taken to the washhouse or the kitchens. When no one comes for me I feel restless and can't settle to anything.

Mrs Gaskell will not come on Christmas Eve. She will be with her family, her daughters, by the fire.

I try to think of it, but the picture has faded. I mind that almost more than the loss of her.

Then I look outside, wondering whether anything will be different at Christmas. I can just see the tops of the tripe works and the catgut factory. I remember the yards, piled high with cow hooves and offal.

I got to know them when I was going out with Ginnie. But even thinking about Ginnie gives me a sore pain in my chest.

So I read my magazines again, lying on my bed, until the light fades.

In the morning there is a service in the chapel. A special choir has come to us, from the *Society for the Improvement of the Working Classes*. It's Prince Albert's society we are told; he is President of it. They sing *Silent Night* to us in German.

Part way through someone starts to sob. We all stare in surprise to see it's Ella Brigg. That's the first I've seen of her since the time in my cell. Then it was me crying and pleading but now she's sobbing as though her heart will break! Of course, she's taken away. But the choir sing on, *Hark the Herald,* and *God Rest You Merry Gentlemen,* and the wardresses glare at us until we join in.

I glance sideways at Emma Flowers, but she's smiling and nodding to herself, not singing at all.

Then we're told to return to our cells and read our prayer books but I read about Libbie Marsh all over again.

It's the best story in my opinion. The others are mostly concerned with telling the poor not to drink. If they behave themselves, they seem to say, all will be well.

I read the part I know by heart now, where Libbie is no longer a 'desolate, lonely orphan, a stranger on this earth', and feel a sad, tugging pain as though nothing will ever be right again.

But at the end of that story the little boy's mother, Margaret, asks Libbie to live with her and be as a daughter to her and is *as tender to her as her own dead mother.*

At last it comes to me why Mrs Gaskell wanted me to read this story. She means me to live with her!

I read the whole story again, then clasp the magazine to my chest and pace about my cell. It's the best Christmas present anyone could ever have!

CHAPTER 25

Elizabeth

CHRISTMAS WAS QUIET because Elizabeth had cancelled all their engagements. They rested and recovered from their colds, but on Christmas Eve, after a thoroughly indigestible meal, they all stayed up late playing Twenty Questions, Spanish Merchant, and a game in which they had to keep a feather in the air by blowing it from one to the other. They were helpless with laughter by the end of it.

It was a good evening, though not without tensions. Julia cried when she was taken upstairs, Polly played the piano but Flossie could not be persuaded to sing and Meta ran out of the room. Elizabeth found her crying on her bed. 'What is it?' she said patiently. 'Polly can play the piano on her own. But don't spoil the party – everyone's so happy!'

'Happy!' said Meta.

'Yes – happy! You were laughing with everyone else.'

'That doesn't mean I was happy. It means I was trying to *fit in*.'

'Well try harder,' Elizabeth said, more sharply than she'd meant.

Meta gazed moodily at her window. 'Don't you ever feel that there's a kind of darkness in everything – at the heart of even the brightest thing?'

'No,' Elizabeth said, firmly.

'I do – it's always there. As if behind everything there's only nothing.'

She was weeping silently now.

Elizabeth felt torn between sympathy and resentment. She'd tried so hard to create a happy Christmas after everyone had been ill. But Meta had been subject to these black moods since she was very young.

Once, when she was six, she'd said she knew what infinity was. It wasn't beyond imagining because she'd seen it. And she'd known then that she didn't matter – nothing did.

Comforting words wouldn't work and certainly she wouldn't respond to being told how lucky she was, how many people were in far worse situations than herself. *That's exactly what I mean*, she would say.

So Elizabeth kissed Meta's hair and told her it was up to her whether she re-joined the party or not. And because she'd done nothing if not pass on a social conscience to all her girls, Meta wiped her eyes and followed Elizabeth downstairs where she sat in a corner looking martyred.

Still, everyone else enjoyed themselves although the roast was charred on the outside and raw within and the pudding had inspired a debate about what might possibly be in it. William said it was good to encourage experimentation . . .

Then immediately after Christmas there was a run of disasters. Relentless rain caused the Irwell to swell, flooding the houses on its banks. Part of a terrace fell into the river and entire families drowned in their cellar rooms. The Domestic Mission worked flat out to find accommodation for the remaining families still crammed into the collapsing slums. Elizabeth helped to coordinate food parcels and blankets, William opened the Cross St Chapel to the homeless and Tottie pitched in, looking after the smaller children in an improvised creche. Elizabeth spent an afternoon sitting with a woman who'd lost all three of her children in the flood and whose husband was missing. She attempted to sweep the remaining water out of the door, crammed rags into the broken window and managed to heat some half-stewed tea, aware all the time of the woman's dreadful stillness, her blank, shuttered gaze.

What could she say? *I lost three children too?* But not like this hammer-blow from heaven.

She'd never been so aware of how limited a thing *help* was.

Although she did remember, when she was very young, taking a piece of cake to her Aunt Lumb who was crying in her room. Her aunt hadn't taken the cake, but she'd drawn Elizabeth to her and hugged her so tightly Elizabeth had wanted to pull away or cry, but she hadn't.

There had been nothing to say then, either. Sometimes she thought it was all the things words couldn't say that made her want to write. But that wouldn't help her now, with this poor woman.

In the end she sat beside her in silence with the dreadful tea, feeling the small exchange of heat from the woman's thigh to her own. Was this it? she wondered. Was this *compassion*? Being there. Suffering with. William would say that was what was asked of them.

But when an outbreak of diphtheria followed the floods she went to find William. He was helping to turn a warehouse into a temporary hospital. His face was yellow, his eyelids red, slightly crusted. How would it help if he fell ill as well? She wanted to say that in the end nothing he did mattered, there was nothing to be done. But all she said was, 'I'm going home.'

'Home?' he echoed, as if he'd forgotten what it meant.

'Yes, home. And you should come too.'

He ran his hand through his hair. 'I can't,' he said. 'There's too much to be done – it isn't finished—'

'It won't finish, Willy, you know that. I'm asking you to come back with me and not bring diphtheria into our home.'

She expected him to argue but he only stared around the warehouse, distracted. 'Yes,' he said, surprising her. 'All right then, yes.'

She didn't know where Tottie was but William said he would find her.

'You go,' he said, 'I'll bring her home.'

'Right,' she said, 'you and Tottie can take the carriage, I'll walk.'

She waited for him to say it wasn't safe, he would find another carriage but he only nodded at her absently. She'd turned to go, pain swelling in her heart, when he said,

'I'll be back when I can – it might be a few hours. Don't wait up.'

They stared at one another then, so many unsaid things between them.

She left him and walked towards the river through the sulphurous glow of the streetlamps. Shadowy, inhuman shapes were crammed onto boats or huddled beneath the bridge. *In a few days that will be Pasley*, she thought, and felt a cold finger on her heart.

Then she heard someone calling her name.

'Mrs Gaskell – what *are* you doing?'

Mrs Carver, who ran the Mission for the Destitute Devout.

She insisted that Elizabeth should get in her carriage. Elizabeth didn't particularly want a lift from Mrs Carver who never stopped talking, but it was more than a mile to her house and still raining.

As she climbed in Mrs Carver asked her, 'Where's Mr Gaskell?' and Elizabeth said, with hardly any bitterness, that he was busy.

Then she had to listen to Mrs Carver singing William's praises, his tirelessness, his selflessness, his devotion . . .

Elizabeth looked at the people wading through the ginnels and alleyways towards the shops. Attempting to loot them, no doubt.

She couldn't allow Pasley to be released onto these streets, but she still hadn't found anywhere for her. Should she take her in, just for a few days?

But then she would have to send her away again. How painful would that be?

Mrs Carver was talking about her Mission, which was already overcrowded, and now this . . .

'Mrs Carver,' Elizabeth said, interrupting her, 'Can I ask you a favour?'

Quickly, she outlined Pasley's case.

'You can see how we're fixed,' Mrs Carver said, and she launched into a tale of overcrowding, under-staffing, leaking roofs . . .

'What if – a small donation were made?'

Mrs Carver said there was no room in her Mission even for a thousand pounds. 'You're not offering a thousand pounds, I take it?'

'No indeed,' said Elizabeth.

Mrs Carver didn't know of anywhere that would have a spare bed, donation or not, but she did say she would ask around. Elizabeth promised it would only be a temporary measure, a few days at most, it might not be needed at all. Mrs Carver said she would see what she could do.

Elizabeth sat back with a tremulous feeling in her stomach. She felt as though small, dark pits had opened in her heart.

Lily is such a good little girl, her aunt's voice said.

She'd always tried to be good, but she wasn't sure she even knew what *good* meant any more.

She did know. It meant that she, who had everything, should give to those who had nothing. Like Pasley.

She could feel the other Elizabeth who didn't want to, unfolding her dark wings.

But that was nonsense, she told herself. She would still do her best for Pasley. And for her family. It wasn't her fault if those things weren't compatible.

'So what do you think?' Mrs Carver said. Elizabeth looked at her blankly.

'About setting up a collection in chapel for the refuges?'

'Oh. Oh, yes. I'll have to ask William,' she said. Fortunately Mrs Carver seemed satisfied with this. Elizabeth sat back, contemplating all the other things she had to say to William when he finally came home.

Surely he would see now that they had to move.

If he didn't . . . but she didn't know what else she could say to persuade him. She'd used up all her arguments.

Then a thought penetrated her like a shaft of ice, a lightning bolt of clarity.

She could leave and take the girls!

To Knutsford, or somewhere else – anywhere. William could stay here.

It seemed so drastic, shocking, and yet, as she thought about it, more and more reasonable. Why shouldn't they? It would be better for everyone. William could get on with his work undistracted, and the girls would thrive. And she could travel to Italy with Tottie and Hearn! The girls would go to school and join them in the holidays . . .

Italy! Even at the thought of it she felt giddy, as though she was soaring into a blue, blue sky. But then Mrs Carver's carriage rattled over a bump in the road and she was jolted back to reality.

Of course she couldn't run away to the continent. What would William say? What would the girls think?

And the congregation, always the congregation. Prying and spying, judging.

Her thoughts plunged downwards like a diving bell. Dimly, she realised they were approaching Upper Rumford Street. Mrs Carver asked if they should take her to her door.

'Oh no, this is fine,' she said. Thanking Mrs Carver profusely she got out of the carriage and hurried home.

She let herself in to the usual clamour. Polly had cut her hand trying to repair the fence that still wasn't mended, the milk had been delivered already sour and Flossie had found a mouse drowned in it. Julia was crying because she'd lost her favourite toy, a small stuffed rabbit called Stumpy because he'd only ever had three legs. No one knew where Meta was.

'Girls,' Elizabeth said, holding her arms out. They came to her and she buried her face in their brown and blonde curls, their sweet-smelling, slightly sweaty necks.

Then Julia started to squirm and Elizabeth let her go. She took a long shaky breath and said, 'Now.'

She bathed Polly's hand in the kitchen and promised Julia they would all look for Stumpy. She told Bessie she would write to the dairy again about the milk and tried to comfort Flossie about the mouse.

In the middle of it all Meta wandered in with a garland of old leaves and bracken in her hair, saying she'd just wanted to be alone.

Gradually everything became calm again because Elizabeth had attended to it. And Polly, her sweet girl, said she would read to Julia and Flossie, Elizabeth should lie down.

She'd thought she would fall asleep immediately but in fact she lay awake, thinking about Italy and and Hearn and Pasley. Eventually she heard muted voices on the landing that could only be William and Tottie.

She waited but he didn't come in.

Was he sleeping in the parlour?

Was he sleeping at all?

Had he gone back to the slums? She wouldn't put it past him. She fought the urge to get up and look for him. There was nothing she could do about it now. She could only hope he hadn't brought the contagion into their home.

Tomorrow was New Year's Eve, and her party.

She'd never felt less like a party but she would have one, nonetheless, for Tottie. Whose stay had been marked by crisis, illness and disaster. It was the least she could do to create some small, pleasant occasion for her friend before she left.

CHAPTER 26

IN FACT THE party was a great success. Susanna Winkworth came with her sister, Catherine, and they played the piano together while William sang with Henry Burnett. Then William danced a jig with Susanna and Catherine while Polly played and Meta and Tottie produced sketches of them all. Finally, they toasted the New Year in. 'To happy times!' William said. It was 1850, half way through the century already. Life was short, short! Where had all those years gone?

Then the Winkworth sisters departed, Polly and Meta went to bed and William excused himself, saying he had to be up early. Elizabeth, Henry and Tottie sat talking around the fire.

Everything was perfect, Elizabeth thought. The glow of the fire, one side of Tottie's face pinker than the other as she sat by it, the glimmer of the candlesticks, the sheen of the piano, all these things made more beautiful and poignant by the sense of how rapidly they passed.

Then Henry Burnett said, 'How is that girl you've been trying to help?'

He'd heard about Pasley from someone at his church. She was becoming quite famous, he said.

Elizabeth exchanged a look with Tottie. *See*, it said. Pasley would never be free while she remained in Manchester.

'She'll be released soon,' she told him, 'and I've got no further – I feel as though I'm running into brick walls everywhere.'

She wouldn't mention the possibility of a refuge in Tottie's hearing.

Henry Burnett leaned forwards. 'You've heard of my brother-in-law,

Charles Dickens?' he said, in his hushed voice and Elizabeth refrained from saying that since she didn't live on the moon, she had.

'Well,' Henry said, 'he's involved in a scheme for rescuing fallen women . . .'

It seemed that Dickens had established a cottage in Shepherd's Bush where destitute girls were fed, clothed and educated, with the aim of preparing them for a new life in the colonies.

'Oh, I've heard of it!' cried Tottie, at the same time as Elizabeth said, 'Isn't that transportation?'

'Not the *penal* colonies,' Henry murmured, mildly shocked. 'They go to respectable households, as domestic servants.'

'But how marvellous!' cried Tottie, as Elizabeth said, 'You mean he might take Pasley?'

Henry frowned. 'I'm not sure they would have any vacancies in the cottage,' he said, 'but if you write to Charles he might tell you more about how the scheme works. And perhaps find a place for her on one of the ships . . .'

'That would be wonderful,' said Tottie, beaming.

'Where do these ships go, exactly?' Elizabeth asked.

'Australia, Canada – any number of destinations.'

Elizabeth's mind whirled like the globe from the sudden expansion of possibility. Not the Lake District or Wales, but – *would they take someone straight from prison?* 'It might take some time to arrange,' she said, thinking about the Emigration Office.

'Oh, but I believe one of the benefactresses of the scheme has some influence there,' Henry said. 'You will have heard of her, I think – Miss Angela Burdett-Coutts.'

Tottie was thrilled. The famously wealthy and philanthropic Miss Coutts was also a patron of art, a collector of paintings.

'I think there is a stipulation that the girls should be accompanied on the voyage,' Henry continued. 'There would have to be some kind of guardian to take care of her and vouch for her behaviour . . .'

There was a pause while everyone tried to think of someone who might want to make a long and arduous journey to an unknown land, merely to return on the next ship.

'Unless they wanted to emigrate as well,' Tottie said.

'Do you know anyone who wants to emigrate?' Elizabeth asked.

'Perhaps an advertisement could be placed to see if anyone who's leaving on that ship would mind looking after her,' Tottie said.

'For a small fee?' said Elizabeth, wondering what sort of person that might attract.

'I believe Charles sends his girls over with a matron,' Henry said. 'I'm sure she could be induced to look after an extra girl.'

'That's a brilliant idea!' said Tottie.

Henry smiled modestly.

So it was agreed that Elizabeth should write to Mr Dickens, there was no possible excuse for her not to. She could hardly say she was afraid he wouldn't reply, or that she'd privately vowed not to ask him for anything again. But this was different, of course.

'Where is he at the moment?' she asked, hoping, unreasonably, that he might be on one of his perpetual tours.

'London,' Henry said.

Elizabeth said she would write as soon as possible. It occurred to her that she should also write to the Emigration Office about the cost of the trip. And what about Pasley's uncle, or mother? They'd shown no interest in her so far, but surely they should be told if she was going to be sent away?

There was so much to do it was hard to know where to begin.

CHAPTER 27

EARLY IN THE New Year Tottie went home, leaving a gap that had to be filled with the business of new dresses and dance tutors for the girls. Then Elizabeth heard from Pasley's uncle.

Dear Mrs Gaskell,

Thank you for your letter. I can confirm that the girl in question is indeed my niece, and that I am her legal guardian, though for some years now I have heard nothing from her.

Although Pasley said she'd written to him several times.

I regret the circumstances you describe but can see no advantage now in visiting her.

No advantage to whom?

I can also confirm that the girl's mother, my sister-in-law, has made a new life for herself, and does not wish to be drawn into an association that could only be deleterious for them both.

Dear God!

I am unfortunately unable to help with the future placement of my niece, since I expect to be travelling for some time.

How convenient for him!

However, I am in receipt of a small fund left to her by my brother; the sum of thirty pounds, with interest, and I will consider releasing all or part of this money for any appropriate scheme conducive to the welfare of my niece.

Elizabeth paced around the room. She was actually shaking.

Thirty pounds! He'd had *thirty pounds* for Pasley, while she'd been in a sweatshop and on the streets and in prison. Even a small part of that money could have been used for bail!

Her first instinct was to write back and tell him what she thought of him, but that wouldn't help Pasley – he might decide not to release the money after all. Then it would be kept in trust until her marriage or until she turned thirty, or subjected to any of the other conditions applied to women and money.

She stopped pacing and sat down again to think.

Few people wanted a servant with independent means who might leave the job if she didn't like it. Even though thirty pounds wasn't an enormous sum and would hardly support Pasley for long, it might help her to marry or set up house and live independently.

Pasley's uncle hadn't specified whether sending her abroad would be an *appropriate scheme*, but surely he'd be pleased to see her go.

Thirty pounds might pay for the ship, if he agreed.

Why would he not agree?

If Pasley could keep the money herself she'd be free to begin again in a new country, but Pasley couldn't keep the money – the law didn't allow it.

So it would pay for her voyage and perhaps also for a guardian of some kind, who still had to be found. Elizabeth still had to write to Charles Dickens. And there was Pasley herself, of course. Elizabeth hadn't told her yet because it might not happen, but she would have to be told. How would she feel about being sent to the other side of the world?

Elizabeth would explain to her that it was in her best interests, that no other opportunities had presented themselves, but what if she refused to go?

Elizabeth sighed, uncomfortably aware that she'd been putting off another visit to the prison, but now she would have to go, to tell Pasley in person and give her the choice. She owed her that much at least.

CHAPTER 28

Pasley

AFTER CHRISTMAS THE governor comes to inspect us, and there is a terrible rumpus for Edie Bent lifts her skirts as he passes and she's wearing nothing underneath. The governor walks away muttering 'For God's sake,' under his breath, Miss Jopson running after him. Edie is carted off to the poky and three of the girls who laughed are given penalties. Miss Hannaway marches up and down the line trying to catch anyone else out laughing. She stares at me for a long time but I keep my face poker straight, thinking how strange it is that what a man will pay to see in one place disgusts him in another.

Then she gives us all extra chores to do. Mine is cleaning the ovens which are black with grease. I do the best job I can, thinking all the time about when Mrs Gaskell will come. She'll have to tell her daughters, of course, and her husband, about me living with them and give them time to get used to the idea.

At the end of that long, horrible morning, Miss Jamieson comes.

'Make yourself decent,' she says, 'you have a visitor,' and my heart turns over. I catch sight of myself in the bottom of a pan. My face is streaked with grease, all my hair escaping from my cap and my hands are black. I rinse them quickly, wiping them on my apron, and pin my hair up again. Miss Jamieson gives me a cloth for my face and I scrub it fiercely, then follow her to my cell where Mrs Gaskell is waiting.

'My dear girl,' she says. 'I'm so sorry I haven't been to see you.'

I want to run into her arms but of course I don't. Now she's here my tongue is all tied up like wool. I hang back for shame.

Miss Jamieson brings us an extra chair and we sit either side of the small table which is covered in bits of yarn. I sweep some of them away, wishing it was neater.

Mrs Gaskell is talking about Christmas and how busy she's been. Then she says, 'Did you get the magazines I sent you?'

I nod at her. 'Yes,' I say, and, 'thank you!' which is all I can manage.

'Did you read them?'

I nod again. I don't even manage to tell her how many times.

'And did you enjoy them?'

'I - they were the - the—'

I seem to have swallowed my tongue.

'Did you read the one I mentioned - about Libbie Marsh?'

'That was my favourite,' I say in a rush.

I've pleased her now. 'Oh?' she says, 'Why's that?'

I swallow. It's so hard to find the words. 'I think Mr Mills - knows how it is - to be alone in the world, and to wish not to be alone - but not to be married,' I say, feeling that I'm making a great hash of it. But she's looking at me differently now. I stop, but she nods at me to go on.

'And he seems to know Manchester very well - only it's not the Manchester I know.'

'How do you mean?' she says, and I see I've made a mistake. She seems less pleased now. I mumble something about Mrs Digby's sweatshop, and that there are many poor people who are not honourable and kind, and she says,

'But you see, Mr Mills may have wanted to set an example and not show people in their worst light.'

I bow my head humbly.

She says, 'Anyway, I have a little secret to confess,' and my heart is banging its foolish drum again, because now, surely, she will ask me to go home with her.

'I am Cotton Mather Mills.'

I look at her blankly. She's smiling and quite pink.

'I wrote the story,' she says.

'But—'

It was a name I adopted because I didn't want people to know it was me. It seems silly now,' and she laughs a little. I'm trying to remember what I said about it, whether I said anything bad or wrong. I should have known it was hers! I hasten to tell her again that it was my favourite of all the ones I read, it was the best by far!

'Oh, if only that were true – I look at it now and wish it better.'

I tell her it couldn't be better and she shakes her head, laughing, so I screw up my courage and ask her how she can write so many words, and such fine ones?

'Very quickly,' she says. 'Too quickly, I sometimes think, but then if I didn't write quickly I would never write at all! There's always so much to do . . .'

'But how do you remember what to say?' I ask, thinking how hard it is for me to remember anything from breakfast to supper.

'I don't – I'm afraid to say I forget a great deal. I always think I should take notes but never do. So what I *do* put down is a poor imitation of what I would like to write.'

And she looks quite sad for a moment, so I hasten to say again how good her story is, but she interrupts me.

'I'm so glad you enjoyed it. I thought about you many times over Christmas and hoped you would find time to read. But I've not come here to discuss my poor stories,' and my skin prickles all over, for now she will ask me. I feel almost sick with hope and fear.

She's smiling at me, but there's something not quite smiling in her eyes.

'I've heard from your uncle,' she says. 'He tells me he's been holding money for you. A small sum left to you by your father.'

I shake my head, not understanding.

'It won't revert to you until you're twenty-one. But he's willing to give some of it to help you on your release.'

'My father – left me money?'

'Yes, with your uncle.'

'No one told me—'

'Well no, they wouldn't, I'm afraid. Your father gave it to your uncle until you came of age.'

'How much?' I say, sharply. She looks displeased.

'I'm sorry?'

'How much did my father leave me?'

I think she won't answer but then she says,

'About thirty pounds, I believe.'

Thirty pounds! My uncle had thirty pounds – for me – from my father!

'But he wasn't supposed to release it until you were twenty-one.'

'But – he will release it now?'

'For a suitable plan—'

'Not to get me out of here?'

She bows her head. 'To be fair, I don't think he knew you were in prison,' she says.

I sit back thinking, *I've been in a workhouse and on the streets and worse*, but Mrs Gaskell is speaking again.

'I've been looking into the possibility—' she says, but I interrupt her.

'Can I have the money when I leave here?'

She doesn't like me asking this. 'As I say, it's to be kept in trust for you until you're of age. But your uncle will release some of it, for an appropriate scheme.'

'What scheme?'

'That's what I was trying to tell you.'

She looks away from me and is silent for so long I begin to be afraid. I'm about to speak, to tell her not to worry, I'm happy for her to keep the money until I'm of age if that's the plan, when she says, 'I have been considering the possibility – that it may be best for you to leave Manchester altogether. To go to another country – somewhere with a better climate – for your chest.'

She looks at me then, but I don't understand her. I shake my head again.

'Australia, perhaps. There is Canada, of course, but the winters are very cold. You have heard of Australia?'

'Where the convicts go?'

'Not only convicts. Many of the colonies are looking for people like yourself, with skills, to make a new life there. I'll make sure you don't go on a convict ship.'

Something inside me is toppling.

'What do you think?' she asks.

I think she's sending me away.

'I – it's very far—'

'Well, that, in part, is the beauty of it. You'll make new friends there, and as long as you don't speak about your past there's no reason why you shouldn't have a new start. I've heard many stories of young girls like yourself who settle there and do very well. They have homes, and families—'

She doesn't want me.

'How will I get there?'

'That's still to be arranged. You would go on a special ship – much bigger than the one you sailed to England on – and I have to find someone to travel with you, to escort you.' As if to herself she adds, 'You can't travel such a great distance on your own . . .'

'What will I do there?' I ask.

'Someone will be there to help you find employment. But I've checked and seamstress is on the list of required trades. I don't think it will be too difficult, finding work.'

I don't say anything. I can't.

She says, 'I realise this is a new idea for you – and very big, and shocking. But my dear, I want you to consider it, I want you to give it a chance. Because the more I think of it, the more I think there's nothing for you here – only misery and squalor and the danger of being trapped into the same way of life as before. I truly believe you can start again, but only if you go somewhere you aren't known. You could really make something of yourself, but not here. Manchester is too full of people willing to drag you back into the gutter – do you understand what I mean?'

I understand she doesn't want me, she wants me to go. I understand my father has left me money I can't use. She says, 'Surely you can see there's nothing for you here?'

My breath comes out in a long, quivering sigh. I close my eyes then open them, looking at her. I see her face change. She talks rapidly then. 'You said yourself that you coped well with the voyage over here – weren't you the only one who wasn't sick? Because if you were sick, I wouldn't think of it – it's a very long journey.'

I look away from her. Tiny pulses are hammering in my head. *My mother knew there was money for me*, I think. There's a bad taste in my mouth. *Who will I talk to? Where will I sleep?*

'Promise me you'll think about it,' she says. 'I know there isn't much time before your release but there are no ships sailing before February. So I'm still looking for somewhere for you to stay – just for a short time. And then, as soon as your papers come through—'

'I won't stay with my uncle then?' I say. *Or with you*, I think, and the bad taste is there again. She dips her head, no. Then goes on quickly, 'But he seems very sorry for everything that's happened – and I think he truly wishes you well.'

'Does he.'

'As I say, I don't think he knew all the circumstances.'

I close my eyes again. It doesn't matter, nothing matters any more. *It's because of everything I told you*, I think.

'Perhaps I should leave you now,' she says, 'to think it over. It's a big decision and not one to be taken lightly. No one can force you to go, if you decide you want to stay . . .'

I turn away from her, not wanting her to see my face, how close I am to crying. 'Suppose I do want to,' I say.

'I'm sorry?'

'Suppose I want to stay here, in Manchester?'

With you, I don't say.

I hear her sigh, then she's silent. But I won't speak, I won't help her by saying what she wants me to say.

'If I ask you something,' she says, 'will you answer me?'

My heart plummets. *This again*, I think. I thought we'd done with it.

'You told me that when you left Mrs Digby's things went badly for you – so badly that you thought about – harming yourself.'

I start to speak but she lifts a hand to silence me. 'I'm not judging you – please believe me. You told me that a man came and helped you, but not what happened after that. You haven't told me how you came to be arrested.'

I try to speak but my jaws clench. I shake my head.

'Can you tell me what happened?'

I cover my face. Gently she takes my hands away. 'Pasley,' she says softly.

I close my eyes. I can't look at her but I do manage to tell her that I went to the workhouse.

'But – how did that lead to your arrest?'

This is it, the question I've been dreading. I feel a liquid terror. I make myself look at her, willing her to see what I cannot say. She takes her hands away from mine. Before I remember not to, I wipe my nose on my sleeve then brush my eyes.

Then I tell her, with many stops and starts, about Ida Quayle and the inn. I don't call it a Molly House – how would I say such a thing to her? I say as little as possible about Silas and Buzz, just that I had to attract punters – customers, by walking the streets in fine clothing.

I don't tell her about the baby. She doesn't ask.

All the time I'm thinking about Ginnie. About trying to escape with the money from the office. And Silas in his tight green dress, like a knife in a sheath.

'What are you up to, Pags?' he said, smiling, and I knew my last moment had come.

Then Ginnie burst through the door, saying 'Pags! What are you – ?'

She stopped as though she'd been shot. I could see her taking everything in at once.

'Your little friend's been helping herself to our takings,' Silas said, so pleasant it sent a dagger of ice up my spine. Then he moved his leg so his skirt parted and drew a real dagger from his stocking.

'But she's going to give it all back, intyer, Pags?' he said.

What happened next is a blur. Ginnie pushed the coat stand and it toppled onto Silas.

'*Run Pags!*' she screamed.

I didn't need telling twice. I bolted through the door, dropping my sack on the way, and hurtled down the stairs fast enough to break my neck if I slipped.

Then I heard Ginnie scream again.

Silas had her by the hair. His knife was at her throat.

'Come back up here, Pags,' he said.

I stood there like washing strung on a line.

And then I moved, but not towards Silas. To the door.

'Pags!' he shouted.

With all my heart I wish I hadn't looked back then. Not seen him draw a red line across Ginnie's throat, her eyes roll back in her head. She toppled over the banister and landed with a *thud* at my feet.

That's the sound that wakes me up every morning.

I tugged the door and sobbed when it wouldn't move, Silas thundering towards me. I wrenched it again and it opened and I was out.

I ran towards Deansgate, my heart bursting out of my chest, bumping into people, pushing through. Then a man caught hold of me.

'Here now, my pretty,' he said, or something like it, but I clawed his face. He swore, then shouted for the police and two of them came running.

He said I'd been thieving, which was true enough although not the way he meant, and that he thought he'd seen an accomplice, so one of the peelers set off after Silas while the other one took my arm. I couldn't speak. I didn't even want to – I wanted to fall to my knees and pray.

And so I was arrested.

I spent two nights in a stinking cell with no window, only a grid in the door, and two old woman singing hymns all night between soiling themselves in a bucket.

They lolled on the bench and I sat on the floor, wondering what would happen to me. I knew thieves could be hung. I felt a twist of sickness at that, the sudden drop and everyone cheering. I knew from the stories I'd heard people didn't always die quick.

I wondered if my mother would come if I was to be hanged? Would I have the chance to write to her, to tell her? Then I thought, *I might as well write to the moon.*

I wondered whether Silas and Buzz had been arrested, what would happen to the Mollies? And Ida and her girls?

Most of all I thought of Ginnie, how she tried to save me. Why I didn't save her. And that red line across her throat. I kept seeing that until I was sick in the stinking bucket.

Then I sank down into myself and wished never to come back up. I closed my eyes and pressed my forehead to my knees but there was no sleep to be had. There was chanting from the next cell and one old woman was still droning hymns and filling the room with her shite.

In the morning I was taken to the courtroom which was full of a great rabble of people, crammed onto benches or standing at the back. The judge had to bang his hammer on his desk and threaten them all to keep them quiet. There was a smell of tobacco and wet wool and worse. I glanced round quickly, half hoping, half fearing to see someone I knew, but there was no one.

The judge was called Justice Day. He had a long face that seemed to be sliding downwards. Pouches under his eyes hung down to his cheeks that hung past his chin. He seemed to be half asleep but I could see him watching me through his crinkled lids. I didn't expect any mercy from him.

An officer read out my crimes. I was accused of stealing and enticement. No one spoke up for me but at the end, when everything had been read out against me, the officer asked the judge to take into consideration my youth and previous good character.

'Give her the whip!' someone called out and someone else cried, 'Shame!'

The judge banged his hammer again. Then he made a speech about how crime was rife in Manchester and urgent action was needed. The culprits should be taught a lesson, he said.

I stared down at my clasped hands, hardly able to see anything but a hangman's noose. I thought my legs would give way.

'I sentence you to six months in Her Majesty's prison,' he said.

I looked up at the judge, then at the officer standing next to me. Would I not be hanged, then?

No one explained anything as I was led away to a black carriage that brought me to this prison.

My head was shaved and I was made to get into a tin bath once more, but by then I didn't care – I'd lost all shame. After that I was led here, to my cell.

And that's the story of how I stopped being a vicar's daughter and became no one, and nothing.

※

I tell Mrs Gaskell hardly any of this, just that I was arrested for parading in my finery and luring men. To stop her asking more I burst out crying,

'Oh Mrs Gaskell, if you only knew the things I've done you wouldn't be here with me now! I've done so many bad things! Stealing – and worse! I drank wishing it was poison – hoping to end it all and be done with it!'

'Ah, Pasley,' she says with a catch in her voice, 'we all make mistakes. I—' but she doesn't finish what she was going to say. What did I think she would say, that she too got rid of a baby, and worked in a whorehouse?

My nose is running so she gives me her handkerchief, then moves a strand of hair from my face. Then she stands and walks away from me to the back of my cell. 'Well,' she says to herself, 'I think I've heard everything I need to know.'

I'm so relieved, I sob again.

'You see, what I've been trying to establish,' she says, turning round, 'is that it isn't safe for you to remain in Manchester – not while people like that are still here.'

And at once I see what she's done. She's led me to see it all the way she sees it, to think what she thinks. And the worst of it is, I do. I know she's right. As long as I stay in Manchester there will be Silas and Ida and Ella and the other girls out looking for me.

'Please don't cry,' she says, taking my hand. I bend over it and sob. 'The important thing is that you have a chance to start again. But there would always be something or someone holding you back here—'

I start to say I would pay no heed to anyone or anything, not if I was with her, but she says, 'So you see, you must go far enough away to leave your past behind, where no one will trouble you.'

Speechlessly, I nod.

'You'll be released next week. Then, if you agree, you'll be taken to a safe place until the ship sails . . .'

I stop listening to the words, only the soft murmur of her voice. When it pauses for a moment, I say, 'Will you write to me?'

'What?' she says, and she looks so nervous I feel almost sorry for her.

'Will you write to me, if I go?'

'Of course!' she says nodding. 'Of course I will – and I hope you'll write to me. I'll look forward to hearing how well you're doing!'

'Then I'll go,' I say, 'if you want me to.'

'You don't have to—'

'No,' I say, and although my legs feel weak I manage to stand, 'I will go.'

Relief glows from her face. She stands too, saying what an opportunity it is and how glad she is that I can see it, not everyone is given a second chance in life. I bear with this patiently and she trails off, saying finally, 'I don't want you to feel rushed into a decision. You can take all the time you want. I'll be happy to answer any questions . . .'

I don't have any questions.

'Anything,' she says, 'anything at all?'

I've turned away from her, staring through the window at the square of sky that soon I won't have to look at any more.

There will be a different sky.

I ask, 'Will you tell my mother where I've gone?'

She says she will write to my uncle with my address as soon as I have one.

'Anything else?' she asks but my mind is quite blank, like the square of sky.

But then another question comes to me, one I've wondered before but didn't know how to ask. It didn't seem quite right or proper, but now I think, *what have I to lose?*

And so I ask her, 'Did you ever have a mother?'

CHAPTER 29

Elizabeth

DID YOU EVER *have a mother?*

I could have told her everyone has a mother, but the words seemed to stick in my throat.

Instead I remembered my Aunt Lumb, my 'more than mother,' as I always call her. She could be stern and crotchety, but she was full of affection. She once stuck a cherry on her nose to make me laugh.

She sat with me all night when I had whooping cough. And chased some boys away like an angry goose when they tried to take my sledge.

She was my mother's oldest sister, nearly sixty when I was born, yet she took me in after my mother died.

My father didn't want me, the youngest child of eight and only a girl. He wanted John, who was the oldest and a son, but not me.

Ah, the bedroom in my father's house! With the mirror and the chandelier that scared me so. Creeping onto the landing to hear the sound of voices and occasional laughter, then back to my own bed to cry myself to sleep.

I would never let my own children feel so alone.

Pasley is staring at me now because I haven't answered her so I tell her in a voice that sounds strange to my own ears, 'My mother died when I was a baby. My aunt took me in.'

'Couldn't you live with your father?' she says.

'I – he had another family.'

I see her taking this in, then she says,

'Was she good to you, your aunt?'

'She – was very good to me, yes.'

'Did she love you?'

She asks so timidly that I can't take offence or find a reason not to answer.

'She did,' I say, faintly, 'and I loved her with all my heart.'

Pasley nods slowly. 'You were lucky,' she says, turning back to the window.

Lucky.

But it's true, after all.

My mother died and my father didn't want me. If I hadn't had an aunt but an uncle like Pasley's, my own story would have been very different. Like Pasley's.

The realisation is like a rushing wind. It's as if I've stepped through a door into another world in which all the events of my life play out differently. I see with a sudden, fierce clarity that so little separates me from Pasley – practically nothing at all.

My father was a minister too.

It seems hot in here suddenly. My corsets feel too tight. I struggle to compose myself, flicking my tongue over my lips. 'But why are we talking about me?' I say with a little laugh, 'when there's your whole future to discuss?'

Pasley says nothing to this. She doesn't turn around and her shoulders are rigid. I feel as though I should comfort her somehow, embrace her, but I can't bring myself to.

'Well,' I say, 'I'll leave you now to think it all over. It's a big decision and not one to be taken lightly. I'm sure you'll see it's for the best. However, no one's forcing you to go so if you decide you want to stay . . .'

'No,' she says, 'I'll go.'

'Well, good,' I say, my voice still sounding strange, as though it belongs to someone else. I hear myself prattle on about what an opportunity it is, how exciting it will be, until Pasley's silence makes all my words dry up.

CHAPTER 30

'LILY,' WILLIAM SAID.
Elizabeth whimpered and stirred.

'Lily,' he said again, tenderly.

For a moment she didn't know where she was, then she became aware of her husband's arm holding her, his body tucked into hers.

Her cheeks were wet.

'What is it? What's the matter?' William said.

'Ship,' she mumbled.

'You've been dreaming,' he said. She could tell from his voice, his touch, that he wanted to go back to sleep. She should let him but instead she started to weep again hopelessly.

'Lily, sweetheart,' he said in the voice he used to console their girls, 'No, no.'

His arm was heavy when she tried to move from under it. As she disturbed the sheets heat came from him and the acrid smell of his sweat. Although she knew if she could reach his feet they would be cold as they always were. As if they were too far from his heart for the blood to reach them.

'What were you dreaming?' he asked in the same consoling tones.

She'd dreamed she'd sent Pasley away on a ship. But as she'd waved her off she'd seen that her mother and her brother John were standing with her on the deck. They were looking out to sea. She'd called out to them but no one heard and the ship didn't stop. None of them looked back.

'They've all gone,' she wept.

William kissed her hair. 'Who's gone?' he murmured, but of

course she hadn't told him about Pasley so how could she even begin to explain?

'Tell me,' he said.

'It doesn't matter,' she sobbed.

William sat up. She could feel him groping for a candle. It took several goes to light it and all the time she was thinking, *this is it*, she would have to tell him everything.

'Now,' he said, turning back to her.

Bit by bit it all came out, the prison visits, Pasley's story, Elizabeth's attempts to find a place for her and the scheme to send her abroad. William didn't interrupt or ask any questions, though she didn't think she was making sense or telling it in the right order.

When she'd finished she waited with a dull dread like a weight in her stomach.

'Why didn't you tell me?' he said.

'Because - because - I thought you would tell me to bring her here,' she said, weeping again.

'Here?' he echoed.

Elizabeth shook her head, meaning *yes*.

'As a maid, you mean?'

'No,' she said. She could hardly treat Pasley as a maid after everything that had passed between them.

'Would you dismiss Bessie?'

'Of course not—'

'Or a cook - we could certainly do with a new cook . . .'

'No, William,' she said, testily. 'If she came here it would have to be - as one of us - like a daughter. And I don't know if I can!' she said, weeping all over again. 'I don't want to, William - I *can't*!'

There, she'd said it. She waited miserably for the recriminations, the weight of shame.

After a while he said, 'Well, I don't think that's a very good idea.'

She glanced up at him but couldn't see his face.

'There's no room, for one thing. Where would you put her?'

'I—'

'How would you explain her to our daughters? Or would you leave her to explain herself, her background, her circumstances - ?'

Of course, she would tell Pasley not to speak, ever, about herself or the things that had happened to her. How unreasonable that was, how cruel!

'And how do you intend to prevent her past following her? Because it would.'

'That's what Thomas said—'

'He's right. It would follow her here. Our daughters wouldn't be safe.'

She felt a rush of relief and at the same time the desire to argue.

'But—'

'But what?'

'I thought you would tell me we should take her in.'

'Why would you think that?'

Because of everything you've ever said, she thought.

'You're always preaching charity!' she said.

William sighed and shifted. 'Our charity is we give out food parcels and clothing and tokens where we can. We don't involve ourselves further - because of the danger of doing damage, rather than good.'

You ladies and your charitable works.

'But when someone needs so much - and we have it—'

'How do you decide on *need*?'

Pasley needed to belong somewhere, Elizabeth thought. To have a family. And she, Elizabeth, could provide her with one. She remembered all the people she'd approached who hadn't responded. She'd thought she was better than them.

'—gets in the way of justice,' William was saying.

'What does?'

'Charity. It saves the government the effort of doing what should be done. What's really needed is a change in society itself.'

'If I could change society, William,' she said, 'I would.'

'Look,' he said, 'what's happened to this girl is terrible and sadly there are hundreds, possibly thousands, just like her. I know you want to help, but the question you need to ask is can you do the same for all of them? Because if you can't then . . .'

'So I should do nothing?'

'Didn't you just say you're going to help her to leave the country?'

'Yes, but—'

'Then you are doing something. You're doing your best.'

It isn't enough, she thought.

'And what about your writing?'

'What about it?'

'You can do more with your writing than Parliament can. Look at Charles Dickens.'

Elizabeth stiffened.

'His books are changing the world – the education system, poor relief, medical care. *Oliver Twist* has reached more people than any number of laws.'

'I know,' she said, 'Mr Dickens keeps telling us.'

But William continued. Four thousand people had attended Dickens' reading in Bradford. In America people had torn his clothing for souvenirs. It could truly be said that Charles Dickens had changed the hearts of a nation.

'Well,' she said, 'I've not been invited to read in America. Or even Bradford.'

'But you might be,' William said. 'You could reach even more people with your novels.'

'Me?'

'Who else speaks for working women like you? Not Dickens – his heroes are all men. Dickens didn't create Mary Barton – you did. Because of you, women like her have a voice. Because of you, other women will write. Possibly even women like Mary Barton will write! And, who knows – our daughters may also feel moved to become writers. Even if they don't, they know they could – because of you.'

He'd never said such things to her before. Her throat was almost too tight to answer. But William went on, 'Your writing will survive long after you or I have gone. It will go on changing the world. No,' he said as she started to protest. He took her face in his hands. 'I'm proud of you,' he said.

'Ah, William,' she said, close to tears again. He smiled at her and she smiled back and in that moment it was as though twenty years had vanished. They were smiling as they used to before they married, before all the children, before Manchester, when she'd first fallen in love with him because of that quality he had of believing the world could be changed.

Then the clock in the hall chimed three times and William yawned. 'I don't suppose,' he said, 'we could possibly go back to sleep?'

He turned to snuff out the candle, then lay down with his back to her. After a moment she curled into him.

They had lain together in this bed for nearly twenty years. At first every touch had been thrilling but then all the babies had come. And some of them had died. They seemed to have reached an unspoken agreement after Julia that they would have no more children. She didn't want another child but sometimes she missed it, that gentle flame, that flared into something more.

Now, when she touched his shoulder his breathing altered to a tiny snort but there was no other response. He was asleep already, and she wasn't sleepy at all. She lay thinking about what he'd said.

After so many years he could still surprise her. He didn't want her to take Pasley in after all!

She should be relieved and she was in a way. But she still felt unnerved by her dream.

Why had Pasley been with her mother and John on the ship? What was it telling her – that she was sending her to her death?

If she died on the voyage it would be Elizabeth's fault.

She felt an impulse to wake William again to comfort her, to tell her that nothing terrible would happen. But she couldn't do that – it wasn't fair.

What he'd said about her work had warmed her but the thought of trying to write about Pasley chilled her again.

What would people think?

Could she bear another furore, after *Mary Barton*?

It would be worse this time, everyone would know who she was.

Dickens could write about Nancy in *Oliver Twist*, but Nancy wasn't the heroine. And Dickens wasn't a minister's wife.

She couldn't give readings like him, speaking to thousands of people.

Then she remembered she still had to write to him. She'd left it so late – she couldn't put it off any longer.

Carefully, without disturbing her husband, she got up and made her way downstairs.

※

My dear Sir, In the first place I am going to give you some trouble, and I must make an apology for it; for I am very sorry to intrude upon you in your busy life. But I want some help and I cannot think of anyone who can give it to me so well as you . . .

She told him about Pasley, her respectable parentage, emphasising the mother's indifference. She told him about the sweatshop, the doctor and the woman whose sole purpose was *to decoy girls into her mode of life*. She said how unhappy Pasley had been, how she'd thought of killing herself, *for no one ever cared for her in this world*.

She paused, holding the quill over the paper until it made a tiny blot, then wrote, *she looks quite a young child (she is but 16) with a wild, wistful look in her eyes, as if searching for the kindness she has never known . . .*

That might move him, she thought. There must be similar stories among the girls he rescued. He interviewed them all personally, his brother-in-law had said.

Pray don't say you can't help me for I don't know anyone else to ask . . .

That would appeal to him, surely.

She didn't know if she'd said enough or too much. She'd not mentioned his most recent book or her own novel, of course. It was best, she thought, to keep to the point.

So she signed off, sending her love to Mrs Dickens and Miss Hogarth.

Then she sat back, wondering whether he would reply and how long it would take him if he did.

In fact, he replied by return of post.

Wednesday 9th January 1850

My Dear Mrs Gaskell,

I am very much afraid I cannot help you in the distressing case you describe. I assist Miss Coutts in the management of her "Home" and have at all times a great deal to do with it. But the voyage out has been and still is, our great difficulty. The ships are, for the most part, disgracefully managed; and the temptations to a renewal of the old life on board, we find a most serious and disheartening circumstance.

I therefore feel that Miss Coutts would not like to take the responsibility of sending out this girl, or allowing her to accompany any of our people; nor could I urge it upon her if I saw her inclined to object, because we have, within our knowledge, some very strange and sad experiences. But I will communicate to her *today* and write to you again tomorrow.

We have no matron to send out with them, because of the distance and the long duration of the Voyage. We have a very reliable correspondent in Australia – a lady emigrant, with whom four of our girls went out – and we are not without some similar help at the Cape. But I feel certain that Miss Coutts would not think it expedient to consign your protegee to either place, unless she first came into the Home, and enabled us to form a personal knowledge of her from our own observation. And I doubt Miss Coutts' inclination to admit her, as she is not altogether a helpless outcast, but may get abroad without her help. However, as I have said, I will see, in the course of the day, whether we can do anything in the matter.

>   Faithfully yours
>   Charles Dickens

Elizabeth's first response was a pang of pleasure that he'd replied so swiftly. She'd left it so late to write, she was always late these days with everything, and Pasley was due to be released today. But he'd replied to her immediately!

Although what he'd said about Miss Coutts and the ships was hardly encouraging.

the temptations to a renewal of the old life on board, we find a most serious and disheartening circumstance –

That was worrying, but she hoped the money from Pasley's uncle might provide Pasley with a better ticket. And she could only hope that Miss Coutts would be more helpful than Mr Dickens supposed. He would write to her today, he'd said, which was yesterday so with any luck he would already have written . . .

Miss Coutts was indeed helpful. She suggested that Elizabeth could write to S W Silver and Co. a firm which acted as shipping agents for people travelling to the colonies. Mr Silver employed a Miss Kaye in a supervisory capacity to assess the suitability of applicants for emigration, and she might be able to find a family willing to take a young girl into their care on the voyage. Miss Coutts also mentioned a charitable association known as the Plymouth Ladies, who had pledged themselves to the spiritual and physical welfare of those preparing to emigrate, and who might take care of a young girl until the ship sailed.

Finally she recommended the services of a Mr Nash of the Ragged School Union who was hoping to travel to Manchester to assess the viability of opening a Ragged School there. She was sure he would be happy to take the young lady back with him to London.

Overwhelmed by this encouraging response, Elizabeth wrote at once to Miss Kaye and to Mr Nash. Then she wrote to Pasley's uncle to inform him of the cost of the passage and to ask him whether he would release all or part the money he held in trust towards the cost of emigration.

Lastly she wrote back to Mr Dickens.

Saturday, Jany 12th, 1850

My dear Sir,
I am exceedingly obliged to you for what you have done about my poor girl. I return you Miss Coutts' letter, (which I only received late last night). It is really and truly kind, for she has taken the trouble to think of several plans, and her suggestions are very valuable. As she is out of town, I have written off at once to the fore-woman at Silver's, choosing out the plan which seemed to me the most desirable, – i.e. placing the girl under the charge of some respectable family, (of the working-class if possible). If Miss Kaye should not know of anyone, then, if you will allow me, I will write again to ask Miss Coutts, through you, if she will kindly write to the Plymouth ladies, of whom I never heard before – I have already received kind offers from Mrs Chisholm in helping out a family of emigrants, but I thought she required those whom she assisted to be of unblemished character. – Miss Coutts is very, very kind – for she evidently thinks as she writes of what can be done . . .

. . . The girl herself is in a Refuge – a literal refuge, for any destitute female without enquiry as to her past life being made – all are received and not classified. So it is a bad place, but what can we do? I am going to see her today to keep up & nurse her hopes & good resolutions.

My best love to Mrs Dickens & Miss Hogarth,

Yours truly
E. C. Gaskell

CHAPTER 31

AND IN FACT she'd had every intention of seeing Pasley that day, but she was interrupted by a deputation of ladies from church. Mrs Hudson's niece, the woefully plain Angelina, had run off with the husband of Mrs Dymoke, another member of their congregation. Mrs Dymoke had retreated into her house and could not be coaxed out of it. The ladies, including Mrs Carver and Mrs Fairlie, begged Elizabeth, as wife of their minister, to write to Mrs Dymoke to assure her that the disgrace was not hers. She was also persuaded to visit Mrs Hudson who was distracted with grief and shame. And she promised to help track down Angelina, although she had no idea how.

In the afternoon there was an unexpected visit from some Christian Socialists who wanted her to distribute their pamphlets. By the time they left it was too late to go to the refuge, so instead she wrote to Miss Coutts about the Plymouth Ladies who might take care of Pasley in London.

The next day Elizabeth gave her talk to the Mother's Association. She spoke about the importance of reading and the difficulty of being a writer and a mother, how determined she had to be to put her husband and daughters first to ensure they never suffered for her art.

Then she paused, looking round at them all, a dozen or so women in a plain room at the back of the Christian Mission. They were all young, although their faces were greyish and lined, their gowns faded and frayed. One woman had no teeth, another had sores around her mouth. Elizabeth thought of Pasley, how she couldn't aspire even to this because of everything that had happened to her.

And on impulse she began to talk about the vulnerability of young girls and fallen women, who were never counted among the ranks of the deserving poor because pregnancy was the manifestation of their shame.

'You should all be angry,' she said, startled by the rage in her own voice. 'You should be furious.'

She opened the single copy of *Mary Barton* she'd brought with her, and told them about Mary, who was pursued by Henry Carson, a mill-owner's son, and Esther, her aunt, who was abandoned by an army officer and became a street-walker to pay for medicine for her little girl. Then, ignoring a sour look from Mrs Pringle, she read the section where Esther, despised by all, returns to warn John Barton about Henry Carson.

How can I keep her from being such a one as I am; such a wretched, loathsome creature! She was listening just as I listened, and loving just as I loved, and the end will be just like my end. How shall I save her?

More than one of the women was weeping as she finished. Several declared they would ask their husbands if they could read her book. As everyone left, the young woman with sores around her mouth hung back. Elizabeth smiled encouragingly at her, and she whispered that the same thing had happened to her sister when she was fifteen. She'd hidden her shame as long as she could then disappeared, and had never been seen since. 'I don't know if she's alive, ma'am, I do hope so, I pray for her every day,' she said. Elizabeth pressed her hand and gave her the copy of *Mary Barton*, and told her she must never give up hope. Then she left, feeling more strongly than ever that she must write about these matters in her next novel. Although who would read it? Not these women, but their husbands. And not Mrs Pringle, evidently, who had thanked her so coolly at the end.

The following day there was a funeral to attend in Knutsford, and she and William travelled back in terrific storms that destroyed what remained of their garden fence and brought down part of the chimney. The parlour was full of soot.

William said as soon as the weather improved he would redouble his efforts to find a house, but the weather worsened if anything. Torrential rain led to fears of the Irwell bursting its banks again. Even William stayed in. Elizabeth felt restless all day with a prickling sensation beneath her skin.

Pasley.

But what could she do? She had to content herself with packing a bag for her.

Since William had made an announcement in church an assortment of items, aprons, bonnets, mufflers, sewing materials, handkerchiefs, stockings, had been donated. All the people who'd not wanted to assist Pasley in any other way now gladly discharged their unwanted goods to her cause. Elizabeth had disposed of some of the less salvageable offerings (*not fit for a beggar,* Hearn had said of some maid's undergarments) but still she needed a bigger bag to fit it all in.

At the back of her cupboard she found an old carpet bag that had belonged to her aunt. Her aunt had made it in fact, out of scraps of material and zeal – her mission against waste. She'd given it to Elizabeth because there were lilies on it. Elizabeth had always been Lily to her aunt.

She pulled it out and pressed it to her face. It smelled musty, of old wool, but there was the faint, lingering perfume of lavender water. That afterlife of scent.

How could she give it away?

But the cupboard was crammed with her aunt's belongings and it was her aunt who'd first impressed upon her the necessity of giving to those less fortunate than themselves. Which at that time, in Knutsford, included almost everyone. All those visits they'd made to the poor, the sick, the needy, the grieving . . .

Her aunt would approve of it going to Pasley. And it would be a gesture of – what? Goodwill? Penitence? Remorse?

Pushing that thought aside she packed it carefully, adding an extra shawl. Who knew how cold it would be on board, especially at night? She hesitated, then slipped in a copy of the American magazine which had published her most recent article about her memories of growing up in a small town. Inside the cover she wrote: *To new beginnings and adventures, with all my hopes and blessings for your future life, Your friend, E. C. Gaskell*

Then she put the bulging bag near the door. She would take it to Pasley soon, whatever the weather.

The next morning she received three letters. The first was from Miss Kaye, who had found a young couple willing to undertake the task of delivering Pasley to her new life. Their names were John and Jane Buchanan. They were both of an industrious, God-fearing disposition and would be sailing for the Cape on 16th February on the *Lady Bruce*.

The Cape.

Elizabeth hadn't considered the Cape, even though Mr Dickens had mentioned it in his letter. She knew nothing about it, but then she knew so little about Australia or Canada either. Would it make a difference to Pasley? Surely she would know even less about it than Elizabeth?

Miss Kaye wrote that Mr Buchanan was of Scottish extraction, a carpenter by trade and a Wesleyan by persuasion. He was hoping to obtain a grant of land in the Cape in order to build his own church. Mrs Buchanan was expecting their first child and they wanted someone who might assist them with the baby when it came, and with general domestic work.

She also said she was happy to handle all the paperwork at her end, which was a relief since Elizabeth felt quite daunted by the forms.

The second letter was from Mr Nash, who said that he and his wife would be more than delighted to act as guardians for the young lady on the London train. He was greatly looking forward to meeting Mr Gaskell, whose sermons he had read so often he knew them by heart, and he would travel to Manchester at a moment's notice to look for premises for a new Ragged School.

Elizabeth was not inclined to favour the Evangelism of the Ragged School Union, but she could hardly afford to quibble at this late stage. The young couple sounded ideal, however. That they were Methodists was only a minor impediment; at least they were devout.

The third letter was from Pasley's uncle saying he would be happy to release the sum of £20.00 for his niece's passage, although he would retain the rest of the money for the specified time.

Twenty pounds. Elizabeth imagined him hunched parsimoniously over his accounts.

But progress at last! For so long she'd met only with obstruction, but now every obstacle seemed to have cleared. She had the sensation of gathering momentum which made her nervous because everything she did from now on was irrevocable, like stepping off a cliff.

She had to act quickly to co-ordinate everything and everyone. And she had to visit Pasley, to tell her about these developments and to give her the bag.

CHAPTER 32

Pasley sat in the small office at the refuge. She looked hunched and miserable, her eyes pink-rimmed. She didn't move as Elizabeth approached but picked at a sore spot on her hand. Elizabeth held the bag out to her but she made no attempt to take it.

'Don't you want to see what's inside?' Elizabeth said. Pasley didn't look up. Undeterred, Elizabeth sat on the bench next to her.

Pasley gazed towards the window which was mottled and mouldy around the frame. The place itself reeked of something sour and stale, like despair. Pasley smelled of it too.

Guilt seeped through Elizabeth. But Pasley would be leaving soon and it would all be over. Elizabeth just had to explain to her where she would go.

'I have some news for you,' she said into the silence. 'You'll be sailing to the Cape. Do you know where that is?'

Pasley gave no sign of having heard. Elizabeth tugged the bag open and removed a book from it. Susanna Winkworth had donated a copy of Mary Ann Parker's *A Voyage Round the World*. It was mainly about Australia, she'd said, but Mrs Parker did describe the Cape, and she wrote with such lively good humour that it was sure to raise Pasley's spirits.

'It's the southernmost tip of a great Continent called Africa – you've heard of Africa, I suppose?'

Was that a nod?

Elizabeth opened the book at a map.

'It is, I believe, a remarkable country, beautiful – not like here. It will be very clean, with big, open skies.'

She was thinking of Cumberland, one of her favourite places, but who knew what Pasley was imagining? She remained partially turned away from Elizabeth, staring at the window. Elizabeth felt a pang of sorrow and impatience.

She told Pasley where she would stay in London and about the Buchanans who would sail with her.

When Pasley still didn't reply Elizabeth told her about Mr Nash and his wife who would take her to London and then about the *Lady Bruce*, which would carry more than 200 passengers and weighed nearly a thousand tonnes. She produced an article about it cut from one of William's papers.

Pasley smoothed the paper on her knee but said nothing.

'It will sail from the London docks,' Elizabeth said, conscious of her voice running on. 'Mr and Mrs Buchanan will meet you there.'

Pasley crumpled the corner of the newspaper cutting.

Elizabeth had known this would be difficult but she'd hoped Pasley would see it was exciting too.

'I should think you'd be pleased to leave this place, at least,' she said, instantly regretting it, because whose fault was it that she was here?

Pasley got up, and walked towards the window.

'Is something wrong?' Elizabeth said.

Pasley shook her head.

'What, then?'

'I wish—'

'Yes?'

'I just wish I could see my mother again before I go.'

Elizabeth felt a stab of pain. 'We've discussed that,' she said, quietly, 'and there's nothing more to be done, I'm afraid.'

Pasley said nothing. How Elizabeth wished she could change things for her! But the pain made her brusque.

'A great many people have put themselves out for you, people who care about what happens to you and wish you well.'

Nothing.

'You know,' she said, 'I can think of many people who would

love to go to another country. Who would relish the chance of a new start in a different world, where nothing is known about them and all the old associations are gone.' An image of her brother, John, rose in her mind. 'It will be like turning a page, a new leaf. Perhaps you can't imagine it—'

'I can,' Pasley said, surprisingly. 'It will be as if I never existed.'

Elizabeth said firmly, 'It will be as if none of the bad things ever existed.'

Silence.

Elizabeth felt stricken suddenly by the enormity of it all.

I'm sorry, she wanted to say. But how could she ask for forgiveness now? In a few days Pasley would leave this refuge and Manchester for ever.

Would she want Elizabeth to see her off at the station?

She felt a strange dread at the thought of it. But if Pasley asked her she would go.

To distract her she opened the bag. She wanted to show Pasley everything that had been given to her, but when she tried to speak she felt a constriction in her throat. She cleared it and tried again.

'This bag belonged to my Aunt Lumb,' she said. 'I told you about her, remember - she brought me up.'

Pasley was listening, she thought, so she carried on.

'I think of her every day.' Her voice was not quite steady, she had to pause again. 'This bag is one of the things she left me and I treasure it. But I'm giving it to you now so that something of my aunt - and me - might go with you on your journey.'

She looked at Pasley. Her own eyes must be as pink as the girl's were, but she held her gaze. She offered the bag again and this time Pasley took it. Elizabeth closed her hand around Pasley's on the handle, the girl's fingers limp and unresisting beneath her own.

Pasley

She puts her hand on mine and then moves as though she will embrace me but I flinch away from her. I see she is pained by it but I don't do anything to make it better.

I think she will leave then but she's not done yet. She says she's sorry that things have turned out this way and if it was up to her, and some other things I hardly hear. *Words*, I'm thinking. Just words, rattling like peas in a can. *I'm sorry too*, I think, for all the things I ever told you. Because you made me live through it all again and because telling it got me nowhere. It made you bigger, somehow, and me smaller. And now you'll make me disappear.

I turn away from her, back to the window. It's clear to me now that there was never any hope she'd take me in; I can't imagine the thought ever entered her head.

But when I hear the door click I want to run after her, to beg her forgiveness and tell her I understand. To thank her for everything she's done for me.

Of course I don't.

The room feels twice as empty as before. I'm struck hard by the sense of what's going to happen to me, how my life will change. My mouth feels dry then it fills up as though I will be sick. I have to hold onto the back of the bench to steady myself then sit down. I hug her aunt's bag to me thinking,

It's done now, it's over.

CHAPTER 33

Elizabeth

ALL THE WAY back from the refuge Elizabeth wept.

For once she was glad of the fog screening her. She could imagine people stopping to stare – *look at that lady, weeping in her carriage.*

I tried! she said to the accusing voice in her mind. *I tried to do the right thing!*

Why was it so hard?

There were so many things she could have said. She could have told Pasley that she understood, that in her place – and she could have been in her place if her aunt hadn't taken her in . . . .

But she wasn't like Pasley. Her aunt had loved her with all her generous heart.

And now she was dead, like her mother, and her babies and her darling boy. And soon Pasley would be gone too.

But Pasley wasn't going to die, she was going to a better life. And Elizabeth was going home to her four daughters, her husband, her house, where she was never alone. She dabbed at her eyes with her handkerchief. If anyone asked she would say it was the smoke making them sting.

Then without warning she saw her brother, John.

He had blonde curls like her son's, and that jaunty walk that no matter what he was going through, said he hadn't a care in the world!

He was whistling the tune he always used to whistle, *The Wind in Our Sails.*

She was about to call out to him, to tell Jim to stop, before she realised it couldn't possibly be her brother. It was a ghost, or the fog giving form to her memories. Her brother wasn't a young man any more, he would be much older now as she was. A much older woman, weeping in her carriage for everything she'd lost.

She let herself in to a house that was mercifully quiet for once, since Hearn had taken Julia out and the other girls were at their lessons. As she closed the door she noticed a letter addressed to her, tucked beneath William's post.

She recognised the writing at once.

My Dear Mrs Gaskell,
You may perhaps have seen an announcement in the papers of my intention to start a new cheap weekly journal of general literature.

I do not know what your literary vows of temperance or abstinence may be, but as I do honestly know that there is no living English writer whose aid I would desire to enlist in preference to the authoress of "Mary Barton" (a book that most profoundly affected and impressed me), I venture to ask you whether you can give me any hope that you will write a short tale, or any number of tales, for the projected pages.

No writer's name will be used, neither my own nor any other; every paper will be published without any signature, and all will seem to express the general mind and purpose of the journal, which is the raising up of those that are down, and the general improvement of our social condition. I should set a value on your help which your modesty can hardly imagine; and I am perfectly sure that the least result of your reflection or observation in respect of the life around you, would attract attention and do good.

Of course, I regard your time as valuable, and consider it so when I ask you if you could devote any of it to this purpose.

If you could and would prefer to speak to me on the subject, I should be very glad indeed to come to Manchester for a few hours and explain anything you might wish to know. My unaffected and great admiration of your book makes me very earnest in all relating to you. Forgive my troubling you for this reason, and believe me ever,

Faithfully yours,
Charles Dickens

P.S. – Mrs. Dickens and her sister send their love.

She felt a rush of heat, a mercurial joy. So he had read her novel after all! Without taking her cloak off she hurried into the dining room and read the letter again.

there is no living English writer whose aid I would desire to enlist in preference to the authoress of "Mary Barton"(a book that most profoundly affected and impressed me).

England's most famous author, saying this to her!

My unaffected and great admiration of your book makes me very earnest in all relating to you.

She clasped it to her chest. Then re-read what he'd said about the journal. The purpose of which was, *the raising up of those that are down, and the general improvement of our social condition.*

Who needed more raising up than Pasley? This would be her chance to write about girls like her. And it would be published *without any signature,* so no one need ever know who'd written it!

I should set a value on your help which your modesty can hardly imagine . . . but she could imagine it! She would clarify the financial arrangements when he came to Manchester.

It was the spur she needed, the answer to her problems about what to write and who for.

Still she felt an impulse to say she couldn't do it. She had to prepare another talk for a Ladies' Literary Society, as well as the lessons for her daughters and the Sunday school children. And Mr Nash would be arriving soon . . .

But she went up to her room and pulled out the box beneath her bed. Somewhere in it was a story she'd begun long ago and never finished. After some rummaging she found it where she'd thought it would be but somehow she'd missed it the first time she looked. Probably because it was on scraps of paper which were all out of order – it took some time to put it back together again.

The story was called *Lizzie Leigh*, after the girl in William's poem: *Pale, pale through the winter nights, Trying to barter her stale delights* . . . Her Lizzie was a young woman, seduced by a factory owner who casts her out when she is pregnant. Her father disowns her and her mother, though grieving, follows his example.

It would need rewriting of course – it was full of crossings-out and only half finished. She'd tried to finish it from time to time but had always been put off by the thought of how it would be received, especially by their congregation.

No fit subject for a lady.

And she a minister's wife!

But in Dickens' journal she would be anonymous. And if anyone would publish it, he would. It might be exactly what he was looking for!

Elizabeth took off her cloak and sat at her dressing table. She began making notes on the story, comments in the margins. But she hadn't got very far when the door clicked open behind her. 'Flossie,' she said, without looking round.

'A bit taller, and not quite so pretty,' her husband said. He rested his hand on her shoulder, looking down at her with a peculiar expression on his face.

'What?' she said.

'I think I've found a house.'

CHAPTER 34

HE WOULDN'T TELL her where it was. He said it wasn't available just yet, they shouldn't view it until it was definite but he wanted her to see it before she made up her mind against it.

So he knew she wouldn't approve!

But there was no arguing with him. He had to go out again to yet another meeting about the Free Library. So Elizabeth suppressed her impatience and the sinking feeling that she was about to be cajoled into something she didn't want and listened to her girls reciting their lessons before bed.

The next day Mr Nash arrived earlier than expected, but he explained that his wife had to visit her sister in Southport and he'd decided at the last moment to accompany her. Elizabeth stared at him, disconcerted, almost forgetting to invite him in. He was a tall, stout young man, already balding but with a handsome beard.

'So – you're on your own?' she said and Mr Nash, anticipating her concerns, said his wife would be joining them at Liverpool. 'You need have no worries on that score,' he said, and of course she protested that she wasn't worried. Although she hadn't anticipated that Pasley might have to travel with him unaccompanied.

Remembering her manners, she led him into the parlour while he talked about the journey, the weather, his wife's sister's ailments, which were many, and his eagerness to meet the young girl; Mrs Gaskell's protégée, he called her.

Slavery, he said, was still thriving in England, despite the best efforts of the Evangelical movement, as this poor young girl's situation so clearly demonstrated.

Not *only* the Evangelical movement, Elizabeth thought of saying, but he went on, 'I have some leaflets for her since you say she can read, from The Society for the Suppression of Vice. There is a very active membership in The Cape and I think it would benefit her enormously to join. She is aware of her condition?'

Elizabeth looked at him blankly.

'I mean the condition of depravity,' he said.

'She's aware *of* depravity, certainly.'

'We are all steeped in depravity, Mrs Gaskell. Awareness is the first step to redemption. Might I ask what's been done about her spiritual welfare?'

'—I've been busy with the practical necessities . . .'

'Once she is born again in Christ, all other necessities will be met.'

Elizabeth thought irritably of William. This was exactly the kind of discussion he would enjoy. But he was out again, teaching an evening class at the New College. Meta and Polly were dining with the Winkworths who would take them to a concert afterwards. Hearn would put Julia and Flossie to bed so Elizabeth would have to dine with Mr Nash alone.

'Even the disciples had practical needs,' she said.

Mr Nash smiled archly. 'I will speak to her on the journey to London,' he said.

He changed the subject to the new school. How many of the children from her Sunday School did she think might attend?

'That will be up to their parents,' Elizabeth said. Then excusing herself, she went to speak to Bessie about food and making up a bed. She hoped Mr Nash wouldn't lecture Pasley all the way to London. She hoped William might come home early for once, to save *her* from being lectured. He didn't, of course. But he did keep Mr Nash occupied for the next two days, looking at possible premises for his school and arranging for him to give a talk about it to members of the Portico Library.

Elizabeth couldn't attend even though William was chairman, since ladies were not allowed to join. It was one of the inequities she hoped would be addressed by the Free Library when it opened.

She wasn't excessively sorry to miss this particular talk, however, although William said it was very well received and there was a good turnout. Mr Nash acquitted himself well, though he spoke for rather longer than necessary, and at one point broke into an impromptu hymn. Elizabeth could believe it. It had been all she could do to prevent him bursting into song at the dinner table.

She thought ruefully about Pasley who would be on her own with him at least as far as Liverpool. Where, hopefully, Mrs Nash would join them.

Nothing would go wrong, she thought, uneasily. But she would certainly go to the station with Mr Nash to see Pasley off.

CHAPTER 35

That week there was an outbreak of measles among the Sunday School children. Elizabeth told Jim to pin a notice to the door saying there would be no school that Sunday in the hope of preventing the contagion from spreading. So after church she went home.

She thought about going to the refuge, to tell Pasley she would be there to see her off and to reassure her that she wouldn't be alone with Mr Nash all the way to London. But then she remembered how Pasley had been with her on the last occasion, not looking at her, recoiling when she'd meant to embrace her, and her heart failed at the prospect of facing her again.

Also, she had a story to write. She was almost sure now of the ending. Lizzie's mother would repent of her harshness and search for her, but she shouldn't find her . . .

Rewriting was harder than she'd thought. It was like altering a garment; one adjustment here meant another there. She gave it a different opening which made it much longer than she wanted, so she rushed the ending a little. She wasn't sure whether Lizzie had been punished enough, although she wept over the death of Lizzie's child as she wrote it. Perhaps she should have killed Lizzie off as well? But she wanted her readers to see that redemption was possible even for the fallen woman.

In any case there was no time to alter it again, she had to send it off. Dickens would have his own opinions about it she was sure. She put down her quill and leaned back on the chair in her bedroom. Her back ached and her eyes were blurred, but she'd finished something at last.

It was too late now to go to the refuge. Elizabeth thought about seeing Pasley off at the station, what she might say to her that she hadn't already said, but as she went downstairs something happened that took her mind off everything else. She heard Polly weeping in her room.

It was so unexpected she could only stand in the doorway in shock. 'What is it?' she asked faintly. But Polly only shook her head, pressing her face into her pillow.

Elizabeth hurried to her, putting her arms around her daughter's shaking shoulders.

'Whatever's wrong?'

But Polly only cried until Elizabeth almost wept with her.

'Please tell me,' she begged.

'He – he doesn't love me!' Polly blurted out.

'Who? Who doesn't love you?'

Eventually Polly sobbed out the name of Henry Burnett.

Elizabeth thought she must have misheard. But it was true, her daughter had fallen for Henry, who was older than Elizabeth.

Appalling prospects ran through her mind.

'But – wh – surely he hasn't? Polly—' she said. 'Has anything – happened between you?'

'He paid attention to me!' Polly wept.

'What kind of attention?' Elizabeth said. *I will kill him*, she thought.

It seemed that Mr Burnett had been calling at Susanna Winkworth's house, as Elizabeth had hoped he would. But often he'd called when Susanna was teaching Polly and had expressed an interest in her talent. Then he'd started to teach her himself.

'I thought he liked me!' Polly wailed.

As it turned out, Mr Burnett's interest seemed to be of a purely musical nature. He'd given Polly some extra tuition and listened respectfully to her ideas on composition. That was all, so far as Elizabeth could determine.

She felt a vast relief, followed by pity.

'Ah, but Polly,' she said, 'you're only fifteen. You can't go attaching yourself to elderly widowers! You'll meet someone else who loves you in return, and very soon, I'm sure!'

'No one will,' Polly wept.

'Nonsense!' said Elizabeth. Polly was beautiful. All her daughters were. And talented. Although real talent, she'd often thought, was no help in securing a husband.

'He *listened* to me!' Polly cried. Elizabeth felt stricken. Had she been so neglectful of her oldest daughter? Between dealing with Meta's moods and Flossie's illnesses and Julia's occasional tantrums - not to mention the ones who'd died, who had nearly taken Elizabeth with them.

Had she always expected Polly to be good, or at least, *all right*?

'Oh Polly,' she said, resting her head on her daughter's shoulder. Then she said, 'Wait.'

She went to find her diary. The one she'd kept about Polly when she was an infant. On the first page she'd written:

To dear little Marianne I shall dedicate this book, which, if I should not live to give it to her myself, will, I trust, be received for her as a token of her mother's love.

Those words, *if I should not live*, were because of her own mother who'd come into her mind so strongly when Polly was born that she'd felt her presence in the room. But the rest of the book was all about Polly. She showed her daughter all the entries she'd made about her first tooth, her first steps, how at six months old she was already kicking and moving on the floor and babbling as though she was ready to speak.

Polly seemed indifferent at first, even fretful, but gradually she began to smile, hearing about the time when she was the sole object of her mother's attention. Elizabeth read the entries aloud with a comic exaggeration, but internally she felt a growing alarm. Where had all those years gone? That year she would be 40, the same age as her mother had been when she died. The mother who had not been able to rejoice in her baby daughter as Elizabeth had.

Although she'd also been terrified after losing her first baby. Every cough, every fever, had thrown her into despair. And now she was worried for a different reason. But Polly was not like Pasley, after all, or Angelina. Henry Burnett was an honourable man at least.

However, when she told William they made immediate plans to send Polly away to school, which meant going to London for a short stay. It occurred to her briefly that Pasley could travel with them, but she dismissed the thought. It would mean altering all the arrangements she'd made with Mr Nash and in London.

Fortunately, Mr Nash been invited to stay with Edward Taylor, who had promised to write a piece about the Ragged School in The Manchester Guardian. Elizabeth told him she would be back in plenty of time to accompany him to the station. Mr Nash said she shouldn't even think of it, he would take excellent care of the young lady.

'I'll be there,' she said.

But there were so many people to catch up with in London: the Shaens, the Howitts, John Forster, Jane Carlyle, Tottie – and so many schools to visit. They rejected one because it was too authoritarian, and another because it had too many pupils, and a third because they didn't like the headmistress, a sharp-faced woman who said, 'So, you have no son – only four daughters?'

William had taken her hand. 'Yes,' he said, 'we are indeed blessed.' And they pressed on swiftly to Hampstead, to the school Tottie had recommended. It was run by a Mrs Lalor, the wife of the editor of *The Inquirer*, a Unitarian journal. This was the one they chose in the end, for its earnest and sober but affectionate atmosphere.

On the day they were due to leave Tottie had an opening for her paintings in a small gallery in Knightsbridge.

They needn't come, she said, if they had to get back.

Elizabeth thought about Pasley.

'She's the important one now,' Tottie said. 'I'll have other exhibitions.'

But really, what would it accomplish, hurrying all the way back to see her off?

Wouldn't it only prolong the pain?

Was she only trying to make herself feel better?

Tottie was her *friend*.

'I'm sure Mr and Mrs Nash will take excellent care of her,' she said.

'No, but she would want you to be there,' said Tottie, and Elizabeth, remembering their last meeting said, a little sadly, 'I'm not sure she would.'

'You've been like a mother to her,' Tottie protested, and Elizabeth felt a stabbing pain.

'No,' she said, I haven't.'

'But you'll never see her again – and you can come to London any time,' Tottie said, looking so sad that Elizabeth said she'd much rather see Tottie's exhibition.

It was true, she realised. She would.

'We've already said our goodbyes,' she said, which was also true. What more was there to say?

'Well, if you're *sure*,' and Tottie went on to say how many people would be there whom Elizabeth knew and Elizabeth reassured Tottie once again that it was no inconvenience and William would love to see her paintings.

It was over, she thought, really over.

She felt as though some burden or weight were physically leaving her.

Only in the hansom cab on the way back to the train did she feel a tugging pain as if she'd lost the chance to say she was sorry – but why? When as Tottie had said, she'd done everything she could.

The image rose in her mind again, the wounded, wary look, the jutting wrists.

Pasley.

Why hadn't she taken her to London with them?

Because she hadn't wanted to.

It would have been too difficult to travel all the way with her then part painfully at the docks.

The hansom cab rattled through the London streets, William read his paper, and Elizabeth's mood sank further.

What had she done?

Everything she could or, if not *everything*, then the best thing for everyone.

Or, if not the best thing, then at least *something*, when no one else was willing to do anything.

Where did it end, what you were supposed to do?

Where did any of it ever end?

She wanted to turn to William for reassurance, but a small snore came from behind his newspaper, so she went on worrying about Pasley. How would she cope with Mr Nash? Would the Buchanans be good to her? How would she get on with the long voyage? Would the storms die down before the ship sailed?

What if the ship sank?

The ghost of her brother seemed to blow through her mind like smoke. How she'd looked forward to seeing him when he returned from his adventures, how she'd wanted to go with him and had cried at being left behind. She remembered saying that she wanted to be a sailor, not understanding why people had laughed when she said it.

And suddenly she understood who she was sending away. Not Pasley, but another girl – the girl she wasn't any more, and never spoke of to anyone. Even William.

She closed her eyes.

The darkness behind her eyelids was where she used to think God was. Now she saw only blackness. She'd rarely prayed since losing her baby boy, afraid of the absence, the emptiness, that God-shaped hole.

That was something else she hadn't told William.

The God on whose stony ears so many prayers had fallen had not listened to Elizabeth in the extremity of her grief, or Pasley either and there was no reason at all why He would listen now.

Even so, she tried to pray that Pasley would be all right, that she might flourish in her new life, that Elizabeth had done some good rather than harm. Because Pasley was beyond her help now but not, surely, beyond God's.

I should have gone to the station, she thought.

CHAPTER 36

Pasley

I LOOKED FOR her through all the steam and noise, the way I used to look for my mother.

Finally, when the whistle blew, I sat back in my seat.

I wouldn't look out of the window again. Nor at Mr Nash, who, with his great beard and stomach reminded me of the man who followed me that time on the streets. The one Noah should've hit and didn't.

I couldn't bear to look at him.

But he kept talking at me, yatter, yatter, yatter, like a murder of magpies cawing over meat.

That was what Miss Vivienne told me a flock of magpies was called. She would be pleased with me for remembering it. Ginnie would say his tongue moved faster than a whore's quim.

But I didn't want to think about Ginnie. I looked down at my hands and thought of all the things Mrs Gaskell said to me.

I should think you'd be pleased to leave this place, at least.

A great many people have put themselves out for you.

There was a bad taste in my mouth, as though I'd been poisoned by her. And by all the words I couldn't say.

Mr Nash pressed pamphlets upon me to read on my journey – a journey of deliverance, he said. He couldn't even see I wasn't listening – or maybe he liked me that way, quiet, like a plank of wood.

After a while I couldn't hear him any more.

I seemed to go somewhere deep down, and shuttered up. I didn't even come out when we came to the house of the lady I was to stay with until the ship sailed.

Her name was Mrs Liptrot. She was a stout lady with hair in two loops around her ears.

I was given some biscuits and milk and a room next to the maid's, up many flights of stairs. Mrs Liptrot also tried to give me a book, 'Some Christian reading,' she said, but I said I'd had enough of reading, thank you. Then I corrected myself and said I had enough to read, as indeed I had – pamphlets, magazines, prayer books and a journal about sailing round the world.

After that she left me to myself.

She didn't come with me to the docks. Her driver, she said, would take me. Miss Kaye and Mr and Mrs Buchanan would meet me there.

Even though I'd seen the docks in Dublin and Liverpool, nothing prepared me for the ones in London.

All was whirl and movement and noise. The clatter of boxes and crates being unloaded, men shouting and the baying of great horns. I had to clamp my hands over my ears. We passed over bridges, then wound our way through crowds of people and bales and bundles and sacks and barrels, all stinking of turpentine and tallow, to the quay where the ships were moored. So many ships! There was the boom of horns and engines, and through it all a terrible wind I thought might blow me straight into the black, billowing sea.

Then a single ship loomed towards us through the fog, a great black ship rearing into the sky like a mountain.

I looked up and up, but couldn't see where the ship ended and the sky began.

When I looked down again I saw two people in front of me.

They were dressed entirely in brown. The man was quite tall and had a reddish beard that ran all the way around the rim of his face. The woman was very short with a pointed bony face. Her eyes were pushed almost slantwise by the bones of her cheeks. I didn't think her pretty until she smiled.

Behind them was some kind of office, or waiting room, full of people. The man barely nodded at me but went into it with the driver. The woman pushed her bonnet back to get a better look at me and I saw she was hardly any older than I was, but round and heavy with child.

I thought at once of my own child who never had the chance to live.

'Hello,' she said. I had to bend forwards to hear her. 'My name is Jane,' she said. 'What shall I call you?'

'Pasley,' I said, then had to repeat it for all the noise.

'—first name,' she said.

I hadn't used my first name for so long. No one in England could ever spell it. But she went on looking at me with her bright, slanted eyes, and so I said it, my name, and she repeated it in the English way. I didn't correct her, I just nodded.

Then the quay swayed and lurched as the booming, grinding noise sounded again. If there is a trumpet on the Day of Doom, that's what it will sound like. I wanted to fall to my knees and clutch the ground but of course I didn't.

Mrs Buchanan gripped my arm. She kept saying, 'Oh I don't know, I don't know,' and I saw then how much more scared she must be than I was, she who looked likely to give birth on board.

Mr Buchanan was talking to a woman in a stiff blue serge. I thought she must be Miss Kaye. He came back and said something to me that was drowned by the foghorn's blast. I looked at him fearfully, then felt something pressing my hand.

Mrs Buchanan.

Jane.

I squeezed her hand in turn.

Then Miss Kaye came and said some things I couldn't hear, giving me some papers, and Mr Buchanan shouted something else and I understood we were to follow him. He pushed and shoved a path through the jostling crowds until we came to a great ramp leading upwards with chains at the sides. It shook as we stepped onto it.

This is it now, I thought, my old life is over. But for Jane clutching my hand I might have run away or jumped into those black oily waters, but her fear made me strong.

It was slow progress among all the other people thrusting their way on board. When my foot slipped Jane held onto me and I to her. Up and up we climbed, towards the sky. There seemed no limits to it and for a moment I felt dizzy.

It will be a new start, she said, *a new life*.

I thought of her then, and my mother. What would they think if they could see me now?

Tell me everything, she said to me. But I didn't tell her everything, I didn't tell her much at all.

I didn't even tell her my name.

PART II

SEPTEMBER 1852

CHAPTER 37

Elizabeth

ELIZABETH SAT AT her dressing table. She'd never had a room just for dressing before, but since moving house she'd used the small room next to their bedroom as her boudoir.

Tonight was the opening ceremony of the Manchester Free Library. The long campaign was over. All the debates, about whether women should enter the same public space as men, or whether it was unsafe or at least unhygienic to allow the labouring classes into the library, had been resolved. All the canvassing and lobbying and petitioning had reached a successful conclusion which would be celebrated tonight.

Elizabeth inspected herself in her aunt's mirror. Her cheeks looked mottled rather than rosy, her forehead had already begun to shine. Had she gained weight? For the first time in years she'd had a dress specially made, but the long, pointed bodice seemed rather tighter than she'd wanted and the skirt was so voluminous she'd had to buy a larger hoop for it. All of which had cost more than she'd anticipated. That was what came of going to an expensive establishment on Deansgate rather than her usual shop in Knutsford.

But she'd fallen in love with the fabric, a lavender silk moire, because of its shimmering watery finish. Now she wondered whether it wasn't just the wrong shade, giving her cheeks a purplish hue. Should she have chosen the lilac instead?

The lace trim made the neckline discreet. She'd rejected the idea of baring her shoulders, or carrying a fan or bouquet – it wasn't the opera. She would drape a silvery shawl over her gown and wear kid gloves in pale grey, which strictly speaking, didn't go. But at the last moment she'd decided against the extra expense of new ones.

Her hair was looped over her ears into a low bun as usual, but she slipped a band of silk flowers over it and pinned a small spray of lily-of-the-valley to her breast.

It was John Potter, now Sir John, who was to blame for these unusual efforts. The former mayor had called in person to tell them about the ceremony that would mark the historic occasion.

'And,' he said, 'I have an announcement to make.'

They waited for him to say that William, who had worked so tirelessly for the campaign, had been selected to give the address.

Sir John looked from one to the other of them with his unblinking gaze and Elizabeth had a moment of misgiving. Surely he wasn't going to ask *her*? It had to be William. No one had done more for the library – she would have to refuse.

'Charles Dickens has agreed to be our speaker,' Sir John said, raising himself slightly on his toes as they gaped at him. He turned to William. 'The committee are hoping you'll look after him on the evening.'

William looked at Elizabeth with such a droll expression she suppressed a laugh. Sir John's already florid face flushed.

'It's an honour,' he said, glancing sternly at Elizabeth as she coughed into her handkerchief. 'And there's no one more deserving of it . . . ' William grinned at Elizabeth, which set her off again. She excused herself, hurrying into the kitchen for a drink, while William led the ex-mayor into his study.

Charles Dickens!

Of course.

William professed himself unconcerned, relieved even, so Elizabeth refrained from saying that he should resign from the committee because how would that look? But this was the reason she'd had a new dress made rather than going in her old blue silk, and was encased in her tightest corset, largest hoop and four petticoats.

Already too warm, already uncomfortable, and who knew how long the ceremony might last?

William had said Mr Thackeray would also be there, which was some consolation. He'd promised she would have the chance to speak to him.

She scrutinised her reflection. The new drops she took for reading had brightened her eyes. Her cheeks were red enough, but although William didn't approve, she dabbed just a little rouge on her lips, then powdered her forehead and nose and touched her aunt's favourite lavender water to her wrists.

She practised her smile, then closed her lips and practised it again. There was something a little defensive or wary in her eyes.

Perhaps the new dress was a mistake?

Too late now.

CHAPTER 38

THE ATRIUM OF the Science Hall was so crowded it was impossible to steer a path through it. Elizabeth was jostled forward then back. Someone caught her arm and she pulled away before realising it was William.

'—at the front,' he said. He had to say it twice before she understood, then he led her through the crowds to their seats.

'I'll be back soon, I just have to speak to Sir John,' and he disappeared before she could stop him.

Elizabeth's skirts billowed out as she sat. She had to gather them hastily as Councillor Acker descended next to her.

'Well, if it isn't Manchester's leading lady authoress!' he said. 'Not on stage, then?'

'No, indeed.'

'I'd've thought you'd be the main attraction!'

Elizabeth said she could hardly imagine herself addressing an audience of so many dignitaries, and would have declined had she been asked.

'Nonsense!' said Councillor Acker. 'I love to see a pretty woman on stage!'

I'm sure you do, Elizabeth thought, but she bent her head, acknowledging the compliment. The councillor wiped his face with an enormous cloth. 'By God, it's warm in here!' he shouted. Elizabeth agreed with him, thinking regretfully about her fan, and suggested a seat by the door.

'There ARE no seats by the door!' he said. 'That's organisation for you. You hand it over to a committee and what do you get? Chaos, that's what.'

He stood suddenly as a gaunt woman with towering hair appeared.

'This is my wife,' he said. 'Here's Mrs Gaskell, my dear – Manchester's leading lady authoress!'

Mrs Acker subjected Elizabeth to a summary stare which reminded her that her dress had been the cheapest in an expensive shop and her hair was adorned with a simple band. 'Should I have heard of you?' Mrs Acker said.

'Probably not,' Elizabeth replied, with the smile she'd practiced earlier.

'Of course you should – she's famous,' Councillor Acker said. 'Her first novel caused a right stir. Fairly flew out of the shops! Never mind Dickens, eh? If you don't mind my asking,' he said, leaning so close she could smell his teeth. 'How much did you make out of that little venture, eh?'

Elizabeth maintained her smile. 'I couldn't say.'

'NO? Haven't they sent any accounts?'

But she was saved from replying by the band. Then John Potter took the stage, wearing a beige frock coat with a gold thread running through it and a gold cravat. He began by saying that although he was no longer mayor the Free Library was his legacy to the people of Manchester. It was the culmination of his hopes and dreams for the city.

Elizabeth smiled and clapped as he took all the credit. Her gaze travelled along the rows. There was Lady Kay Shuttleworth, who must be with Dr Kay although she couldn't see him at the moment. But Mr Burnett was with some woman who was not Susanna Winkworth. She nodded coldly at him. He could invite who he wanted, of course, but was it only naïve to call on a spinster like Susanna?

Further along was Edward Taylor from *The Manchester Guardian* with Harrison Ainsworth, who would not be speaking, although some said his books sold even better than Dickens'. And was that Friedrich Engels? He was sitting next to a woman with a froth of dark curls spilling over her forehead and a large fan obscuring her face.

Elizabeth had met him once, briefly, at a fund-raising event for the library. He'd bowed stiffly, then said, 'Ah, the celebrated author of *Mary Barton*, the novel where everyone regrets their revolutionary impulses and dies of remorse.'

And she'd been too taken aback by the implication that he'd read it, as much as the aspersion, to come up with a satisfactory response.

She'd heard he was a womaniser, and in fact he was leaning closely towards his companion, both of them laughing as she batted her fan. Elizabeth wished once again she'd brought hers. With an effort, she returned her attention to Sir John.

'Manchester,' he was saying, 'has a particularly rich tradition of writers from the working classes.'

'None of 'em here though,' Councillor Acker said. Elizabeth glanced round, but she couldn't see any of the writers from the Sun Inn, who'd campaigned so hard for the library with William. She'd thought Samuel Bamford would have been invited at least, or Elijah Ridings.

It was an oversight, surely.

Who was responsible for the invitations?

She was distracted enough to miss the end of Sir John's speech, but it had gone down well, judging by the applause.

Edward Edwards spoke next. He would be chief librarian of the new library, but he appeared to be overcome by nerves. His shock of silver hair trembled over his pince-nez and his mouth worked silently for a few moments before he spoke. And then, disappointingly, he delivered only statistics.

The library was already substantial, he told them. It contained more than 18,000 books, purchased at the unprecedented cost of £4156.00. The collection donated by Prince Albert alone amounted to almost £1000 . . .

'Waste of good cash, if you ask me,' Councillor Acker said. She tilted her face away from him.

Mr Edwards continued to stutter through the statistics. They should have asked William, she thought. He would have made a much better job of it.

Just as she was thinking this her husband appeared, making his way along the row with some difficulty and many apologies.

'Mr Thackeray isn't well,' he said. 'I've had to call a carriage for him.'

'Oh, no!'

'It's probably just lack of air.'

'Told you - it's like the Black Hole of Calcutta in here!' Councillor Acker said.

'So - he won't be speaking?'

'I'm afraid not - I'm going to accompany him back to his hotel.'

Elizabeth felt a crushing disappointment. She'd hoped to talk to Thackeray about her new book. In this imaginary encounter, he would be more than happy for her to send it to him and delighted to provide a quote.

Although it wasn't anywhere near finished yet, but she'd hoped that the interest of the great writer might spur her on. She would have said that to him, that he was an inspiration to her and so many others.

William touched her shoulder. 'I'll be back as soon as I can,' he said. *Bear up*, the touch said, *not much longer to go*.

Elizabeth glared after him as he left her with Councillor Acker. He must have known about the seating arrangements.

Councillor Acker leaned towards her again as Bulwer Lytton took the stage.

'You know my opinion about books,' he said.

'I do.'

'Most books are written by folk with beef in their bellies and good roofs over their heads. Like that nice new house you've moved into, eh? Plymouth Grove, is it?'

Elizabeth smiled warmly. 'Or, indeed, your own,' she said, because Councillor Acker had moved into a mansion in Hale. But he was smirking at her, because she'd risen to his jibe.

She remembered when William had finally taken her to see the house. As the carriage had entered Plymouth Grove she'd said, 'We might as well turn around right now.'

'At least look at it,' William said.

It was built in a classical, Georgian style (though in fact it was quite new), dignified but not austere, not too imposing. As they entered the short drive William gave her a boyish look, almost bashful, full of expectation.

'We can't afford it,' was all she would say.

Inside, the rooms were spacious but not grand. Two large reception rooms, a dining room, kitchen, scullery, pantry. And a separate room that Elizabeth knew at once William would claim for his study. It had a large window looking over the drive and a fireplace. Even as he stood in it he seemed to relax.

Upstairs there were so many bedrooms and attic rooms for the servants she began to feel dizzy with possibilities.

But it was the garden that sold it to her. There were vegetable beds, somewhat overgrown, and peas climbing the wall. There were two fruit trees already starting to blossom. They could keep chickens and even a cow in the outbuildings. Fresh milk! They could make their own butter and cheese without depending on the erratic deliveries of the dairy company.

But she wasn't going to give in so easily. 'And the rent?' she said.

When William told her, she had to lean against the wall for support. 'Dear God,' she said.

'Yes,' he teased her. 'It's a good job you're earning now.'

Dickens had sent twenty pounds for *Lizzie Leigh*. William had pocketed it immediately, laughing at her when she tried to snatch it back. He'd said she could have it back once they'd moved, if everything worked out.

Elizabeth objected that they would need more staff, but William explained how it could be done. They would use the legacy from her aunt, he would take on more students, her cousin was investing for him in the docks and there was her writing, of course.

'It will be a new start for us here,' he said, gazing earnestly at her. 'We'll be able to do so much more . . .'

She knew he was thinking about his study. Or the guests she would entertain while he was in it. 'It would be a *new start*,' she said, 'in the country.'

'Yes, but look,' he said, waving an arm towards the window, through which she could see gardens and fields. You'd hardly know you were near the city. The girls would love it. They could invite more people, introduce them to a wider social circle . . .

This was his compromise: she wanted to live in the country, he wouldn't leave the city. 'It's the best of both worlds,' he said.

She asked him how they could possibly live in such a fine house so near the city slums, where so many of his students and the Sunday School children lived.

'I've been thinking about that,' he said. He threaded her arm through his and walked her through the rooms again, pointing out that he could train new ministers here without having to pay for a room. And she could teach some of the Sunday School children – it would be good for them to have their eyes opened to a different way of life. There would be room for all their books. She would have more space, which meant more time, for her own writing.

As always when she listened to him his vision became her own. And cunningly, he suggested a short break in Silverdale, to think things over. There, she produced another story for Dickens and agreed to write a Christmas book for Chapman. She wrote to Tottie, *My dear, it's 150 a year, and I dare say we shall be ruined; and I've already asked after the ventilation of the new Borough Gaol and bespoken Mr Wright to visit us . . .*

And so they'd moved, more than two years ago now. She'd hired a new cook and a gardener. Slowly she'd come to inhabit the house, or it inhabited her. One morning, when the garden was flossed with spiders' webs, each tiny filament shining with rain drops so that it looked as though everything was webbed with light, she felt a profound peace. Now she couldn't imagine herself anywhere else.

Guests arrived in a steady stream: the Kays, the Howitts, the Carlyles, the Forsters and the young writer, Charlotte Bronte, who had recently become her friend.

It was a pleasure to entertain there. The space made it all so easy – that and the new cook, who was excellent, and whose plum pudding was largely responsible for the tightness of the dress she now wore.

She'd become a different person there, someone who loved gardening and entertaining, throwing parties, teaching the girls to dance . . .

Behind Elizabeth, someone coughed and she realised that Thomas Carlyle had been on stage for some time but she'd missed almost everything he'd said. He was describing the library as a holy phenomenon, creating a *perpetual priesthood of men of letters* . . .

And women, she thought, clapping with the rest. She could feel the heat from the room, an animal stench rising from so many bodies. How much longer would it go on?

Monckton Milnes spoke next. He did at least mention women, the great and glorious tradition of women writers, particularly in Manchester, who would at last have equal access to the halls of learning. In this, he declared, as in so many other ways, Manchester led the world!

Elizabeth clapped more enthusiastically this time.

Then Sir John returned to the stage.

'Wait for it!' said Councillor Acker, into a hush. Sir John blinked owlishly, looking round.

'Now,' he said, 'here for you tonight, we have the greatest star in England's literary firmament.'

A muffled moan rose from the crowd.

Elizabeth couldn't help wondering what it must be like to be Charles Dickens now. He'd interrupted a series of readings to appear at this event, and although it wasn't open to the public rumour of his arrival had generated such excitement that the committee had stationed guards at the entrances.

'Author of such inestimable works as Oliver Twist and A Christmas Carol, the poor man's champion, from whose charmed quill no dull word ever flowed, the *inimitable* Charles Dickens!'

Elizabeth's editor ran onto the stage to thunderous applause. He was wearing a peacock blue jacket, gold waistcoat, frilled shirt front and peach-coloured sash. *Punch* had already described him as a dandy, but he had enough presence to carry it. He moved and even stood with alacrity; the air around him seemed to bristle as he spoke.

He began by thanking them all for the beacon of hope that this library undoubtedly was. Manchester, he said, was the crucible of the world, and this library would be the crucible of Manchester. 'A furnace, in which a new race of men would be forged!'

Then he told them a story about a factory child who lived in a slum, devoid of hope, of light, *as closely imprisoned as any criminal in solitary confinement*. But one day a window opened for him onto the world of books. A world of wonder and delight, stimulating the imagination and stirring his soul.

It was a curious thing, Elizabeth thought, that no matter how successful Dickens was, in his mind he always remained the impoverished child he'd once been.

But the audience were rapt, seeing it all through his eyes. On his last tour he'd been mobbed, a dying man had asked to shake his hand. In foundries and factories, on building sites, labourers clubbed together to buy instalments of his latest novel. *Bleak House* was his ninth, while she'd hardly got started on her second . . .

She'd read the opening instalment eagerly, but the description of London had stopped her in her tracks.

Smoke lowering down from chimney pots, making a soft black drizzle . . .

Fog everywhere, fog up the river . . . fog down the river . . .

It was good, it was powerful – it was exactly how she'd described Manchester in her new novel!

She'd decided then that she would set it elsewhere. She wouldn't be accused of imitating the more famous author. Norfolk, she'd thought, or Wales. It would be better that way – she'd always believed in the power of a beautiful setting. And it would be very different from *Mary Barton*, which was a good thing.

And she'd started it all over again.

On stage Dickens was changing into a succession of different characters: the smug bourgeois, the aristocrat, both of them outraged as Mr Down-and-Out proved less meek than they would like. He lampooned the vindictively righteous who thought the poor got what they deserved, the complacently righteous who thought that God's special favour protected them from misfortune, the sanctimoniously righteous who took it upon themselves to judge those in need and the self-serving righteous who displayed their virtue like a badge of superiority.

The crowd roared in recognition, Councillor Acker most uproariously of all. Even his wife seemed entertained and Elizabeth laughed too, while wondering uneasily which kind of righteous she was. The audience's response was creative fuel to Dickens, spurring him on to greater heights of parody. She'd heard he would ask for readers' suggestions about his novels and re-write them accordingly, while Elizabeth had enough trouble pulling her own ideas together . . .

But did she want to be like Dickens?

Sometimes when he spoke to her she knew he was still performing, as though he never left the stage. She thought he must be the loneliest man in the world.

'That was summat like!' Councillor Acker said, wiping his eyes as Dickens finished. Elizabeth clapped, and went on clapping because the applause continued for several minutes.

Finally Sir John declared the library open in a speech so long that Councillor Acker said it would be shut again before he'd finished. Several aldermen joined him on stage, there was a vote of thanks from the new mayor and more applause. Then the first notes of the national anthem sounded and everyone rose.

'Well, it's to be hoped they know what they're doing,' Councillor Acker said.

'I think some of them must,' said Elizabeth, and before he could engage her in further debate she said, 'If you'll excuse me, Councillor, Mrs Acker, I must find my husband.'

It was almost impossible to get through the dense crowd surging into the atrium but she pressed on, fending off a sense of disappointment and failure. She wouldn't meet Thackeray, she wasn't happy with her new dress, she'd been patronised by the councillor and his wife, she had a headache and her husband was nowhere to be seen. Perhaps he wasn't back yet from escorting Thackeray to his hotel. She should have offered to go with him – but Mr Thackeray would hardly have wanted her there, stuttering out her appreciation. And she had to see Charles Dickens because he was returning immediately to his tour. She would have to congratulate him, and Sir John of course, on a highly successful event.

Sir John was standing with the new mayor, Robert Barnes, and another gentleman. Elizabeth approached them intending to be gracious but as she reached them the third gentleman looked at her strangely and left. Elizabeth congratulated Sir John, and Robert Barnes, then she asked, 'Who was that with you just now?'

'Oh,' said Sir John, peering vaguely into the crowd, 'some doctor, I believe. Dr Billington, I think he said his name was.'

CHAPTER 39

'I'M SORRY?' ELIZABETH said. As he repeated the name, she turned abruptly and started to press through the crowds once more. 'Please - excuse me - please!'

Several people stared at her as she pushed past in a fever of determination. But she couldn't get through the sea of cloaks and shawls and feathers.

She would never find the doctor - she would pass out from the heat first. She needed some air. Then she glimpsed the back of a head that might be his, heading towards an exit. She squeezed through a small knot of people and saw the door close behind him.

'Excuse me!' she said, almost falling over someone's bag.

A breeze fanned her as she opened the door and there, towards the bottom of the steps, was the doctor. He was facing away from her, his hand on the back of a woman dressed in blue, but Elizabeth was sure it was him. She gathered her skirts and ran down the steps.

He was approaching a carriage. She couldn't go fast enough, not in these shoes, and the steps were slippery with rain. So she called out to him, 'Dr Billington!'

He must have heard her, of course he had - she saw him falter in his stride but then he helped the woman into the carriage. Elizabeth hurried down the next few steps, then, abandoning all etiquette, bellowed aloud, 'DR BILLINGTON!'

And he turned.

She almost fell down the final steps. She must have looked ridiculous, a middle-aged woman waving one hand frantically and clutching her skirts with the other, but he waited at least. 'Mrs Gaskell,' he said.

How did he know who she was?

He was just as she'd pictured him, spectacles, greying hair, bad teeth.

She wished she wasn't quite so out of breath. 'I believe we have an acquaintance in common,' she managed.

The doctor looked bland. 'I'm sure we have many,' he said.

'A young girl, known as Pasley. You visited her, I believe, in the New Bailey prison.'

'I visited many of the girls there – I was the surgeon there, for a while.'

'But you'd seen this one before.'

'Really?'

'Do you not remember? You said, "Good God, what are you doing here?" I believe those were your exact words.'

The doctor took his glasses off. His eyes appeared smaller, his face softer.

'Mrs Gaskell, I see so many girls—'

'Do you seduce them all?'

The words rang out, their harshness startled even her. The doctor looked horrified. 'Mrs Gaskell!'

From the carriage a woman's voice called, 'Is something wrong?'

The doctor half turned and said, 'Nothing, my dear – I'm coming.'

'Your wife?' Elizabeth said, nodding at him. She moved towards the carriage as if to say – what? But the doctor moved as well, blocking her.

'Mrs Gaskell,' he said gently, 'I don't know what you've heard about me, but I can assure you—'

'You *destroyed* her!' Elizabeth said.

'I haven't the faintest idea what you're talking about.'

He stepped away but Elizabeth said, 'Then why were you asked to leave the prison?'

His expression was different now, less benign.

'Mrs Gaskell,' he said. 'I don't know what you imagine I've done, but I do know how unwise it is – dangerous even – to make such outrageous allegations in a public place. It might cause people to speculate about you.'

She was speechless. As his gaze flickered over her, she saw herself through his eyes. She was dishevelled, unkempt, and many people must have seen her running after him shrieking for all she was worth. Dr Billington nodded. 'Forgive me,' he said, and she hadn't even the wit to ask, *for what?*

'Shame on you!' she said as he walked towards his carriage. *'Shame on you!'*

He didn't look round. The driver flicked the reins and they set off.

Elizabeth stared after them. She felt winded, blood pounding in her ears.

More people were coming out of the Science Hall now, she was attracting attention. She turned and hurried back up the steps. *William*, she thought. She had to find William and tell him about the doctor.

How dare he deny it, when she *knew* – she could see his guilt.

So distracted was she that as she re-entered the atrium she bumped into someone without seeing who it was until a familiar voice said, 'Are you lost?'

Dr Kay. He extended his arm to her and she clutched it. 'Are you all right?' he said. 'You look a little warm . . .'

'No,' she said. 'No, I'm not all right. I've just seen him – the doctor!'

Dr Kay shook his head.

'Dr Billington – the doctor from the prison!'

'Oh – that doctor.'

'He was here! He left just now!'

'Well, I dare say he would have been invited.'

'Invited?'

'Because of his work with the poor.'

She stared at him. 'You don't mean to say he's still working with them!'

'Why wouldn't he be?'

'Why?'

'No charges have been brought – not that I know of, at any rate.'

Elizabeth removed her hand from his arm. 'James,' she said, 'Are *you* still working with him?'

Dr Kay looked discomfited. 'I believe he may have done some shifts at the Dispensary,' he said.

'No!'

'Do you know how difficult it is to get doctors to work with the poor?'

'*Work*,' she said, 'is that what you call it?'

'Keep your voice down,' he said, looking round.

'I will not,' she said. 'You know what that man's done. How can you let him loose on other girls?'

'He isn't unsupervised,' Dr Kay said. 'There's always a nurse present.'

She raised the tips of her fingers to her forehead feeling tight bands of pressure and pain.

'I don't believe this,' she said.

'Elizabeth—'

'No,' she said, walking away from him, 'I need to find my husband.'

CHAPTER 40

'I'LL SPEAK TO the Board,' William promised. In the carriage he put an arm round her to comfort her, but she wasn't comforted. She'd failed, she thought. She'd failed herself and Pasley.

'How did he come to be invited here tonight?'

'I don't know,' William said. 'No one would know about him, of course.'

'They will know,' said Elizabeth. 'I'll tell them. I'll tell everyone.'

'Lily,' he said, 'it's late. And you're tired. You don't look well.'

She didn't feel well. Her headache was worsening, but if she started now she could post a whole raft of letters in the morning.

'You can't do anything now,' said William. 'You need to rest.'

She rubbed her forehead. She could feel a kind of congestion, almost a pain, in her chest. She did need to rest but there was too much to do.

She'd pushed Pasley to the back of her mind but now she returned vividly, as she'd first seen her, the drooping head, the jutting wrists, her white face in the window of the train. But that was her imagination – she hadn't seen Pasley on the train.

All the pain and guilt came flooding back. She hadn't gone to the station, she hadn't written to Pasley as she'd promised, she hadn't done enough for her.

William helped her down from the carriage and she hurried into the house.

'Where are you going?' he said, following her.

'To write to the trustees.'

'Why don't you let me speak to Dr Kay first?'

'I've already spoken to him and he's done nothing.'

'You don't know that.'

Elizabeth started to protest but he said, 'Promise me you'll wait until I've seen him. You don't want to offend him.'

'Are you afraid of him?'

William's expression changed. 'Of course not. I just think we won't get very far without him and we want him as our ally.'

'But—' there were so many arguments raging in her. She saw William glance towards his study, then back to her. 'It's late,' he said. 'At least leave it until the morning. Get some sleep.'

'What about you?'

'I have a sermon to write.'

Elizabeth closed her eyes briefly. She was tired, as William had said, she was exhausted. 'Fine,' she said.

When she opened them again he'd already disappeared into his study.

The house had been designed by an eccentric bachelor with no family and only his own needs in mind, so that all the rooms flowed into one another. Apart from William's study.

Elizabeth didn't have a study; she wrote in the dining room.

She could have written in her bedroom, of course, but the new house didn't run itself. There were problems with the water supply and with the cow, which kept escaping and trampling through the neighbouring gardens. On one occasion she'd got as far as the Mechanics Institute and William said she must have been trying to sign up for a course. And then the new cook had a quarrel with Bessie, who'd said if they couldn't eat the meat she'd roasted they could at least sole their boots with it. Cook was halfway down the road, bag packed, before Elizabeth caught up with her.

In the end she'd set up a small table in the dining room with her inkstand and quills. From there she could minister to the children, consult with Hearn, attend to any visitors and slip out into the garden to collect the fruit she was storing to ward off winter chills. But she'd got no further with her novel.

Charles Dickens and Edward Chapman were both pressing her,

she'd had letters from fans of *Mary Barton*. Even members of the congregation had asked whether they could expect to see a sequel soon.

'I'm so busy with the new house,' she said to them, 'and settling the girls.'

They accepted this of course – it was an acceptable thing for a wife and mother to say.

When the fog worsened, Elizabeth had taken the girls to Windermere. She'd completed a long story there and managed to send the first few chapters of her novel to Chapman who'd said he was eager to see more. But there wasn't any more, just pages and pages of scattered notes lying on the small table like a reproach. Reluctantly, Elizabeth walked towards it. The room was dark but there was a dim light from the window. She stood beside the heap of paper without touching it, feeling a nervous agitation that was almost fear.

There were so many problems with it! The story kept shifting slyly inside her, it wouldn't take root.

As soon as she'd started writing she'd realised how little she really knew about Pasley. The doctor, of course, and the sweatshop. And the moment of desperation on the bridge over the river, which was a problem in itself – the worst sin. She'd imagined a picturesque scene – her heroine floating away like the Lady of Shalott or stumbling along the banks, mourning what she'd become.

She'd called her *Ruth*, which meant pity or regret and thought it might make a good title. She wanted to drive the point home to all those readers who would judge her, all those men who wouldn't let their wives read *Mary Barton*. People would still be shocked, but she needed to show the extremity of the situation. Ruth had to at least consider drowning herself because she was pregnant.

Elizabeth didn't know whether Pasley had been pregnant, or actually had a baby, or what might have become of it, but in her story Ruth had a little boy whom she loved more than anything in the world.

It was her own, her darling, her individual baby, already, though not an hour old ... a pure beautiful innocent life, which she fondly imagined in that early passion of maternal love, she could guard from every touch of corrupting sin by ever watchful and most tender care.

She'd wept writing those words, remembering her own son in his tiny casket, the months of madness afterwards. *I do not believe such pain can ever be healed*, she'd written to Tottie. And it hadn't healed; the wounds opened again so easily and the grief flowed.

No one, so far as she knew, had written about such things before. And she couldn't mention the pregnancy in her novel, so in her story Ruth was saved from her unlawful death by a minister, Thurston Benson, who only learns about her condition from his sister, Faith: *Why, Thurston, there is something so shocking the matter that I cannot tell you.*

Then Thurston and Faith take Ruth in, showing true charity and forgiveness, which was what she hoped to inspire in her readers.

It wasn't Pasley's story, of course. Only when she stopped trying to write Pasley's story and thought instead of all the girls in a similar plight, like the sister of the young woman at the Christian Mission, could she make any progress at all.

But there were so many things she couldn't say, so many words she couldn't use. *Abortion, prostitution, rape.* She felt almost poisoned by them.

And she still hadn't decided on the ending.

Her new friend, Charlotte Brontë, had been quite outspoken about that. Elizabeth had met the younger author at Dr Kay's house in the Lake District, and had been delighted when Charlotte (who was *so* shy!) agreed to visit Plymouth Grove. But when Elizabeth had told her the ending she'd planned for her novel the younger author had responded fiercely, 'Why should she die? Why are we to shut up the book weeping?'

Which had thrown Elizabeth into doubt all over again.

Whenever she tried to write the faces of William's congregation floated before her. She heard the voices of all those who'd criticised

Mary Barton and felt reproached by the example of other writers, Charles Dickens, Charlotte Bronte.

It was so much easier to write her other stories, or her letters, to teach her girls, and the Sunday School children, entertain . . . anything rather than work on her novel.

If only she could learn to shut the door like William . . .

Elizabeth yawned suddenly, hugely. She was so tired there were black spots in front of her eyes. Her thoughts were whirling around without conclusion. Pasley, Ruth, the doctor. What he'd said, how he'd *threatened* her! And denied everything . . .

She should have written about him in her novel! But in the chapters she'd sent to Chapman, Ruth, a beautiful orphan, is sent to a ball to mend any dresses torn in the dancing. There she meets a handsome squire, Henry Bellingham, who takes her to Wales, then abandons her.

The last thing people wanted to hear was that a doctor, in whom such trust was placed, could abuse that trust so abominably.

There is the truth you can tell, and the truth people can hear. Dr Kay had said.

Elizabeth pressed her fingers to her eyes. William was right, she was too tired to write any letters now, and certainly too tired to tackle her novel. Even the sight of it defeated her, that white, accusing pile.

CHAPTER 41

AND SOON SHE was caught up in the gravitational pull of her social world: concerts, lectures, exhibitions. The Tetlows visited, then the Shaens and the Greens. Then, despite all the fruit she'd collected, everyone was ill because of the Manchester fog, which settled around ten in the morning and only began to lift when the factories closed. She still felt a small knuckle of resentment about that, especially when everyone got better apart from her. Her cough persisted, her neuralgia worsened, she had bad dreams. She took a few drops of laudanum each night and went to bed early, but still didn't sleep.

Whenever she saw William he looked exhausted from running his classes or training new ministers in his study. She didn't want to add to his burdens but the thought of the doctor aggravated her like a stone in her shoe. She would go to see Dr Kay herself, she thought, when she was feeling better.

Then one day William came to her as she was reading in bed to tell her that Dr Billington had left the dispensary and Manchester.

Elizabeth put her book down. 'Where's he gone?'

'I'm not sure.'

'You didn't ask?'

'I didn't think it mattered . . .'

'Did Dr Kay tell him to leave?'

'I would assume so.'

Elizabeth felt a spark of irritation.

'Has he gone permanently? Or just for a holiday? Will he come back?'

'I think that's unlikely.'

'Is he going to practice somewhere else?'

'How would I know?'

'Someone must,' she said. She thought of her brother-in-law, Sam Gaskell, who worked at the Lunacy Commission in London. She could ask him if he'd heard anything of a Dr Billington and warn him against hiring him. And Sam could warn other people.

She got up and went to the bureau.

'What are you doing?' William said as she took paper out of the drawer.

'You can see what I'm doing.'

'How long are you going to keep this up?'

'As long as that man's still out there.'

'There'll always be someone out there. You can't stem the tide of evil.'

Why not? she thought resentfully. *Why couldn't God? What was God doing about it?*

'Lily,' William said, 'I'm worried about you.'

She looked up then. 'Why?'

'You're not eating properly or sleeping. What's wrong?'

'Nothing,' she said.

William sat on the bed.

'Tell me . . .'

She looked away from him, towards the window. 'It's just – I can't bear the thought of *that man* setting up somewhere else – destroying more lives!'

'You don't think you're getting a little obsessed?'

'What do you mean?'

'I mean you got what you wanted, he left the dispensary. You won.'

'Won,' she said.

'You know what I mean. Nothing travels faster than rumour, you've said so yourself. To all intents and purposes you've won. Yet you persist in turning this into some kind of personal campaign.'

He'd denied any knowledge of wrongdoing and even threatened her. *I know, as, I suspect, you do, how unwise it is – dangerous even, to make outrageous allegations in such a public place.*

'Lily,' William said. He placed a hand over hers but she snatched it away. She should have said more, she thought, she should have done more to stop him.

William was looking at her with a worried expression. 'You're making yourself ill,' he said.

Outside the sky was dark already, though it was barely four. The Manchester fog had set in. She could see her reflection in the window. Who was that old woman looking back at her? Her face looked pinched and narrow.

'You think I'm mad, don't you?'

'No!' he said. He seemed genuinely shocked. 'Of course not.' he took her hand again. 'But I do think you need to rest. Perhaps you should go away for a while to recuperate.'

Out of the way, said that needle-sharp voice in her mind.

'Didn't you promise Mr Dickens to send him a story?'

She had promised that. And she'd still made no progress with *Ruth*.

'I can't go away,' she said. 'There's too much to do.'

'It won't get done if you make yourself ill,' he said. 'We'll manage here without you.'

How? she thought. But she did long to be away from Manchester. She felt a familiar yearning for something just out of reach. Her childhood.

William was talking again.

'Dr Kay has been campaigning for a new Public Health Act. He wants to set up a Council to monitor and regulate all medical practitioners, so they have to be registered and they can be struck off if they break their code of practice. He's going to present it to Parliament.'

'Parliament!' she said. They took so long to do anything, and in the end nothing was done.

'We have to work through constitutional change, Lily. In the end, that's all we can do.'

'I have no say in Parliament, William, but I can ask Dr Kay to find out where he's gone.'

'I don't think he'd take kindly to that. He may have helped him find a position elsewhere.'

Yes, she thought, *he would do that*, and for a moment the two doctors merged in her mind.

'So I should do nothing – say nothing?'

'There are limits to what we can do.'

'Apparently.'

'You're tired,' William said. 'Go to bed. I'll get Bessie to bring you a nightcap.'

'You needn't speak to me as though I'm a child,' she said, staring at him.

William's eyes grew cold. She was the first to look away, picking up her papers and quill.

'Where are you going?'

'To find somewhere I can write in peace.'

'Lily—' he said, but she didn't look back. She went downstairs, putting the paper and quill on her table, then realised the inkwell was empty. But in any case, she was so cross she couldn't even think about the letters she planned to write, let alone her novel.

There were too many things she couldn't say.

CHAPTER 42

ELIZABETH WOKE SUDDENLY. She could hear, above the drumming of the rain at the window, the beating of her heart. An urgent, desperate pounding.

It was a dream, that was all, a terrible dream.

She was standing at the pulpit of the Cross St Chapel in full view of the congregation who knew, as she knew, she shouldn't be there. It was her husband's place, but she couldn't find him among so many accusing faces. They were all there, Councillor Acker, Dr Kay, Dr Billington.

And Pasley, who hadn't gone away at all. She sat, ragged and pale, looking at Elizabeth with hopeful, sorrowful eyes. Her lips were blue.

Elizabeth was reading but the words wouldn't come out right. She tried to tell her audience it wasn't ready yet, it was only notes, but she couldn't, her tongue was too thick and swollen.

She woke up sweating, feeling as though she was clawing her way out of earth. Her heart was still pounding as though it belonged to someone else. She was afraid of it, remembering her mother who had died when she was younger than Elizabeth was now.

Beside her the bed was empty. Where was William?

He sometimes slept in Polly's room now she was away, or the guest bedroom, or even in his study.

He didn't want to disturb her, he said.

She lay very still, sensing the new house around her, the rooms where Julia and Flossie, Bessie and Hearn and Cook lay sleeping. She heard the clock chiming twice; it seemed far away. She still wasn't used to the distances, the space. They had so many rooms now that both Polly and Meta had gone. Meta had missed her sister so much that they'd sent her to the same school.

They could have given a room to Pasley.

Pasley.

In her dream she'd had blue lips like a corpse.

But surely Elizabeth would have heard if something had happened? If the ship had sunk?

She'd never heard about her brother, but this was different. Such a big ship would have been reported in the papers.

It couldn't have sunk – they must have all arrived safely on that distant shore.

And there was no reason to think anything bad had happened to her afterwards. But would Elizabeth know if it had?

Will you write to me? she'd said, but Elizabeth hadn't written. Better, she'd thought, to sever the connection now.

Better for whom? said the small, nagging voice in her head. She shifted restlessly.

The clock struck the quarter hour. Had she given up on sleep altogether? She could feel a warning pressure from her body. She curled onto her side drawing her knees up, although she knew she would have to get up in the end.

Reluctantly she pushed the bedclothes back, pulled the pot from beneath the bed.

Of course, by the time she'd finished, she was thoroughly awake.

She lit a candle and opened the door with a small click. And there she was, on the shadowy landing.

Even a new house looked ghostly in candlelight. Shadows leapt and flickered in alcoves, the glass bowl of the lamp was like a face bending towards her own.

She was reminded sharply of her father's house, how she used to creep out onto the landing, listening to the sound of voices and laughter, how she was forbidden to go down. But apart from an occasional click or creak startling her, this house was quiet. Flossie had fallen asleep eventually, after being given a few drops of Ipec for her earache, Julia had been persuaded to go with her. The servants had finished their clearing up, their stacking and sweeping. It was so quiet she could hear the ticking of the clock in the hall.

Elizabeth went downstairs towards the dining room. There was a gleam of light from the glass cabinet, the candle flame shimmered on the polished wood. On the small table near the window lay her novel. She went towards it, feeling like a criminal returning to her crime.

She put the candle on the table and began sifting through her notes, *sweat-shop, man with a crooked back, his sister, baby?* On one page in the margin, she'd drawn a quick sketch of Pasley from memory. It wasn't a particularly good sketch. She was not, like Tottie or Miss Bronte, a gifted artist, but she had captured something of the sweetness and trouble in Pasley's face. She touched the sketch lightly with her finger.

Was she never going to be able to forget?

Was she ever going to finish this novel?

She'd told Tottie she was going to give up the unequal struggle to write. She wasn't like Dickens, whose wife and sister-in-law looked after his ten children for him, who couldn't understand why her stories were always so late.

Women must give up leading an artist's life she'd written, *they are too much pressed upon by the daily small Lilliputian arrows of peddling cares* . . .

That was her lot, those Lilliputian arrows. She should bear them patiently, like St Sebastian, and give up these bigger projects that took up so much time.

Yet her other writing was doing well. Especially her stories about Knutsford.

She'd begun writing them when she'd visited the Greens the previous autumn. She'd looked out of the window and seen their girls paddling in the stream. The light was bright and clear, but with a silvery tone to it and the stream ran in a rapid flow of light and shade. Then she'd looked across the field to where starlings were clinging like dark buds to the tips of trees and felt something leave her, some tension or darkness. Life was so easy here. There were no 'poppers in', she wasn't responsible for anything . . .

And she began to think about her own childhood. All those ridiculous, admirable old ladies – the one who drove her little dogs around in a carriage, and the one who made pyjamas for her cow after it fell into a lime pit and became quite bald. She remembered the endless tea parties, the social conundrum of who invited whom, the little economies and petty resentments, the way they all stood together in a crisis.

Dickens was delighted with the new stories, and her readers loved them. So many of them wrote to her, sending her their own anecdotes, begging to hear more about her characters.

She couldn't imagine them begging for more of *Ruth*.

Why couldn't she just be that other kind of writer?

Ah, but Pasley. She'd looked so wounded when Elizabeth had said she was sending her away . . .

She *had* to finish *Ruth*. She felt it as a constant pressure, from herself as much as anyone else.

We are only vessels for something that wants to be born, Charles Dickens had said – as though he knew what pregnancy was! But in fact she did feel it growing inside her – like a tumour rather than a birth. It was making her ill.

Here she was, a woman in her middle years sitting alone in an empty room, afraid of the future, haunted by the past. Oh, she knew the darkness Meta had talked about! She'd said she didn't, but it wasn't true. The numbers of the dead behind her almost equalled the numbers of the living: her mother, her father, her brother, her aunt, her baby son and the two infants who had never lived. And all those empty pages in front of her, those terrifying, blank sheets waiting to be written on.

It was as if that was where her God was, not on the streets, but in the white spaces between the lines . . .

But that was blasphemous. It must be the night and the solitude that was doing this to her, allowing phantoms to rise.

Outside, beyond the curtains, all was darkness and rain. The kind of rain that fell with a persistent, steady intent, dislodging the paving stones, shifting slates from the roofs, making the streets run with sewage. Undoing all the works of man.

In the streets and alleys, under the bridges, were the lost people of Manchester, with their stories of tragedy, abandonment, betrayal. She couldn't write them all. It was *Ruth* she had to concentrate on, to bring the novel somehow to a close.

Ruth should die at the end, there was nothing else for it. But she should die nobly, after nursing her seducer to health. A martyrdom of sorts . . .

I see the Light coming, she would say.

Elizabeth felt her flesh prickle. Her readers would have no doubt that Ruth had been admitted to Heaven. It would make them weep. Never again would they judge a fallen woman so harshly.

More thoughts came, swiftly now, almost too many.

Ruth's seducer should return at her funeral. He would be filled with remorse.

How beautiful she is, he would say. *Do all dead people look so peaceful – so happy?*

She wouldn't remember all this tomorrow, because in the morning she had to go to Preston to campaign against the employment of children as chimney sweeps. And the day after she'd invited the Sunday school children to her home . . .

So despite the hour and the madness of sitting up so late, risking a chill, Elizabeth lit two more candles from the first one. The house was so quiet she could hear the soft scratching noises of her quill on the paper as she began to write.

ACKNOWLEDGEMENTS

I WANT TO thank the many readers who have supported me through the years it has taken me to write this novel, including the members of my writing groups: Sophie Claire, Jennifer Nansubuga Makumbi, Mary Sharratt and Cath Staincliffe; Elizabeth Baines, Carys Bray and Ailsa Cox. Other friends who have provided invaluable feedback include Bernadette McConnell, Liz McIlroy, Anna Pollard, Ian Pople, and Theresa Tomlinson.

I owe special thanks to Chris Foley for her expert reading and advice.

And, as ever, to my agent Charles Walker, and my editor Christopher Hamilton-Emery, for having faith . . .

And all the team at Salt, including Adela Polankova, for going the extra mile . . .

If I've left anyone out then I apologise heartily. Please take my thanks as read - it wouldn't be the same novel without any of my readers!

Finally I would like to thank the team at the Elizabeth Gaskell House for being unfailingly welcoming and helpful. The House is an inspiration, transporting you directly into Elizabeth Gaskell's world. If you haven't visited, you should definitely go!

This book has been typeset by
SALT PUBLISHING LIMITED
using Neacademia, a font designed by Sergei Egorov for the
Rosetta Type Foundry in Czechia. It has been manufactured
using Holmen Book Cream 65gsm paper, and printed and
bound by Clays Limited in Bungay, Suffolk, Great Britain.

CROMER
GREAT BRITAIN
MMXXVI